FROM EARTH AND SKY

A NAPPY SCIENCE FICTION & FANTASY SHORT
STORY COLLECTION

FROM EARTH AND SKY

A NAPPY SCIENCE FICTION & FANTASY SHORT
STORY COLLECTION

BY GERALD L. COLEMAN

BLACK MAGIC BOOKS

ATLANTA

BLACK MAGIC BOOKS
ATLANTA, GA
GERALDCOLEMAN.COM

Publisher's Note: This is a work of fiction. Names, characters, places, and incidents are a product of the author's imagination. Locales and public names are sometimes used for atmospheric purposes. Any resemblance to actual people, living or dead, or to businesses, companies, events, institutions, or locales is completely coincidental.

FROM EARTH AND SKY. – 1st ed.
ISBN 978-1088041932

COVER ART BY ERICA WILLEY
COVER DESIGN BY ERICA WILLEY AND GERALD L. COLEMAN
LAYOUT BY GERALD L. COLEMAN
HONORARY EDITOR SM HILLMAN

CONTENTS

FOREWORD

PROLOGUE

and this is how it begins

once upon a time
in that only place
beyond seven mountains
beyond seven forests
seven rivers
seven seas
on one thousand
and one nights
there was
and there was not

here is a story
story it is
having been said
and said and said

from earth and sky

listen to it
and tell it
to teach it

and if they didn't
die
they're still alive
today
the cat in the vail
lost its tail
end
of the fairytale

FOREWORD

The preceding poem is called a *Cento*. A Cento is a poem made up of lines from other poems. I've played with the form a bit here because these aren't lines from poems, they're traditional cultural alternatives to *Once Upon a Time*. Most believe *Once* has its roots in a tale from 1380 called *Sir Ferumbras*. Interestingly, it's a Middle English romance made up of ten, 540 lines of poetry. It's from the Carolingian Cycle about the history of France.

It begins—" *Onys..uppon a day..he slow kynges three.*

The phrase has been the beginning of many narratives in the western canon. We associate it most with fairytales and their attendant mythos. When you hear that dulcet phrase, you know to settle in for a story that you know is untrue but likely has something to teach you about life and the world around you. Whether it's a warning about the "other" in your midst, a warning against wandering away from the tribe or clan on your own, or failing to heed the wisdom of the elders in your village or home.

This collection seeks to remedy the ongoing circumstance in science fiction and fantasy in which black folks are left out of those stories. I thought it apropos to open with alternatives to the ubiquitous *Once*.

What I found was a rich tradition, around the world, of openings to fairytales and myths spoken by many different communities. The poem includes the rote openings and closings of traditional tales in Farsi, Tamil, Arabic, and Telugu—from Germany, Iceland, Chile, Nigeria, and more.

I loved these touchstones so much I chose one as the title of this collection—From Earth and Sky.

I have endeavored in writing science fiction and fantasy to include myself, and people who look like me, in stories written in the genres I love. That love began in elementary school with the Scholastic Book Fair and titles like Mrs, Frisby and the Rats of NIMH, and Watership Down, which in turn led me to the Lord of the Rings, Elric of Melniboné, The Black Company, the Faded Sun series, and so much more.

I reveled in swords, magic, spaceships, and alien planets. But I never saw characters, especially heroes, who looked like me. So, when I finally sat down to begin writing in these genres, I had a single aim—to show black characters in these settings and environs. These short stories are just some of that work. I hope you enjoy them. Know that there are many more authors like me. Black men and women writing what I call the *Black Fantastic*. I've been dreaming of the day when this would become a reality. Thankfully, that day is here. Enjoy.

Sincerely,
Gerald L. Coleman

November 2022

FROM EARTH AND SKY

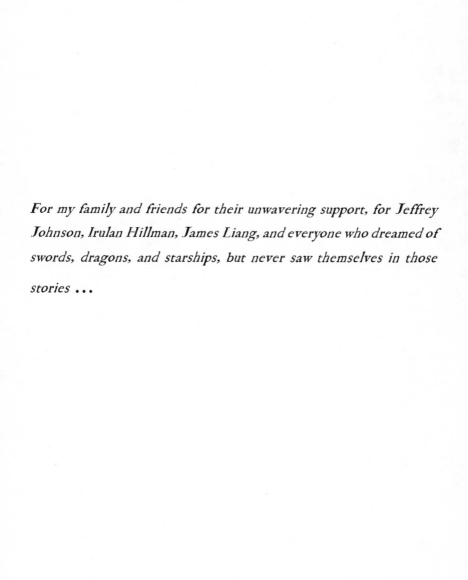

For my family and friends for their unwavering support, for Jeffrey Johnson, Irulan Hillman, James Liang, and everyone who dreamed of swords, dragons, and starships, but never saw themselves in those stories ...

FROM EARTH
AND SKY

PROLOGUE

The Death of Captain Kirk: Why the Illusory Singularity of the
White Hero Must Die

By Gerald L. Coleman

So long as an educated minority, living off all previous generations, hardly guessed why life was so easy to live, so long as the majority, working day and night, did not quite realize why they received none of the fruits of their labour, both parties believed this to be the natural order of things, and the world of cannibalism could survive. People often take prejudice or habit for truth and in that case feel no discomfort: but if they once realize that their truth is nonsense, the game is up. From then onwards it is only by force that a [person] can be compelled to do what [they] consider[] to be absurd.

~Alexander Herzen, From the Other Shore

It does not do to leave a live dragon out of your calculations, if you live near him.

~J. R. R. Tolkien

The jig is up. I use that phrase understanding its lexical and cultural baggage. There's a tension in its etymology and I have summoned it, like an old family secret, for that very purpose. I've also conjured its particular history so I may say, we aren't dancing to that tune anymore. Especially with a fake smile plastered on our faces intended to feign unequivocal acceptance of a fate of white America's making, while simultaneously making its adherents and apostles feel comfortable. The banjo has fallen silent. We are no longer stepping and fetching. Making ourselves smaller for the comfort of others, or invisible altogether, has come to an end.

Welcome to the undiscovered country.

I get it. This probably feels confrontational to some of you, and that's ok if that's where you are. But let's back up for a moment and talk about context. Let's enter this conversation by way of misogyny.

In 1973, Paula Smith coined the term *Mary Sue* after seeing what she thought of as placeholder fantasy characters in stories submitted to her Star Trek fanzine. According to her, the young female characters in these stories were all so exceptionally sweet, beautiful, and good, that every other character in the story automatically loved them. Once the term filtered into the general consciousness of fandom, fans—mostly men—began using the term pejoratively. I vividly remember the term being thrown about the moment Star Wars: The Force Awakens dropped in the theater. It's used as a way of delegitimizing the female protagonist.

But here's my question. And it's always been my question whenever the term comes up. What about Captain Kirk? How about Superman and Batman? Dare I mention James Bond, Ethan Hunt, and Sherlock Holmes?

Flash Gordon was a jock. Yet, somehow, he was able to thwart a master tactician with an entire space empire at his disposal.

James Bond—and listen, I'm a fan—was one guy who was able to beat criminal masterminds with all the resources and well-armed henchmen in the world with nothing but an easy smile and, in some iterations, a few gadgets from Q. And can we talk about the white male revenge fantasy that is Batman?

Again, I'm a fan, so this critique doesn't come from someone outside the fandom with no appreciation for the canon. But the lone orphan whose only superpower is his wealth who can beat people with actual superpowers by out-prepping and out-spending them? Have you seen the memes and their painfully on-point critique of the caped crusader coming out of nowhere to break the arm of the Gotham security guard who is working a double shift to buy his kid Christmas presents, rather than using his wealth to stop homelessness and wealth inequality in Gotham?

That critique and so many others are arising out of a genuine backlash against the unquestioned superiority of the white male hero in our fiction, put in sharp relief by the ever-present criticism of abilities, motivations, choices, and characterizations of heroes of color.

But let's circle back to Paula Smith. Because she, and Sharon Ferraro—who launched the fanzine with her—also threw around the term Marty Sue and Murray Sue, for the placeholder male fantasy characters they saw in stories. Yet, for some reason (add a judicious amount of sarcasm to your reading here)—for some reason, those terms didn't stick.

In his foreword to Jean-François Lyotard's, *The Postmodern Condition: A Report on Knowledge,* Fredric Jameson writes,

> *This seeming contradiction can be resolved, I believe, by taking a further step ... namely to posit, not the disappearance of the great master-narratives, but their passage underground as it were, their continuing but now unconscious effectivity as a way of 'thinking about' and acting in our current situation. (xii)*

This isn't a paper I'm writing for the master's degree program. That was decades ago. But the point Jameson is making about the way master-narratives have changed how they function in our culture is relevant.

We have been predisposed to accept the white male protagonist, in all his forms, from knight in shining armor to deplorable human being tolerated for his "giftedness," no matter how overpowered, unbeatable, and superhuman he may be. We do it without question. When no one can outsmart Sherlock, we cheer. We no one can beat Kirk we nod with approval. When Batman can defeat any enemy because of "prep time" we don't bat an eyelash at the utter idiocy of the notion. But the moment that character is a woman, or black, or queer, or anything outside the established norm of the western cultural industrial default character—i. e. white male—a certain corner of fandom rears its ugly head to cry foul.

In elementary school, my favorite time of the year aside from Field Day was when the Scholastic fair arrived. It was absolutely magical. I loved it. They were just small mass-market paperbacks with a price tag of a couple of dollars each, arrayed on wire racks, but it was joyous.

I discovered *Mrs. Frisby and the Rats of NIMH*, *Watership Down*, and so much more. Even after the fair came and went, my teacher would pass around a thin color catalog from which we could order more books. We'd race home with our selections and get our parents to fork over five or six dollars so that we could place our orders. And then we'd pester our educational shepherd for weeks about when our books were going to arrive. Eventually, we'd return from recess one day and there would be an unremarkable, brown, cardboard box resting atop her desk. Around fifth hour, she would crack it open and hand out our books. She waited until our work was done for the day, because she knew once we had our books, we'd be unteachable.

We were a generation of readers who loved books.

Those small magical treasures led me to *The Three Musketeers, Lord of the Rings, The Dragonriders of Pern, Elric of Melniboné, The Faded Sun, Dune, The Black Company, The Wheel of Time, The Sleeping Dragon, Jhereg (Vlad Taltos)*, not to mention comic books, video games, sci-fi movies, and Dungeons & Dragons. And through it all, one constant remained: the white male hero.

No one ever questioned their heroism, their abilities, their charisma, or the pedestal the culture erected for them. In hindsight, you can almost hear Shelley's Ozymandias whispering in the wind, "Look on my works, ye Mighty, and despair!" Kirk outsmarts Khan, Sherlock runs rings around Moriarty, Paul Atreides comes to Arrakis, is brought into a native tribe, and becomes their long-awaited messiah, with the ever-present trope of being more adept at the traditions of the natives than they themselves, and all the while fandom cheered.

As a Black man, I cheered less and less over time.

The current zeitgeist was inevitable. Fandom could have seen it coming. In the same way all those characters made white fans feel empowered, made them want to wrap one of their mom's good towels around their neck like a cape and run through the neighborhood pretending to be their favorite hero—all the people seen as sideline people when seen at all, every person who didn't see themselves represented in the canon, who always had to take an extra imaginary step to see themselves in the story—wanted to feel that same euphoria. We wanted heroes that embodied our heroism, our valiant streaks, our daring, and ingenuity.

At some point in college, while reading yet another installment in the *Wheel of Time*, it dawned on me that I wanted to write science fiction and fantasy. The preeminent reason was a love of the genre, in particular, and writing in general. But the subtext of that desire was to write sci-fi and fantasy with protagonists that looked like me. When I finally did and broadened my participation in fandom to include conventions as a guest author, a participant in podcasts, zines, anthologies, and all the rest, I discovered that the idea of capable, charismatic, genius protagonists of color (of ALL peoples pushed to the margins, but I'm focusing on how for every one Ben Sisko there are fifteen hundred womprat-shooting Skywalkers)— that idea was dismissed by some as unrealistic, overpowered, illogical, "just self-inserts" and not worthy of being taken seriously as heroes and heroines in good stories. I'm still wondering how anyone can see those as anything other than ridiculously laughable arguments.

Well, I'm afraid I have to announce something some might find unpleasant. Captain Kirk is dead. I don't mean that he died in *Star Trek: Generations* helping Picard beat Soran (notwithstanding a "resurrection" by the Borg in a novel). I mean as a stand-in for the unfettered reign of the infallible white male hero. Marty Sue, Marty Stu, Murray Sue, or whatever you wish to call him… is facing a cultural curtain call. While there will almost certainly be a grimy corner of fandom that continues to try to sell the rest of us on a world where only the white guy gets to be unbeatable, there are far too many new writers and creators who love science fiction and fantasy, who look like Benjamin Lafayette Sisko, Michael Burnham, Rey, T'Challa, and Shang-Chi, writing and creating strange new worlds, boldly going where no white male protagonist has gone before. And as much as that may bother some, it's making many more rejoice.

The jig is up. And not a moment too soon.

FROM EARTH
AND SKY

FOOL'S ERRAND

The French infested Alhamara like rats on a herring drifter. First it was the Dutch looking for trade on the Continent. They were dislodged at Goree by the Portuguese. And then, the French arrived.

A cooling breeze raced down the Senegalese coastline, blowing softly into the city, off the harbor, taking his mind off the heat and the French.

If only we'd known what the arrival of Europeans would bring. If only, he thought. *A hyena does not change its spots even if it moves to a different forest.* But the enticement of commerce and an inability to comprehend their savagery had blinded them to what was to come.

Hannibal could hear his father's deep, rough voice rattling off another proverb; *If you pick up one end of the stick you also pick up the other.* So, though Alhamara sat on the western coast of the African continent, French could be heard being spoken from the docks to the Provincial Governor's office—even if the face doing the speaking was brown.

Hints of spice, molasses, and the odor of briny saltwater filled the air. But the sun was creeping over the horizon, so the sweet aroma of freshly, baked bread fought to overshadow all of it. His stomach growled so loud that he looked around to see if anyone heard it.

Though it was early, Hannibal passed merchants headed toward the docks. Most were fussy Frenchmen in brightly colored silk straining at the seams. They huffed and puffed down the street, dabbing sweat from their brows with soft, cotton handkerchiefs they pulled from their sleeves. A few had their arms wrapped around bundles of rolled parchment, while others chewed at kowtowing servants.

Hannibal sucked his teeth at the sight of it. A tall, pale fellow, with a double chin, wearing a ridiculously oversized black hat with a red plume, caught his eye. A frilly, red, silk shirt puffed out of the top of his black coat. White stockings stuck out of black pantaloons, ending in black, leather shoes, with a large, silver buckle. The man looked Hannibal directly in the eye as he approached.

He was berating a young woman carrying several packages, while she ducked and bowed her head apologetically. Hannibal scowled darkly and the man swallowed hard before pointedly crossing to the other side of the street. The oaf hurried the woman along in hushed, but sharp, tones. Hannibal sucked audibly at his teeth again and considered his level of tolerance for spending a few days in the city jail. Ultimately, it was the cost of leaving his ship docked and the commotion his crew would cause that made him keep walking. But he filed the fussy man's face away in his mind for another day.

Hannibal rounded the corner and passed a bakery, cheese shop, and wine merchant, all nestled together on the cobblestone road like loaves of bread stacked together on a shelf. They marked his proximity to his desired destination. A small smile, slowly, washed the scowl he was wearing away. He took a deep breath before ducking into *Quête Incensée*. It was time to quiet his stomach.

Ebrima was an odd, but likeable, fellow. Hannibal prided himself on being clean and keeping a clean ship, but he had never seen anyone like Ebrima. The bar's dark, stained, wooden surface was so bright it had a glossy shine. The windows sparkled in the early morning sunlight. The floor was neither sticky nor littered with refuse. The tables and chairs were aligned in perfect rows.

Hannibal appreciated a clean tavern and, were that the extent of it, he would've thought nothing of it. But then, there was the man himself. The Mandinka proprietor was of average height, heavily muscled, and several shades darker than Hannibal's own golden-brown complexion.

The man had one of the easiest smiles he'd ever seen. Maybe it was a hazard of being a barkeep. His brilliantly white teeth shone even brighter against his glistening, dark skin. The winning, come-on-in grin beamed beneath the most meticulously groomed mustache he'd ever come across, made more remarkable by its upturned ends.

His bright green shirt and sea-blue apron were pressed. There wasn't even a hint of a wrinkle. His sleeves, though rolled up, formed perfect, matching folds on each forearm.

Did he measure them with a stick?

His pantaloons were steel-gray, and though Hannibal could not see his boots, he had no doubt they were polished to a shine so pure you could see the reflection of your face in them. Gold

3

GERALD L. COLEMAN

rings adorned fingers on both hands and glinted circumspectly in the lamplight as the man wiped a pristinely white towel across the bar, as if there was even the ghost of a speck of dust on it. The only thing about the man that wasn't pressed, folded, or tied down was his hair.

It was long, thick, and adorned his head like a lion's mane. Hannibal always thought it a small reminder that he was, beyond his French dress, still Wolof – even if it was not a traditional cultural style. It was unavoidable, which seemed more to the point. Ebrima nodded at Hannibal when he looked up from wiping the bar.

Hannibal returned the nod before finding an empty table on the far side of the room, where he could sit with his back against the wall. After lowering himself into the padded chair, he removed his wide-brimmed, gray hat and placed it gently on the table. He turned it so its large, purple plume curved away from him. He, unconsciously, adjusted the cant of the set of wheel-lock pistols, stuck in the thick, purple sash at his waist. A quick tug on the large, silver buckle of his brown, leather belt made the hilt of his saber point forward. He sighed and dropped his booted foot in the chair to his left. The shine on their brown leather would make Ebrima proud.

A serving maid appeared instantly. The young, brown-eyed woman had high cheek bones, long hair twirled into an intricate lace of braids, and skin nearly as dark as Ebrima. Her short-sleeved, green blouse, which tied up the front, was tucked into a long, brown, pleated skirt with blue stripes. Leather bracelets, covered in tiny shells, were stacked up her wrists and made a soft clicking sound as she moved her hands. She smelled of frankincense. The scent reminded him of home.

Like Ebrima, there wasn't a wrinkle or stain in sight. After proclaiming that her name was Nyima, she listened intently to his

4

breakfast order. With a curtsey fit for a French court, she flashed him a please-keep-spending-coin smile before disappearing into the kitchen. It was not long before Hannibal was sipping coffee out of a small, glass cup, nestled in a polished silver holder.

Soon, breakfast followed. Nyima brought him a plate with a large square of sharp, yellow cheese, a thick slice of dark bread, and a small bowl of hot oats with a bit of milk and honey. The plate was small making the meal seem larger than it was. He chuckled at Ebrima's business sense.

Hannibal glanced around the mostly empty main room while he ate. The drapes on the windows were tied back so there was plenty of light. It also made it easy for him to see who was coming. He appreciated that even more than the extra light. The walls were covered with melancholy paintings of forests, hills overlooking valleys, and ocean inlets, done in browns, grays, and blues – they all looked like the work of the Flemish school.

Several young women were cleaning, cooking, or serving tables while young men carried supplies into the back, mopped the floor, and washed windows. A large, brooding fellow sat near the door struggling to keep his head off his chest. It was funny watching him lurch awake and turn to see if Ebrima had seen him.

Taverns were usually darkly lit, cramped, smelly affairs a few beers away from a brawl. They had sticky floors and serving maids who could be purchased for the night, or a few minutes. While Ebrima had taken on a few French airs in dress, and décor, he had not adopted the French inclination toward neglect and exploitation. Quête Incensée was run with pride. Everyone under its roof seemed happy.

Nyima appeared out of nowhere to refill his cup with coffee. He returned her warm smile as she turned to leave. He took note of the other patrons while he stirred in a bit of sugar and cream.

Alhamara was a port city, so it was no surprise the clientele was diverse.

Hannibal spotted two French sailors, three Senegalese men who might have been from the countryside, and a few merchants who looked unmistakably British. Everyone seemed busy with their own discussions – though the French and British didn't look happy to see one another under the same roof. He noticed smoked fish, olives, and wine at one table and soft, boiled eggs, cheese, and mead at another.

When Hannibal finished his own breakfast, Nyima was there to whisk away his dirty plate and pour more coffee. Before his cup reached his mouth, a young couple in traditional Berber robes entered the tavern. The woman was on the small side, but she moved with squared shoulders, and an even gait.

The young man accompanying her was a bit taller. He wore a large, red kaftan, covered in gold brocade, over a blue shirt with matching, billowy pants. His soft, red shoes curled sharply at the toe. A red and gold headwrap covered his head down to the back of his neck.

The young woman was dressed just as colorfully. Her shirt and long skirt were blue with gold brocade woven in an intricate design that made Hannibal think of square flowers. She wore a very short jacket with long sleeves. Gold brocade covered them from wrist to elbow and covered the jacket's shoulders in thick embroidery.

Her black hair hung down her back. A headdress of gold chains, with tiny gold coins hanging at equal lengths across her forehead, covered half her face. Gold bracelets and rings adorned her wrists and fingers.

They stood in the doorway holding onto each other like they'd lose one another if they let go and gazed around the room. The woman pointed to an empty table in a quiet corner, and they made their way there avoiding eye contact. Hannibal watched as one of the serving maids made her way to their table.

The young couple looked into a small, leather pouch before speaking briefly with the woman in hushed tones. The maid smiled warmly, nodded, and headed for the kitchen. Hannibal turned his attention back to his own cup. After all, it wasn't polite to stare, especially at someone who seemed self-conscious about their presence.

When he looked up again, he noticed a small group of men through one of the one front windows. They stood in a tight huddle on the street. When the huddle broke up, they stumbled into the tavern. Three of them nearly fell. They shoved each other and steadied themselves. Once they had their feet under them, they turned their attention to the customers. Their combined gaze landed on the young couple, and they passed toothy grins among themselves, leering in the couple's direction. Hannibal sighed.

He placed his hat on his head, grabbed his fresh cup of coffee, and rose quietly from his chair. He moved calmly toward a spot between the young couple and the oncoming sailors. He wasn't sure why the young couple had gotten their attention, but they had it. It was probably her jewelry. Maybe it was that the grubby little band of unwashed water rats were drunk, fresh off the boat, and itching for some excitement. Whatever the reason, they had decided to do something about it.

They were a half-dozen paces from the young couple's table when Hannibal bumped into the first two, spilling his coffee on the man in the lead. He made sure to throw the coffee forward as he feigned bumping into the man by accident.

He certainly didn't want to get any on his clean coat. He was particularly careful to avoid staining the purple embroidery on his sleeves and lapels. Purple was a difficult color to make, according to his clothier, and it was expensive to clean. He wasn't sure how difficult it would be to remove coffee stains, but he didn't want to find out. They smelled of rum and the need of long overdue baths. He'd seen the type often enough. So, what came next was as predictable as the tide.

They stumbled to a halt. The fellow he spilled his coffee on, presumably their leader, looked down at his filthy shirt, as if he could tell the difference between the coffee stain and the other grime. It must have been white at some point, but that was a long time ago. He was nearly as tall as Hannibal. His dull, brown hair was matted. His teeth were rotting in his mouth. His clothes were frayed around the edges. When he spoke, it was with the kind of British accent that chewed up most of the words.

A hand on a British merchant ship then, he thought.

Their captain was likely a small cog in a larger merchant wheel. Had their ship's master been an independent contractor they would have been paid better. He gave Hannibal a shove.

"Awright then, gob'nah. Whot 'ave we here? Ah ruddy fool, whot doesn't look where 'e's goin, ay' lads!?"

The man took a step toward Hannibal and poked him in the chest for emphasis.

"I'va righ' mind tah teach you ah lesson, blackamore. 'aven't I?"

The man's companions, who were just as seedy looking as he was, spread out to flank Hannibal on either side. There were five of them.

Hannibal smiled and said, "How about a bath first?"

They looked at each other as their faces turned red. Hannibal ducked under a sloppily thrown right, smashed his cup in the man's face, and kicked the leader in the groin. His boot made a hard *thump* in the man's crotch. He crumpled to the floor like an empty burlap sack.

Hannibal took two, full steps back, to give himself room to move. He pulled both of his wheel-lock pistols from his sash, cocking them in the process. The *click* of the hammer's locking into place seemed louder than usual. He aimed one at the head of the man on his knees, who was clutching his groin and aimed the other at the groin of the man to his left, who was wiping at the blood on his face from where Hannibal hit him with his cup.

They froze, with their rusty sabers half-drawn. Hannibal had only seen one pistol among them. It was still tucked in the leader's waist. The rabble stood there, slack-jawed and wide-eyed, trying to look at their leader and Hannibal at the same time. No one moved. The sound of a blunderbuss being cocked broke the spell. Hannibal saw Ebrima, standing behind the bar, with the short barrel aimed at the head of the man nearest to the bar.

Hannibal paused to let them figure out they were in an untenable situation. They looked anxiously at each another. He smiled calmly, giving each of them a good, hard look. They were bilge rats not hardened soldiers, or even pirates. They were the kind of men who liked a fight only when they had their target outnumbered. It was likely they saw the young Berber couple on the street and decided they were easy pickings.

Hannibal looked down at the leader and showed his teeth. It wasn't a grin. It was more like an animal revealing fangs. A little gleam in his eye added just the right touch.

Once he had their undivided attention, he said, "I haven't shot anyone in a while. Maybe it's time, if for no other reason than an excuse to clean my guns. What do you think?"

The leader looked around at his fellows with a darting glance, saw Ebrima with his blunderbuss, and said, "Now, we was jus' havin some fun, wasn't we, gob'nah? No need ta loose them pistols, Cap'n. No need."

He waived a hand in surrender. His head dropped down, he grimaced in pain, and held his groin with his other hand. Hannibal leaned down, lowered his voice, and imagined it was a knife's sharp edge.

"You have about as long as it takes Nyima to bring me another cup of coffee to be out of this tavern and on your way. Or we start shooting."

His head jerked up, his face flushed red, and his eyebrows climbed his forehead as if they were trying to escape. Hannibal motioned toward the door with the pistol he was aiming at the man's head, and, without a moment's hesitation, they all ran for the door, climbing over each other to get out. They left their leader to bring up the rear, hobbling for the door while still clutching his crotch.

Hannibal watched them go with a wry grin and a shake of his head. He uncocked his pistols and slid them back in his sash once he was sure they were long gone. Then, he walked back to his table, dropped his hat on it, and lowered himself back into his seat. Nyima was already there, with another cup of coffee and a soft chuckle aimed squarely at him.

"You do be ah rascal, ready for trouble, eh Captain Black? Yer sure it don't be following you 'round?"

He held up his hands in feigned surrender and said, "Who me?" Then he chuckled right back at her.

She shook her head ruefully, placed the cup in front of him, and started back toward the kitchen.

She stopped after two steps, turned back and said, "Ebrima say, you be charged for anyt'ing dat woulda' been broken." Her laughter followed her to the kitchen.

Hannibal looked over at the bar and Ebrima gave him a curt nod, rubbed his fingers together, and then held up his hands in mock frustration. The message was clear. *You break it, you pay for it.*

I'm trying to make a living here. When Hannibal nodded and held up his hands in surrender again, Ebrima flashed him a big grin and swiped at the air as if to say, *go on you roudy fool.* He chuckled and went back to wiping at invisible dirt on his bar.

Hannibal knew Ebrima was only half-serious. The man took the safety of his clientele seriously and would suffer no harm to come to any of them while they were under his roof. He would've tanned the sailor's hides and then extracted the coin for any damage from them or their ship's captain. But he wouldn't tell Hannibal that.

He reached down, picked up his fresh cup of coffee, and barely got it to his lips before the young couple approached his table. They bowed their heads, but only the young man spoke.

He continued to bow, placed his hand over his heart, and said, "Our thanks, *Bwana.* We are in your debt. They must have seen us disembarking from the ship we took passage on. I believe they followed us from the docks."

Then, the young woman chimed in. Her voice sounded like music. It was light, soft, and lilting as she bowed her head again, copying the young man's hand over the heart.

"Thank you, Bwana. Thank you. You are most kind."

Hannibal smiled warmly at them both.

"No thanks needed. I have seen their kind often enough. It's my pleasure to give them a taste of their own medicine. Please, join me."

He stood and motioned to the other chairs at his table. They bowed again and moved to join him. The woman's gold headdress made a soft jingling sound as she moved. The sound told Hannibal it was pristine gold decorating her brow. It was only after they sat that she raised her head and looked at him. When their eyes met, he inclined his head and smiled again. She returned his smile with shy one of her own, revealing beautifully perfect white teeth.

11

Nyima returned to ask after them. There was a lot more bowing and pleasantries as they asked for tea. Hannibal sipped at his coffee and watched while they talked with her.

When they finished, he cleared his throat and said, "I'm Captain Hannibal Black."

They nodded and the young man placed his hand over his heart again.

"Salaam, Bwana. This is my sister, Massinissa. I am Anaruz. We are blessed to make your acquaintance. Peace be upon you."

Hannibal nodded. "And with you. The blessing is mine. May I ask why you took passage?"

The young man's face changed. The smile slowly slipped away. It was replaced by a grim frown.

"Yes, Captain. We are from Sali, in southern Morocco. We thought we were safe from slaving raids, but the Barbary pirates have been raiding farther and farther south. They had never come so far down the coast before. Two days ago, they sacked Sali. Our village was devastated. Many were carried off to their ship. It is our understanding that they will be taken to the Canary Islands to be sold into slavery."

The young woman's head dropped again. This time the jingling of her headdress sounded solemn. Anaruz stared off past Hannibal's shoulder as if he was hiding his face from some shame.

Hannibal spoke softly. "So, why did you come south?"

Massinissa raised her head. Her eyes had hardened, and her lips were pressed firmly together.

"We came to find men who would help us retrieve our family. We drove what was left of our village's cattle to the market at the port and sold them. We also sold much of our family's ancestral jewelry. I would've sold even all that I wear but Anaruz would not have me be … unadorned as is our tradition. We have money. All we need are sailors willing to take the job and a ship to carry us."

Hannibal leaned back in his chair. He had never heard of the Barbary pirates raiding so far south either or the taking of Berbers. But it didn't surprise him. At some point pirates discovered how lucrative the slave trade could be. Some of them even began working directly for countries involved in the trade, though unofficially. Every European power was invested in the pillaging of the continent.

He drank from his cup and did the calculations. It was likely their fellow villagers were already on the Canary Islands. But they might not have been put on ships bound for their final destination yet. He looked across the table at the young woman.

"Did you happen to hear the name of the ship, or see the colors they were flying?"

Massinissa nodded slowly.

"We hid at the village edge. We were on our way back from the fields when they attacked. I was so afraid, but we forced ourselves to watch. I saw the flag on their ship. It was red with a black skull and two white roses crossed underneath."

She crossed her arms to mimic the image.

Hannibal leaned forward so fast he nearly spilled his coffee. He gave Massinissa a hard stare. The woman didn't flinch from his steady gaze.

Hannibal spoke so low it was almost a whisper.

"This is important, Massinissa. Are you sure that's what the flag looked like?"

She pressed her lips in a hard line, locked eyes with him, and nodded.

"I am sure, Captain Black. I have never seen anything like it before. I will never forget it."

Hannibal sat up straight, tilted back his cup, and finished his coffee in a single gulp.

"Then we haven't any time to spare. Come with me."

13

He stood, dropped some coin on the table, and flipped Nyima a full *piece of eight* on his way out with the two Berbers in tow. Nyima smiled and waved at him as he left. His own smile disappeared once he was several paces down the street. Hannibal did not believe in omens. But maybe the name of the tavern should have given him pause. *Quête Incensée*, was French. It meant, *Fool's Errand.*

He despised the pirates of the Barbary Coast. They didn't hunt merchant ships on the open sea. They were slavers. They raided the coast from northern Morocco to Tripoli and sold those people into slavery. People called him a pirate, too. But, Hannibal, and his crew, didn't hunt merchant ships, depriving them the of molasses, wine, silk, or porcelain in their holds. He hunted pirate ships that had turned to slaving.

They freed the captured and plundered the ships for their gold, silver, and rum, or whatever other treasurers they carried. It was lucrative business, of course, but the treasure was never Hannibal's true motivation. It did, however, keep his ship well-supplied and repaired, and his crew well paid. Hannibal's reward was seeing human beings set free, and slavers made to pay for their choices.

But for as long as he'd been hunting pirate ships, there was one that had managed to elude him. The *Whydah Galley* was the most notorious pirate ship in the entire Atlantic. She raided up and down the Barbary coast. Her crew was as notorious as it was brutal. Her captain was cunning. And Massinissa had seen their colors.

Hannibal turned toward the docks. He was no longer paying attention to his fellow pedestrians. He had a scent in his nose, now, and he wasn't about to lose it. Time was not on his side. He reached into his coat and retrieved his long-stemmed pipe. After filling it from a pouch secreted in a coat pocket, he looked around at the nearby street vendors. A lovely, plump woman, in a green tunic, was grilling fresh fish. It smelled heavenly. Only a full stomach allowed him to resist.

He did, however, prevail upon her for a long, thin, piece of hay, which he lit in her fire. He held it over the bowl of his pipe, and puffed away, until a thick plume of smoke rose into the air. With a flick of his wrist, he smothered the flame, leaving the half-burnt piece of hay smoldering on the ground.

Alhamara was a typical city along the Senegalese coast. It sat on a rise, overlooking the ocean, with its dull, reddish-brown, stone walls dotting the landscape. You didn't see the brightly colored Senegalese aesthetic until you entered the city-proper and walked its streets.

There were arches everywhere and the residents of the city were unafraid of color. Building fronts were inset with colored stone arranged in squares and rectangles. A dark-stained door was surrounded by an arch of white stone. The white stone, in turn, was enclosed by a square of red, which was then circumscribed by a rectangle of blue tile. A few paces farther down the street and the walls exploded with bright yellow, green, and blue tile, arranged in dozens of small circles.

Even the streets were laid with stone in amazingly brilliant colors and complex patterns. The city, seen up close, was breathtaking. Just when you thought you were getting used to the architecture, you turned a corner to find an asymmetrical fountain in twelve shades of blue, or a hidden courtyard with landscapes embedded in the walls in purples, greens, blues, and golds – every bit of it in tiny pieces of tile.

Hannibal liked Alhamara for two reasons. It was far enough south that it was generally beyond the regular sailing lanes – especially for pirates. And there wasn't a single piece of trash anywhere in sight. He enjoyed being able to walk down the street without smelling days-old refuse or having to weave around horse droppings. He certainly didn't miss people heaving dirty water from second story windows. Thick puffs of smoke trailed behind him as he walked. He wasn't trying to ignore his new companions, who talked in hushed tones as they followed him, but he needed time to think. Even the beauty of Alhamara's colorful presentation was lost on him at the moment. It was time to hunt.

Overhead, arctic terns flittered about. The birds were white with black heads and beaks. Soon, they would be darting from the sky, dashing into the water, to catch lunch. Hannibal watched one hit an updraft, shooting straight up in the air with barely a flap. As he watched it climb, his mind drifted back to a late night, several months ago.

He and Ebrima were just beginning to get to know one another. The Gambit had dropped anchor late causing Hannibal to arrive at the tavern just as it closed. Ebrima was kind enough to let him in. He fixed Hannibal a late supper and sat with him, drinking rum, late into the night. With rum heavy on his breath, Ebrima told him how no one had supported his dream to open a tavern near the sea. He was told again, and again, that it was a fool's errand. The family that had herded goats for generations expected him to continue the tradition. While it was a good and noble living, he'd always wanted to live in a great city, near the sea.

So, with his mother's secret blessing, he'd left late at night, made his way to the sea, and worked until he could open his own tavern. When he did, he named it *Fool's Errand*, so he would never forget. The search for the Whydah Galley had often felt like his own fool's errand. But like Ebrima's tavern, it might finally be in his grasp.

When Hannibal arrived at the docks, three of his crew were waiting for him. Just before he reached the pier, he left Massinissa and Anaruz on the street and ducked into a nearby sundries shop. There were candles everywhere and the place smelled like flowers.

But he was only interested in writing materials. He placed a piece-of-eight in the husband's hand and the wife obliged him with a piece of parchment, a quill, and black ink. When he finished writing, he picked up his companions at the front door and continued to the docks.

When he arrived, there were two crewmen seated in a small launch, oars in hand, and his First Lieutenant standing at the end of the pier watching his approach. Safiya's eye was on the street behind him. On any other ship she'd be called a Quartermaster. But Hannibal preferred lieutenants. The Gambit's Quartermaster answered to a third, and second lieutenant, and finally Safiya.

The dark, brown skinned woman, with eyes to match, was born at sea, on her mother's dhow. She was the toughest chess opponent he'd ever faced, was deadly with the cutlass at her hip, and would have stepped in front of a cannon to save his life. There wasn't a sailor on board the Gambit who wouldn't do the same for her.

She snapped-to as he approached, brushing back her long, black, wooly hair in the process. Pirates didn't knuckle their foreheads like officers on war ships, but she liked the show of respect for her captain. When he nodded in her direction, she relaxed her tall frame. She absently checked that her white, silk shirt was buttoned to the neck before brushing her hand down the front of her light-blue tunic.

It had thick, red embroidery around its buttonholes, and she wore a red, silk scarf around her neck, tucked into the collar of her shirt. It matched the much larger, silk sash around her waist. Brown, leather bracers covered her forearms, matching the spauldrons on her shoulders. Her forearms rested easily on the butts of the flintlock pistols tucked into her sash. Their meticulous woodwork was accentuated with steel, covered in flowery engraving.

She had gushed over the craftmanship of his own pistols. It had gone on for more than an hour, one night, as they prepared to raid the Danish slaver ship, *Fredensborg*. He'd only managed to get her to stop by promising Safiya her own pair. The next time they made port, he went straight to his gunsmith, with her in tow, after selling the sugar and rum from the Fredensborg.

She played with them for hours – spinning them in her hands, then putting them in and pulling them out of her sash. It had been like watching a kid play with a new toy. No one was allowed to touch them – ever. She also carried three knives and a gracefully curved cutlass hanging from a leather belt, buckled on over her sash.

Hannibal nodded at his First Lieutenant. She returned his curt nod with one of her own and stepped into the slowly rocking longboat. He took a few moments to speak with the dock master before passing the sealed pieces of parchment, along with a gold coin, to the man. Janic was not above a bit of grift on the docks, but he was a man of his word. The missives were safe in his hands. After a quick handclasp with the man, Hannibal crossed the pier to the longboat. He motioned to Massinissa and Anaruz to hop in while Safiya fill him in on the other two longboats he sent ashore for supplies. They were already on their way to the Gambit.

As the longboat approached where the Man-of-war, and former British ship-of-the-line, lay at anchor in the bay, Hannibal puffed on his pipe and took in the view. No matter how many times he saw her, it still gave him pleasure.

Three masts, each with four sails, rose into the sky from her deck. Seventy cannon hatches hung closed around her hull. Anyone counting would note thirty-one on each side, four fore, and four aft. There was a cannon resting behind each. The Gambit could carry more, but Hannibal preferred her fast. A little more than three-hundred women and men were moving about on board.

The Gambit had room for another two hundred crew, but he liked the added space, and so did his crew. There was room to bathe and sufficient space to sleep without having to step over someone.

As the longboat closed on the Gambit, Hannibal could see the crew preparing for departure. The other longboats were stowed, which meant that the supplies were already stored. Safiya had things well in hand. It wasn't long before Hannibal was stepping down onto the deck.

Safiya barked, "Captain on deck!"

The brown faces of the women and men of the Gambit swung in his direction. A handful had come with him from his posting on the *Resolute*. The rest still carried the scars and memories from the pirate ships that had intended to sell them into slavery before the Gambit appeared on the horizon. The overwhelming majority of the people Hannibal freed went home. But sometimes they chose to join his crew.

He walked past the main mast, and up the steps to the stern castle. The crew smiled at him as he passed. They weren't half-hungry, inebriated, or barefoot. They wore clean clothes, were well-fed, and could leave at any time with a purse full of coin. While they liked having wool tunics and leather boots, most of them stayed because they got to burn slaver ships to the waterline. It was his favorite part of the job, too.

Hannibal found Quartermaster Salke standing amidship. With some quickly whispered reassurances, he turned the two Berbers over to the man with instructions to provide them a cabin and anything they needed. Massinissa gave the Gambit and the crew a quick once over and seemed pleased with what she saw. Then she tried to pass Hannibal a leather pouch that jingled as she held it out.

He raised his hands and said, "No, no. That's unnecessary."

She gave him a hard look, but Hannibal continued, "We've been looking for the Whydah Galley for some time. Your information about her whereabouts is payment enough."

He watched the lines around her mouth soften. She stared at her brother for a moment and finally turned back to him and inclined her head in acquiesce. When she lifted her head again, a bright smile had replaced the brief frown. Her brother dipped his own head and they allowed Salke to lead them below deck.

The main deck was clean. Ropes were being coiled, and the crew moved about the ship with purpose. Hannibal made his way to the stern castle, just above the short deck, where the ship's wheel stood. He leaned against the rail, puffing on his pipe, and watched his crew. Safiya came into view below him and took her place before the mast. She looked up toward the stern castle as if she already knew he was ready. Hannibal pulled the pipe from him mouth.

He raised his voice and bellowed, "Weigh anchor!"

Safiya turned to the crew and barked, "Weigh anchor! Prepare to get underway!"

With a practiced ease, the crew of the Gambit jumped to their stations. Within moments, the anchor was raised, the sails were lowered, and they billowed taut, filling with wind. He felt the Gambit surge under his feet. In the meantime, Safiya made her way to the helm. She was standing just behind, and to the right of the helmsman. From that perch she could see most of the main deck.

Hannibal said, "Set your course north, by northwest. Seven knots please. Make for the Canary Islands."

Safiya barked, "Aye, Captain! Helm, make your course north, by northwest."

At her instruction, the helmsman turned the wheel.

Safiya crossed the three paces to the rail of short deck and shouted down to the main deck, "Hoist the main mizzen and make for seven knots!"

"Aye!" echoed back up to her and the crew scrambled across the deck.

He looked on, taking another draw on his pipe, as the main mizzen dropped into place and snapped full of wind. The Gambit picked up speed. Seawater sprayed into the air. His ears filled with the sound of ruffling sails above him and boots thumping across wooden decks below him. He couldn't have stopped broad grin spreading across his face, even if he'd wanted. There was nothing like a stout ship and a brisk wind to sail her by.

He made a few vain attempts at puffing on his pipe. The bitter taste on his tongue let him know the tobacco was burned out. He stepped to the back of the stern caste and emptied it over the rail. The water below churned as the Gambit cut through it. He could tell they were nearly at speed just by the feel of the deck beneath his feet.

Over his shoulder, the coastline of Alhamara began to recede in the distance. It thinned into a fine line before, finally, disappearing altogether as he watched. Soon, there was nothing to see but vast stretches of blue water in every direction.

A quick glance down to the main deck assured Hannibal that everything was in order. So, he made his way to the steps and headed down, past the helm.

As he passed it, he said, "Safiya, you have the helm."

She gave him a sharp nod and said, "Aye, aye, Captain."

Hannibal hit the main deck and took a sharp right. He opened the door that led to the rear section, aft, just beneath the stern castle. There were cabins on either side of the narrow hall, which ended at his quarters. He opened the wooden door and stepped inside.

It was the biggest cabin on the ship – a captain's prerogative. His bed sat along the wall, to his right. He'd relieved the captain of the *Queen's Revenge* of the new Queen Anne bed, to his chagrin. It had a dome-shaped, carved head decorated with lions, and footboards, with cabriole legs. He slept like the dead in the thing.

The rear wall of the cabin was also the hull of the ship. Small, square, glass panes, inset in wood, made for a large window. In front of it was one of his prized possessions – a French writing table, made by Charles Cressent in Paris. It was a full four paces long and two wide, made of oak and pine, veneered with satiné rouge and amaranth. The mounts were gilt bronze, and it had a leather top. It was one of the most beautiful pieces of furniture he'd ever seen.

Every now and then, when he captured a slaving ship, there were a few surprises in the cargo hold. It was, undoubtedly, headed to some wealthy man's estate in the colonies. The armchair sitting behind it was Italian, made from rosewood and kingwood, with looping armrests and blue, inset cushions, covered in a finely woven thread. Against the wall, to his left, was a small blue and gold Turkish bed, which he used as a couch. The floor was covered in Persian rugs that had been bound for a sugar plantation in the Caribbean.

Hannibal closed the door behind him and went to his writing table. It was covered in maps. His plotting tools were strewn about it, holding them down like paperweights. He sat down and took a deep breath. It had been a long, but exciting morning. He reached for the crystal decanter perched on the right corner. It contained a lovely Armagnac. He'd relieved the captain of the *Salty Dog* of a dozen bottles he'd hidden in floorboards of his cabin.

It would've cost Hannibal a heavy bag of gold coin to buy such a stash. If Dandy Rand Doggert hadn't been busy swimming for his life, he might have cursed Hannibal. If he'd been better at naval tactics, he might not have lost his ship and his Armagnac.

Hannibal poured a glass of the amber liquid into a heavy crystal glass. It went down smooth as a freshly sanded deck. A warm glow spread across his midsection. He sighed and began sorting through his maps. It only took a moment to find what he was looking for – *The Canary Islands*. After another sip of brandy, he set about looking for an edge.

Hannibal was twirling his steel divider by one of its legs when someone knocked on the door.

He leaned back in his chair and said, "Enter."

The door opened and Safiya stepped in. She closed the door behind her and hopped to attention.

He smiled at his First Lieutenant and said, "As you were, Safiya. How are our guests?"

She relaxed and strolled over to his writing table in that fluid trot he'd recognize across the decks of three ships. She leaned his desk and glanced down at the maps and charts.

Her voice was as calm as the sea without wind or wave. "They're doing well, Captain. The young man keeps to himself, but he's pleasant enough when you speak to him. The woman is as curious as a school of dolphins. She asks twenty questions in a quarter as many minutes. But the crew doesn't mind."

Hannibal took another sip of brandy and nodded.

Good, he thought.

His crew was always well-behaved. Safiya would tolerate nothing less. The last thing any of them wanted was the sharp side of her tongue. She ran a tight ship and did not tolerate fools gladly. He decided to talk shop.

"What's our course and speed?"

Safiya dropped a curt nod and an easy smile as if to say, *ok, shop talk it is.*

23

"Aye, Captain. We're maintaining our heading: North by Northwest. And we're continuing at seven knots. I just checked our speed before coming down. The wind is good, no storms on the horizon, and no ships sighted."

He dropped his divider onto the stack of charts with a soft *clink* and said, "Very well. Now, let's talk about what's to come. Time to get an edge."

That made her eyes light up. She loved it when he got tricky.

Safiya listened intently as Hannibal explained his plan. She pointed to the map a few times, and, unsurprisingly, asked some incredibly insightful questions about her captain's plan. But, once they were finished, she was clear about what needed to be done.

She stepped back from his writing table and asked, "Will that be all Cap'n?"

"Yes, Safiya. That will be all. Continue on our present course until it's time for our first course correction and make for twelve knots."

A fool eating grin was plastered across her face as she gazed at him across the desk.

"Aye, Cap'n. This is going to be fun."

Her attitude was infectious. The door closed softly behind her, and he realized he was grinning too. He poured himself another finger of brandy and stood.

He turned from his desk, leaned on the window inset in the rear hull, and stared at the wake of his ship. It wasn't long before he heard the sound of pounding boots on the deck above. As Hannibal watched the foaming water in the wake of the Gambit, he could feel her pick up speed. Things were going to get dicey. But Hannibal had a crew and a ship he trusted. He just hoped his plan worked.

Several hours passed with him in his cabin. He tried to read only to be drawn to his desk to check and recheck his calculations. Finally, as the sun dipped low in the west, he made his way topside.

When he reached the stern castle, Safiya bellow, "Captain on deck!"

The evening air was brisk, but invigorating. The sound of the sea, as the hull cut through the water, made Hannibal feel alive. He leaned against the forward railing and watched his crew keep the Gambit trim. Safiya was leaning over the side with the *common log*, measuring their speed. She pulled the long rope with large knots, at even intervals, along its length until she had the wooden pie-shaped piece at its end in hand and nodded up at him letting him know they were at twelve knots and holding.

He took a moment to fill his long-stemmed pipe with a fresh bowl of tobacco. Safiya appeared at his side with a long, lit, piece of straw. She covered the bowl with her hand, while holding the flame over the top. Hannibal puffed until the tobacco glowed bright red. She walked to the port side of the ship and tossed the burning straw overboard.

He reached down to the pocket of his vest and tugged on the gold chain hanging there. His watch came free. It had a gold back, impressed with intricate circles. The face was clear glass, revealing the watch's gold-plated inner workings. Clock makers called them *complications* for some reason. One glance told him it was time.

He gave Safiya a single nod. It was going to be a long night.

The Gambit sat about five hundred yards off the shore of *Lanzarote*. The Canary Islands weren't, actually, a single entity. While there were two different provinces, Las Palmas for the western islands, and Tenerife for the eastern, each island had its own *Cabildo Insular*. It also meant each had its own economy and concerns.

The major islands made wine and sugar cane, trading with England and the Americas. But the poorer islands, like Lanzarote, situated at the northern most tip of the islands, were left out of that lucrative trade. Sadly, they'd decided to take part in the slave trade to make up the difference. So, Hannibal brought the Gambit up past the most western point of the island chain, past Valverde, around the tip of La Palma. But he kept her well out at sea.

The Gambit's sails were black, for just such an occasion. They were running dark and quiet. Earlier in the day, he'd plotted their course for maximum coverage of the islands. They moved the Gambit, using dead reckoning, from point to point, searching for any sign of the Whydah Galley. His crew lined the rails of the main deck, spyglasses in hand, scanning the sea.

They wove their way around Gomera, up the coastline from the south, around Tenerife. And quietly, sailed south past Canaria, before swinging east – voices would carry across open water. They took a wide birth around Fuerteventura, staying closer to the African coast, than the eastern shoreline of Puerto del Rosario and Arrecife, and finally ended up north of Lanzarote, just before dawn. Peering south, they found her. The Whydah Galley sat at anchor, just off the shore of Lanzarote. Hannibal set the Gambit, with her port side to the Whydah, guns loaded, upwind from where the pirate ship lay at anchor.

As the sun came up in the east, one of the mates, a charming, young man named Issa, climbed the steps to the stern castle. He brought Hannibal coffee, in a porcelain cup with a matching saucer. The set was white, with blue and green flowers winding their way around the exterior. He thanked the young man, who knuckled his forehead, and returned below deck. Hannibal walked to the rail, on the port side, and took a sip of coffee while he gazed out across the calm, morning sea at the Whydah.

She was a *Carrack* class ship with four masts, built to cross an ocean. She was sturdy and her captain was notorious. Randall *Jolly* Redhook had refitted her to carry both cargo and cannon. The man gave up some of the space he could've used for quartering slaves, if you could call stacking people like cords of wood quartering, in order to better arm his ship.

It worked. The Whydah didn't make the trip to the Americas but spent her time along the Barbary Coast. Hannibal knew what that meant. Redhook made more runs to make up for the smaller numbers in the hold of his ship. But that was all about to change.

Hannibal would have preferred to just sink the Whydah and head for open sea. The likelihood of captured people in the hold stopped him. He had one other reason, which he kept to himself. Any other crew would have questioned his plan, maybe even been on the verge of mutiny. But the crew of the Gambit trusted their captain.

Hannibal took one final sip of his coffee and said, "Safiya, give her a single shot across the bow. Let's get her attention."

Safiya replied, "Aye, Cap'n."

She turned, walked to the rail, and barked, "One shot, across the bow."

Hannibal couldn't see the Quartermaster from where he was standing by the port rail, but he heard the man relay the command. He set his cup down on its saucer just as a loud *boom* echoed from beneath him. Cannon smoke drifted up past the rail, dissipating in the breeze. The sea erupted in a violent explosion of water just past the Whydah Galley. The cannon ball had passed over their main deck before splashing into the sea. He smiled as the deck of the Whydah flailed to hectic life.

He waited a few heartbeats before telling Safiya, "Send the message."

She grinned and said, "Aye, Cap'n."

She relayed his order and a woman standing on the foredeck began signaling the Whydah with a flag in each hand. The message said they were to surrender or be sunk. Hannibal was pretty sure he knew what the answer would be, but he wanted to try. He waited while the crew of the Whydah scrambled to get her anchor up and her sails lowered. He sipped his coffee calmly while he watched.

When the Whydah lurched forward, with her sails filling with wind, Hannibal shouted, "Raise the colors!"

Safiya echoed him. "Raise the colors!"

"Make for seven knots!"

She shouted again. "Make for seven knots!"

The flag of the Gambit shot up the line from the deck, unfurling overhead, as the ship lurched forward. When the flag caught the wind, it snapped taut. Hannibal didn't fly the Jolly Roger. He left that to traditional pirates. The Gambit flew a skull, but one made of shards of various colors, on a field of red. A set of black shackles, broken in the middle, were emblazoned beneath it.

He watched as the Whydah tried to gain speed. She was downwind. Her captain knew they were at a serious disadvantage.

Hannibal barked, "Port-side guns, fire at will. Hard to port! Lay in a pursuit course. Bring us up on her rear."

Redhook hoped he could get to speed in time to be out of range of Hannibal's guns. He shook his head as the Gambit's port guns boomed away with a sharp cracking sound and the smell of gunpower filling the air. The Whydah's main deck exploded along its fore section. It wasn't long before the Gambit was in full pursuit. The Whydah, rather than heading south, along the coastline, made for what appeared to be open sea. But Hannibal knew she was headed straight for Tenerife.

He should have laid down raking fire. Generally, ships were the most vulnerable to attack from the rear. Just like the Gambit, they had large windows in the officer's quarters. Raking fire would run through the ship, lengthwise, from stern to bow, causing maximum damage. But Hannibal was trying to damage the Whydah as little as possible. Cannon fire exploded into the sea to the port side of the Gambit. The Whydah was firing her aft cannons. There were only four cannons in the Gambit's fore, while Redhook likely had as many as six in the Whydah's aft. Hannibal would have to rely on the second part of his plan.

He shouted down to Safiya, who was standing next to the helm, "Keep us outside the range of his cannons!"

Safiya nodded. The Gambit slowed as Safiya gave the helmsman orders. The Whydah stopped firing after several volleys from their aft cannons fell short. Redhook focused his efforts on running.

Hannibal sent for another cup of coffee while he watched the Whydah tack for wind. She was fast. They were making about ten knots. The Gambit could still overtake her, but Redhook wouldn't know that. Man-of-wars, fully outfitted, generally rated for eight to nine knots. The captain of the Whydah would have no idea that the Gambit was only outfitted with half the guns and crew, and that she was sailed by a captain who knew how to get a few extra knots out of his ship.

He let her run. It was a waiting game now. Redhook knew there would be other slaver ships in the Canary Islands, or at least a few Spanish or British Galleons he could call on for assistance. He was running his Carrack full out trying to reach the waters near Tenerife. Even Hannibal knew there were likely other ships offshore there. And even if there weren't, there would certainly be cannon along the shore.

Issa returned with another cup of coffee and a nod. He gave the young man his cup in exchange for the fresh one. He saw the young man, out of the corner of his eye, staring at him just before he left the stern castle. He was measuring his captain. Hannibal chuckled softly to himself. If all went to plan, Issa was going to have a story to tell.

It took another twenty minutes, but the call Hannibal was expecting came down from the crow's nest.

"Sail ho!"

He looked in the direction the crewman was pointing and, sure enough, there was a ship making for the Whydah. Hannibal barked for a mate from the main deck. A young woman came running up the steps. He handed her his cup and saucer and took her spyglass. He raised it to his eye and homed in on the approaching ship. She was already flying her colors.

It was a skeleton, dancing on a field of black. Hannibal smiled. It was the Salamander, captained by Percy *Three-fingered* Vane. It didn't take long before the Whydah began tacking, to come about. Redhook had found his support. He was turning to fight.

Hannibal put down the spyglass and pulled out his pocket watch. He closed his eyes and ran the numbers. He could feel Safiya's eyes on him. It was a sure bet that, nearby, other members of the crew were watching too. He knew what they would see.

Sometimes, he moved his lips while he ran the numbers. He could hear the ticking of the pocket watch in his hand. He could smell the salt water of the sea, as spray leaped into the air. He could hear the snapping of black canvas as the sails of the Gambit played in the wind. But his focus was on the numbers. Wind speed, current, longitude and latitude, all ran through his head. The

Whydah and Salamander would be in range of the Gambit in moments.

Wait, he thought. *Just wait.*

Hannibal's eyes snapped open. "Now!" he shouted down to Safiya.

The Gambit fired seven shots, then three shots, then seven more, in quick succession.

He barked, "Come about! Hard to port!"

Rigging strained and canvas snapped in the wind, as the helmsman made the course-correction. The crew scrambled on the deck and in the rigging, adjusting the sail. The Gambit leaned into the turn. Hannibal held onto the rail and watched her. The sea exploded with cannon fire where the Gambit had just been.

She started to straighten, and Hannibal roared above the noise of the sea and cannon fire, "Starboard cannons, fire!"

The starboard side of the Gambit exploded as she spit out a heavy cannon volley. The Salamander took a direct hit to its fore deck. The Whydah was hit on her starboard side.

Hannibal bellowed into the wind, "Make for twelve knots!"

Cannon fire hit the water all around them. The black sails of the Gambit filled with wind. The cat had become the mouse as the Salamander and Whydah chased the Gambit. He had the aft cannons fire without stopping. And then, as the numbers popped up in his head again, Hannibal lifted the spyglass to his eye and laughed. Given their bearing, he knew he was seeing Las Palmas ahead, on the horizon.

As soon as he saw land, he turned the spyglass south. And there they were.

"Come about!" he shouted. "Come about!"

The helmsman hesitated. Safiya pushed the man aside and spun the wheel herself, yelling up toward the rigging as she did. The Gambit leaned into the sea again. When she was fully turned and heading directly for the Whydah and Salamander, Hannibal had another message sent. When she finished the complex dance of waving flags, the cannon fire stopped. Hannibal slowed the Gambit to just a few knots as the *Wanderer*, *Flying Dragon*, and *Fortune* came alongside.

When he decided to go after the Whydah, he'd sent messages to their captains asking them to meet him at dawn off the coast of Las Palmas. He'd sent three invitations, in the hope that at least one of them would show. He was surprised to see all three, though he shouldn't have been.

The Whydah was the most notorious ship in the Atlantic and a prize catch for any captain looking to fill their hold with treasure. Hannibal's reputation for filling his own likely helped entice them to join the hunt but the Whydah's reputation had done most of the work. The Salamander was an added bonus.

The Salamander and Whydah signaled surrender. Their captains weren't fools. They'd done the calculations. They knew the reputations of the ships arrayed against them and were certain that continuing to fight would end in being sunk to the bottom of the sea. They were likely hoping for parlay – maybe that a payoff would set them free with their ships intact.

It was only when Hannibal boarded the Whydah that he realized her crew had mutinied. Randall Redhook was trussed up, before the mast, like a pig for slaughter. In short order, Hannibal had freed the one hundred men and women chained below deck and his crew had looted the Whydah's hold. They pulled the ship close enough to the shore of Las Palmas and let the Whydah's crew swim ashore. Hannibal had Redhook placed in his brig on the Gambit and set the Whydah on fire. He let the Wanderer, Flying Dragon, and Fortune raid the Salamander as their prize.

Hannibal stood on the stern castle of the Gambit and watched the Whydah burn to the waterline. Safiya oversaw dividing the spoils from the Whydah's hold among the crew. Hannibal had retrieved the only thing he'd wanted from the Whydah himself, while its crew was being thrown overboard. He flipped through the pages of the Whydah's slave ledger, slowly, with trembling finger, until he came to his father's name.

THE MESSIAH CURSE

T he dream was always the same. It began with the impertinence of a rising street covered in uneven, cobbled stone, followed by the intemperance of its aimless winding as it passed between two and three-story houses, which were huddled together as if they were seeking comfort from one another.

A vibrant throng of angry voices emanated from the mob lining the street. Every texture of human emotion was in the air as the mob surged and receded around a stooped figure like water as the tide was coming in. Antipathy resounded above all the others. The hostility was so palpable, he could taste it. It was all shoving, and fists in the air, mixed with curses and spiting. What did anger taste like? Burnt toast? Sour milk?

He was weak—a shadow of a man, easily swayed by the will of others. So, he joined in. The air was hot with the smell of cheap wine. The stale odor of old sweat mixed with fear.

What does fear smell like? The coppery scent of blood? A sharp, twinge of lemon peel in the nose? It was clear, upon hindsight, that the thick cloud of hostility had been borne of fear, not anger.

It had not been remotely justified. But human beings feared what they did not understand and despised even more those who held up a mirror to their ugliness. Out of it all, though, those penetrating brown eyes haunted him the most.

They pierced him to his core, like a hot knife inserted between his ribs and plunged into his heart. He felt naked. Not the kind were one's clothes sat in a haphazard bundle on the floor.

No, it was the kind of naked, where all your secrets are laid bare. The taunts he was shouting suddenly caught in his throat. And then, the beleaguered man spoke.

Azriel jerked upright in bed, flinging his blanket off in a confusion of pillows and sheets as he reached for something that wasn't there. It took him a moment to realize that it was just a dream.

No matter how many times it happened, he could never remember that it was a dream. It was as if he had fallen through time and landed in his bed. His heart raced in his chest. Sweat clung to him like an oil slick on the ocean's surface.

Breathe, he told himself. *Just breathe.*

The dream never changed. The moment hunted him, while he slept, like a hungry wolf in a familiar forest he could not escape. He slid to the edge of the bed, dangled his legs over the edge, and placed his feet on the thick, white rug below them.

In, hold, and out—was how he breathed for the next few minutes until his heart rate slowed. He reached over to the white nightstand, grabbed his cell phone, and touched the screen. When it glowed to soft-white life, he was able to see the number five glaring back at him. It was way too early, but there was never any going back to sleep after the dream. He rubbed his hands over his face and decided to get up.

Azriel crossed the bedroom to the bathroom and turned on the shower. White striations, swirled through the gray tile behind the full-length, glass door. Shower jets were imbedded in the ceiling and walls creating a cross-stream of spraying water.

He set it to a heavy mist before stepping in. When he had the place remodeled, an instant water heater was installed, so there was no need to wait. He placed his hands on the wall and let the steaming water wash the last echoes of the dream away along with the night sweat. He wasn't sure how long he stood there, but, finally, he reached for soap and a washcloth.

After cleaning up, he threw on a white tee and blue, stripped, pajama pants. He changed the sheets and made his bed before heading downstairs. As he drifted down the stairs, he slid his hand across a clean-shaven head and jaw.

He shaved at night, before bed, so his mornings were less pre-occupied with personal grooming. The kitchen-dining-living room was a single, large, open area demarcated by how the furniture was arranged. The kitchen and dining area were separated by a long, wide, island with a white marble top, streaked through with gray lines. The marble sat on a stainless-steel body filled with drawers. The rest of the kitchen matched the aesthetic of the island – *modern chic.*

By the time Azriel began fixing breakfast the sun was creeping through the floor-to-ceiling windows lining the right wall. The golden light created a soft, warm glow in the living room. He cut a

37

thick piece of crusty ciabatta bread, sliced an avocado, and added two eggs over medium to the rectangular plate with rounded edges. He sprinkled the eggs with a shaved parmesan that was aged for ten years, a bit of extra-virgin olive oil, and a dash of salt and pepper.

The most expensive thing in his kitchen was his espresso machine. It had a double boiler, rotary pump, digital thermostat, pressure gauges, spring-loaded steam and water valves, as well as insulated steam and hot water wands.

It was a work of art shape from stainless steel. But even the best espresso machine is an utter waste without a machine capable of grinding your espresso beans properly. His sat on the white, marble counter beside the espresso machine, right between the sink and the stainless-steel refrigerator.

The grinder cost nearly as much as the espresso machine. He ground his fresh, roasted beans with the sound of spinning burrs churning inside the grinder. Next, he tamped the grounds down in the shining basket of the portafilter, before twisting the portafilter into place inside the ring of the head of the espresso machine.

It was an involved ritual. Grabbing the stainless- steel pitcher, which had been sitting in the refrigerator to keep it cold, he turned on the pump on the espresso machine until a thin stream of whistling steam came racing out of the long, thin steel steam arm. Soon, he had worked the steam into the milk until he had a thick micro-foam.

Azriel lifted the lever that started the brew-cycle and watched as the thin, creamy lines of dark-brown espresso poured out into the waiting cup below. Mixing the espresso with the sugar he spooned into the cup, he poured in the micro-foam mixed with steamed milk until the cup was full. With his coffee made, he placed the cup on its saucer, grabbed his plate, and walked over to the dining table.

Sometimes he ate with the television on, but he'd recently stopped watching the news. The Americans had elected a buffoon as their new chief executive, and he did not care to watch the circus. While it wasn't the first time, he'd witnessed someone utterly unqualified being given authority, this time seemed more egregious than most.

This morning, like most mornings following the dream, he ate with soft music playing in the background. Tapping a few virtual buttons on his cellphone, he elicited sounds from the wireless speakers installed throughout his home. As Marvin Gaye crooned, *I come up hard baby, but now I'm cool,* and *Trouble Man* echoed through the room, Azriel focused his attention on how crusty the thick bread was, and how the rich olive oil mixed with bits of shaved parmesan complimented the buttery flavor of the avocado slices mingling with the soft-cooked egg.

He washed it all down with the caramelly-sweet intoxication of the espresso mixed with foamy, steamed milk. Slowly, the haunting memory of his recurring nightmare faded, even as the glow of the early morning sunlight flooded in brightening everything around him. By the time he was staring at the bottom of his empty cup, coated with the last dregs of brown espresso crema and white, milk foam, he was ready to get dressed and start the day in earnest.

Just like traveling over land was so much faster—you could go from one side of the world to the other in hours rather than months—coffee tasted better, and dentistry was exponentially superior, clothes were also made better. It was somewhere between late fall and early winter in Atlanta.

The air was cool, though not yet cold. Even though it was Saturday, he still had a meeting. Azriel went back upstairs and slipped into black, fitted jeans, a black polo, and black, dress boots. He slid a black, leather belt with a small silver buckle, through his

39

pant loops and the leather loops of a black holster tucked into his pants, just behind his right hip. Then, he grabbed his *Sacramentals*.

The first one lay in an antique, Persian box sitting on his white dresser. It had been called a *Gentleman's Box* when he first began using it to store his weapon. The box was brown wood with middle eastern inlay in mother of pearl and Syrian marquetry.

It was covered in geometric designs of Moorish origins. It was a work of art and nearly two-hundred years old. Azriel smiled as he ran his hand over its carved surface. He lifted the lid and pulled out the modified Wilson Combat 1911 laying on a padded bed of purple silk.

The scrollwork running along the slide and down the frame was in a language no longer spoken by men. Finding the materials for the ceremony that would change it from a simple firearm to a metaphysical weapon had been difficult. Locating a mystic for the ceremony was an even more arduous proposition, but ultimately worth it. Though, he would not be going back to the Sahara anytime soon.

For some reason, he was crazy enough to follow a Benine Voodoo Priestess into the *Eye of Africa*, deep in the heart of the Sahara, at midnight. It was something he would never forget. While golden grains of sand howled around him like a whirlwind, Azriel was comforted by the fact that he had seen things that would turn a hardened soldier's hair white.

But what that woman did, standing in the middle of the blue spiral known as the *Richat Structure* by astronauts who could see the formation from space, changed his understanding of darkness. When she was done, she handed the black gun back to him, with smoke rising off it, covered in ancient runes, which looked like decorative embellishments if you didn't look too closely.

According to her, the kind of bullets no longer mattered. Where he had once relied on blessed bullets that had been conjured over, he could now fire any ammunition that was the right caliber for the gun, and it would do the job.

Holding it in his right hand, he pressed the release, ejecting the magazine into his left. He checked to see that it was full of the .45 ACP tactical rounds he preferred, before sliding it back in place with a solid *click*.

The barrel made a nearly identical sound when he pulled it back and released it, feeding a round into the chamber. With it loaded, he thumbed the safety on, and tucked the gun into the holster strapped on at five o'clock, just behind his right hip. Behind his left hip, at eight o'clock, he snapped on two, black, leather, magazine pouches and slid a seven-round magazine into each.

After lowering the lid on the box, he reflexively checked to make sure the small, gold, Akkadian medallion still hung around his neck. It was inscribed with the eight-pointed star of Anunnaki. Assured that it was still hanging there, he opened the second box sitting on his dresser and pulled out a black, Rolex submariner, along with the large, gold ring sitting next to it.

The ring was engraved with the Eye of Heru, bound between a falcon and a serpent. He slipped it on his left-hand ring finger before securing the watch on his left wrist. Assured in the comfort provided by the Sacramentals being on his person, Azriel threw on his leather jacket, grabbed his cellphone and wallet, and made his way downstairs.Once he hit the main floor, he walked through the living room over to the door in the far wall. He pulled open the door to the garage and step through it.

During the renovation, he decided to keep the delivery bay of the business that was once located on the lot in order to turn it into a garage. Closing the door behind, to what was once an office, he strolled past his weights, benches, treadmill, and heavy bag to where his car was parked.

He glanced over at his café racer, but then decided to take the car. There was a chance of rain later in the day. Riding a motorcycle in the rain was not his idea of a pleasant experience.

A turn of the key and the seven-hundred horsepower, Edelbrock-supercharged, Coyote crate engine in his nineteen sixty-six mustang Fastback roared to life. The car was rebuilt by a small outfit in Wisconsin, which specialized in customized restoration. It was a thing of beauty.

The stance was lower and more aggressive than its stock alternative. The paint scheme was a unique blue-gray for the body with a black hood, roof, and grill. Bits of red adorned it, here and there, as a highlight. Large wheels with satin-black rims, red brake calipers, and matching red rotors, finished the look.

Azriel clicked the garage opener hanging on the visor and revved the engine while the door slowly rose. The garage opened onto the back of his home. Once he pulled out, he clicked the opener, so the garage door closed behind him. By the time it had, he was already turning onto Atlanta Road. The area was a semi-warehouse district halfway between downtown Atlanta and Vinings.

There were two reasons he chose to renovate a property in the area rather than buying something already finished. It was sparsely populated and only subject to traffic for a brief span in the late afternoon. The rest of the time it was fairly private and out of the way. He liked his privacy.

It was also safer for other people for him to live in a less populated area. Driving down Atlanta Road, he passed the headquarters for the Atlanta Ballet on his left. There was also a Pepsi bottling facility, several non-descript small businesses, two trucking companies, and a strip club.

Had he turned left onto Atlanta Road instead of right, he would have passed a defunct gas station turned mini-mart, a couple of self-storage companies, and a cemetery on the corner. He crossed a small bridge before turning left onto Marietta. The small, winding backroad took him to his destination.

As he drove down Marietta road's small hill, he could see the spires of downtown Atlanta in the distance. To his immediate left, stood new luxury apartments. They were well-located but overpriced—though he would not have minded being able to leave his home, cross one street, and walk into a coffee shop, or any of the several restaurants in the immediate vicinity.

The area was very much like Midtown but without the hassle. Azriel parked on the street, exited his car, and stepped onto the sidewalk. The air carried a hint of winter. Today was the first day of fall where the temperature dropped into the low sixties.

He didn't mind. In fact, Azriel enjoyed being able to wear jackets, coats, and sweaters. Colorful leaves crunched under his boot as he strolled into the tiny parking lot that fronted Octane Coffee Bar. He passed the small, bespoke, men's shop next door, called Thomas Wages, and stepped through the propped-open door to the coffee shop's interior.

The coffee bar layout opened up to the right of the door, but Azriel continued walking straight ahead. Entering the short hallway to the left of the register, he stepped past the two bathrooms on his right, and walked toward the blank wall dead ahead.

To mortals that's exactly what it was—a blank wall. But, to Azriel, or any of the others like him, it was much more. There were many names for those who would be able to see a door that remained invisible to mortals. They were called the Fallen, the Fairie, Extramundane, Fae, or even Immortals—though many were not, in fact, immortal.

Some knew them as Shadowwalkers, or the Undying – even, the Cursed. Many, over the centuries, had simply called them monsters. Most of the names were reductive or insufficient to describe everything, or everyone, that lurked in the shadows, filled the books of lore, haunted the dreams of men, or went bump in the night. The only one Azriel ever got comfortable being called was the *Long-lived*.

There it stood, at the end of the small hallway nearly everyone saw as the way to the restrooms. The door was simple wood, but painted red, with a gold sigil in the shape of the sign for infinity. They all looked the same. Azriel turned the golden knob, pulled the door open, and entered.

As he was closing it behind him, a young woman turned into the hallway, presumably heading for a bathroom. Her face went from startled to alarmed as it dawned on her that she had never seen the door Azriel was walking through. He smiled at her and closed it behind him. He knew what would happen next.

The giant, red ruby, embedded over the door, would fill the hallway with a flash of light invisible to the naked eye. He did not have to open the door again to know that the door, and the sight of him holding it open, had been erased from the woman's memory. At that very moment, she was likely standing in the hallway wondering why was there before suddenly remembering she was on her way to the bathroom.

Azriel made his way down the hidden stairwell behind the red door. Three flights down and he was walking into a very different bar, but one with the same name. It had become easier, over time, to simply call the *Hidden Places* by the same names as their fronts.

The Octane was his favorite haunt. Like the one above it, it served coffee, other drinks, and food. It also served more exotic forms of nourishment meant for the various kinds of beings who lived in the *Otherworld*—the one that existed behind the world of mortals—the one right in front of them, which they could not see.

The other difference between this Octane, and the one above, meant for mortals, was a much more luxurious décor. Instead of small café tables that wobbled, and hard, wooden chairs, there were wide booths with oversized, leather couches, heavy, wood tables with large, plush armchairs, and discreet sections hidden behind diaphanous curtains. The floor was covered in a lush, blood-red carpet. The lighting was warm, but dim. And there was a long bar with red, leather sides and a black, marble top.

It was early, so it was no surprise that there was no one else in the main room. Azriel was early for his meeting, so he grabbed his favorite table on the far side of the cafe. It put his back against the wall and gave him clear sight lines of the entire bar. Epiphanus approached the table with a double espresso.

Azriel smiled and nodded at the tall, thin man. He was pale, pleasant, but quiet. He wore blue velvet pants, and a powder-blue shirt with Italian cuffs. A quick glance down revealed brown, wingtip brogues, with a two-tone, brown patina stain. A white hand towel hung neatly folded over his forearm. His voice was much deeper than might have been expected.

He rumbled, "Good morning, Wanderer. I made your usual doppio. Can I get you anything else?"

Azriel replied, "Good morning, Ep. The chessboard?"

With a smirk, Epiphanus sat the cup and saucer down in front of Azriel. He returned to the bar and retrieved a chessboard with a game in progress. It was beautifully carved wood in silver, brown, and gray.

The spaces alternated between heavily carved blue, gray, and brown squares and plain, brown ones. The pieces were light-gray and brown on one side and tan and gray on the other. Their weighted wood was sculpted to match the board. All in all, it was a lovely board, though it was nothing like the cast-iron antique set he had at home.

His was one of five sets made in Germany in 1850 by the master craftsman Gerhardt Klausman, shortly after the failed 1848

45

March Revolution, and just as Prussia was entering the industrial revolution before Bismarck achieved unification in 1871. The Klausman had tall, slender, delicately rendered pieces that were fashioned from heavy, cast-iron—an anachronism the artisan had prided himself on.

The man was a genius with his hands and was gifted with a high tolerance for dark, German beer. The pieces matched the chest table they came with. Also made of heavy iron, the top was round, with the square board inset – both heavily engraved with scrollwork in brown, gray, burgundy, and gold. Azriel had spent countless hours sitting at that table working on his game.

The chest board showed the standing match between Azriel and Epiphanus. They were a full year in. Today, it was his turn to move.

Epiphanus thought he was going to put Azriel in check in twelve moves, and mate shortly thereafter. But Azriel was running a long con on him. The man thought he was on the verge of victory. Only, when Azriel finally *castled,* it would become clear to Epiphanus that he was on the verge of losing – in three moves.

As Epiphanus carefully sat the chessboard down on the table in front of him, with no attempt to hide a smug grin, Azriel schooled his own features. He narrowed his eyes, while pressing his lips firmly together as though troubled by what the board was showing him.

In the next hour, he sipped espresso, made it look like he was trying out different moves in his head, and waited for his meeting. Soon enough, Hopscotch McGavin slid into the chair across from him like a slimy snake slithering through high grass.

There were few men Azriel knew as odd, or shifty, as Hopscotch. He put the shade in shady. The scrawny man earned the nickname Hopscotch by always being on the move from one place to the next – and always being willing to jump sides at the first sign of trouble, or after being paid to do so.

Dirty-blonde hair fell into his blue eyes as he scratched at his thick beard. The suit was an expensive British label in jort-blue with a soft sheen. The jacket was cut high at the waist with a single button, peak lapels, and a single vent up the back.

The black shirt looked like Italian silk patterned with blue, silver, white, and red flowers. It had a wide, spread collar, French cuffs without cufflinks, and was buttoned to the neck without a tie. He was also wearing black, double monkstrap, leather boots. A white-gold, diamond encrusted, Audemars Piguet Chronograph hung loosely on his wrist, like it was still the nineties. For all of that, he smelled like cheap cologne.

Hopscotch smiled lazily at Azriel and ordered a drink; it was Grey Goose on the rocks. The smell told him that the man was more than a few drinks into the day. Azriel put up with Hopscotch because the man could get just about anything you wanted for the right price. You just had to remember never to turn your back on him, especially when money was changing hands.

Sliding the chest set over, out of the way, he said, "Hello, Hopscotch. I'm glad you could make it. You look like you're in the middle of something. Are you in the middle of something, Hop?"

Hopscotch unbuttoned his jacket, shaking his head a little too much, as his drink arrived.

He downed it in one swallow, waving his free hand erratically, and said, "No, no, no. Not at all, Wanderer. Everything is copasetic."

Azriel tried not to roll his eyes. Hopscotch liked slang that was way past its use-by date. He thought it made him sound hip— *retrograde*, he called it, as if it was a fashion forward movement, or avant-garde.

GERALD L. COLEMAN

The man grinned widely, leaned back in his chair, and
continued, "Azriel Stone. So, how are you, my guy? Looking good
as usual. You still driving that pristine-ass mustang? I keep telling
you I can get you a hundred thou' easy, maybe more?"

Azriel shook his head, "How many times do I have to tell you,
Hop. The car is not for sale. Now, do you have what I asked you
for?"

The slender man leaned forward, reached inside his suit jacket
to the small of his back, and produced a sheathed knife.

He laid it on the table and said, "Tah. Dah. Motherfucker."

Then he smiled, indicating the knife with both hands, like an
infomercial salesman. It was a Persian Caucasian qama, also known
as a double-edged dagger, from the 18th century.

It had a broad, straight blade that was embellished with lotus
palmettes, scrolling lines, and golden clouds giving the steel a black
sheen. The hilt and wood scabbard were covered in similar
ornamentations.

It once belonged to a powerful Mazdayasna Magi, who fought
a dozen Shades at the ruins of the Zoroastrian temple of *Pir-e-
Narak* near Yazd, and lived to tell about it. The dagger had been
old even then. Azriel heard whispers about it for years but felt no
need to seek it out until he lost his last dagger fighting a
Shadowwalker in Seville, Spain the month before. He needed a
replacement, so he put Hopscotch on the trail of it. The man had
actually produced.

Azriel said, "How much, Hop."

Hopscotch pulled his chair closer, wet his lips, leaned over the
table, and was about to launch into his sales pitch when Azriel held
up his hand and interrupted.

"No."

Shaking his head, he continued, "No, Hop, don't even try it.
Listen to me. You have one shot to make this deal. I'm not going

to haggle with you. I have two other feelers out on similar artifacts, so I don't have to have this one. Here's what we're going to do. You're going to give me a number – one number. And I'll either pay it, or I'll get up, leave, and buy one of the other artifacts that I have no doubt are on the way. I suggest you make it a good number."

Hopscotch clamped his mouth shut, swallowing whatever bullshit he had been about to spit. Narrowing his eyes, he stared at Azriel, no doubt trying to ascertain whether he was bluffing.

After a moment, he swallowed hard again, waved his hands over the table like a magician doing a reveal or a maid indicating the table was clean, and said, "Thirty thousand."

Azriel looked at the dagger sitting on the table again.

He stared at it for a moment, looked back up at Hopscotch, and said, "Sold."

He reached into his leather jacket, pulled out an orange envelope, and removed three stacks of bills. Sliding the envelope back into his jacket pocket, he pushed the money over to Hopscotch and grabbed the dagger.

"Nice doing business with you, Hop. You take care of yourself."

Without waiting to hear the man's response, Azriel headed for the door. As he passed the bar, he slid Epiphanus a ten for the espresso. The man flashed him a salute with two fingers before he went back to wiping off the bar. Soon, Azriel was back on the street headed for his car. His stomach growled when he reached the driver's side door, so he decided to head over to Café Intermezzo in Midtown for lunch.

The sun was up, and the weather was still right between warm and cool, but it was pleasant. Atlanta was alive with its usual bustling ambivalence. Thankfully, Café Intermezzo was only ten minutes away without the need to get on a highway or interstate.

It was Saturday, so he could avoid the normal downtown traffic. He pulled out onto Marietta, made a left onto Northside, and a right onto 10th. When he reached Peachtree, eight minutes later, he turned left. One block up and he was parking.

Café intermezzo was once located further down Peachtree toward Lenox mall. Azriel had enjoyed that location. In his mind, it had more character. Now, the quaint bistro's new location was a bright, glitzy spot with a lovely patio, tucked into the base of one of the many nondescript buildings closer to the center of Midtown.

He still missed the old place, with its dark corners, high tables, and a bar that looked like something out of the nineteen-twenties. Nevertheless, the food was still delicious. He sat in the main room by the wall of windows and ordered a Caesar salad, Viennese Salmon, and a decadently sweet piece of cheesecake covered in mixed-berries and offset with a swirling dollop of whip cream on top. It left him satiated in the best way.

The rest of the day was all errands. He stopped at his UPS post office box to retrieve some mail and a few packages, including some new cigars and roasted espresso beans.

He did not receive mail at home. Its location in a commercial district, along with not receiving mail there, was part of keeping his whereabouts hidden. After leaving the UPS store in midtown, he stopped in Channing Valley at Sid Mashburn.

A text had informed him that the hand-tailored suits he ordered were ready. While he was there, he grabbed a pair of green foilage, diadora sneakers, which looked a bit like a pair of seventies-era nike cortez.

It was on his way back to the car that he noticed the black Mercedes. Putting the three suit bags and the sneakers in his trunk, Azriel tried to remember if he had seen the car earlier. Sid Mashburn was located in a kind of warehouse-style building on the second floor.

Its blue walls and dark gray awnings stood out against the painted, white, brick walls of the rest of the building. The parking area fronted the entire lot. And though there were other specialty shops in the complex, it was situated in such a way that it was difficult to be inconspicuous.

With no other parking available, they had chosen to park in the far-left corner near the street. The tinted windows, the running engine, and the fact that they never got out of the car were all warning signs that set off his senses.

Azriel did not let on. He simply got in his car and pulled off. The sun was going down, so he turned onto Marietta NW and drove the two miles to Five Points. A left on Peachtree, a right on Ellis, took him to Freedom parkway and Ponce De Leon.

Barnett took him to Virginia and he pulled over to park beneath the trees, a few hundred yards from the corner of Virginia and Highland. Sure enough, the black Mercedes cruised by, rolling through the light in order to park further down on Virginia. Azriel got out and made like he was walking to Murphy's for dinner. But then, he turned onto North Highland.

By the time the sun was down, he was walking around the right side of a small, local coffee shop called Press and Grind. It had a small, three-car lot in the front. Azriel walked through it and down the sloped drive on the right side of the building. He walked to the back and waited in the shadows. It was dark, quiet, and out of the line of sight to the sidewalk. It was perfect.

Three, large men in dark suits came lumbering around the corner. When Azriel was sure they were also out of the direct line of sight from the sidewalk, he stepped out of the shadow. They froze. He spoke calmly.

"Let me guess. Hopscotch tipped you that I was going to be at Octane, and you followed me from there."

They did not bother denying it. They were all white men. One was blond, the other two had black hair.

Hired help?

They must have been. They moved like the kind of former soldiers often employed by private security companies. The cheap suits, faux-dress shoes with lugged soles, and ill-fitting overcoats screamed hired muscle.

Azriel knew Hopscotch had been acting odd. He made a mental note to have a nice little chat with the man. He continued, "So, now that we know how you found me, who sent you?"

The blond fellow in the middle spoke up.

"Our employer wants a word with you."

He grinned. "A word? A word concerning what?"

The man replied, "She told us to bring you to her. That is the extent of the information we were given."

Azriel tilted his head, loosening his neck.

Then he said, "I don't think that's going to work out for you. It would be better if you returned to your employer and told her you couldn't find me."

The blond man smirked and said, "Oh, you're coming with us, one way or another."

Just as the blond-haired thug stepped forward, a high, whining sound cut through the evening air. The black-haired goon to the blond fellows right slumped to the ground with a grunt.

When he fell forward, Azriel saw the knife sticking out of his back. Before he could shout a warning to the other two, they were all surrounded by men in black suits. These suits were much nicer. But it was the red cloth tied around the biceps of their left arms that caught Azriel's attention. When he saw it, he immediately thought, *Asmodeus.*

He looked over at the blond man and said, "Run. Now."

The man shook his head and replied, "Sorry, our employer warned us that if they came, we were supposed to protect you."

Before Azriel could say anything more to man, he pulled his gun and fired. His remaining colleague did the same. The black-suited men swarmed around them like an angry, disturbed beehive. The bullets did not seem to affect any of them. The hired henchmen screamed as they were cut to shreds by the black-suited men wielding long, wickedly curved, jewel-encrusted knives.

It wasn't until Azriel slashed one across the chest with his newly purchased knife that they reacted. The man he cut howled in pain as he spun away. The flesh around the cut sizzled. Even as the wounded man backpedaled, Azriel was among them.

He twirled the knife in his hand, darting left and right. At what looked like six feet two or three on average, they were all a couple of inches taller than him – most were even heavier. But, Azriel stabbed, sliced, and cut, running through them like an obstacle course. They shrieked at the wounds inflicted by the ancient dagger. He broke through them, and headed for the street, slipping his dagger back into its sheath in his belt.

As he reached the sidewalk in front of Press and Grind, he heard five shots ring out. His back erupted in fire as three of the gunshots hit him. They spun him around before two more shots hit him in the chest.

Had he not already sheathed his dagger, it would have tumbled from his hand. As he fell, he saw a woman on the sidewalk drop her coffee cup and pull a gun from the holster on her hip. She fired down the drive toward the acolytes. Azriel was out before he hit the ground.

He came awake with a start. It took a moment before Azriel realized he was being rocked gently, back and forth, like a baby in a sleeper. It took another moment to realize that it was the movement of a car. He was laying in the backseat.

He sat up and said, "What is happening?"

The woman driving screamed, swerved the car, and then steered it back into the right lane, barely avoiding the oncoming traffic.

She stared, wide-eyed, at Azriel in the rearview mirror, and said, "What *the* hell?! What. The. Hell. I thought you were dead. Wait, why aren't you dead? You were shot five times. You had no pulse. I checked. You were clearly dead. What the fuck is happening right now?!"

She pulled the car over, slamming on the breaks, and throwing it into park. With a shaky hand, she grabbed onto her gun, but she did not raise it. She just sat in the front staring over the seat at Azriel like he was a ghost.

After a few seconds, her eyes narrowed, and she said, "Goddammit. You better start talking, or I will shoot you again, myself. The men who attacked you disappeared into the night after I put two of them down. When it was over, you were lying on the ground dead. Explain."

Azriel adjusted his shoulders, leaned back into the seat, and held up his hands in surrender.

"Look, I know this all looks odd, but I can explain. You are?"

The woman stared at him hard for another moment before taking her hand off her gun. She flipped open a black leather wallet revealing a shiny, gold badge on one side and a picture with a seal on the other.

She said, "I'm Special Agent in Charge, Teresa Hernandez." Flipping her badge closed with a snap, she just stared at him. Her eyebrows were raised. Her lips were pursed. Everything about her expression said, *explain yourself.*

Azriel said, "It's very nice to meet you, Special Agent in Charge. And let me thank you for your help."

The agent shook her head and said, "Un uh, nope. I was not helping you. I stopped to grab a cup of coffee before heading back to the FBI field office over on Century when, suddenly, I started taking fire. I only saw you after I returned fire and those men in black suits faded into the night like something on fucking Netflix or the Syfy channel. I should still be there to meet the agents who are on their way to investigate the incident, but I needed to get you to a hospital, if for no other reason than to have you declared officially dead before I return to the scene. So, I'm going to ask you again, what the hell just happened, and why aren't you dead? In fact, while you're explaining that I had better get you to the hospital before you do die."

Azriel spoke calmly.

"Agent Hernandez, that won't be necessary. I'm fine."

She blinked.

"What do you mean, you're fine? You took three bullets to the back and two to the chest – specifically to the heart. You should be dead. Now, I'm trying to process why you aren't, and how you're just sitting there like fuck it, I'm good, but you're going to need to give me more than, I'm fine. The hell you are."

He took off his jacket and shirt. He turned around and then back to face her so she could see.

When he did, he heard her say, "What. The. Fuck!? Where are the bullet holes? You had five bullet holes in you. And they were all bleeding. Now all you have is dried blood on you? Un, uh. Nope. I'm not doing this. Not today."

He said, "I understand this is all going to be hard to believe, but if you really want answers, drive me home. I'll explain everything when we get there."

Agent Hernandez stared at him for a while. Azriel saw the moment when curiosity beat out caution. It was a dark twinkle in her eyes. She turned back around and slowly placed her hands on the wheel. They were in a standard, black charger, which likely had government plates.

While gazing out through the windshield onto the street ahead, she said, "Address. And when we get there, you'd better start talking."

Azriel gave her his address. When she balked, he explained that, yes, it was in a commercial district, but it was where he lived. She pulled off into the night as he shrugged back into his bloodstained tee and jacket. The tee-shirt did not bother him.

The three bullet holes in his leather jacket did. It was his favorite. He tried not to think about it as he rode in the backseat. It was not long before they were on his section of Atlanta Road.

She pulled onto the lot, giving his building a visual once-over. She was probably trying to figure out what kind of business it housed. What was once a small parking lot out front was now a simple lawn of close-cut grass. The front door and windows were bricked in to make a solid wall. There was nothing about the front of the building that invited you to enter, and he liked it that way.

"Pull around back, Special Agent."

Hernandez followed the blacktop driveway around to the back, while muttering something about, *in charge,* before parking in front of the garage door. Azriel waited for her to turn off the engine, step out, and open the back door for him.

It was locked like a police car so that anyone in the back seat could not get out on their own. She popped the door open, while looking over his backyard. Her saw her note the landscaping, the tall, manicured hedges and the wooden fence preventing anyone on either side of his property, or behind it, from looking into his yard.

A narrow, cut-rock path wove its way through the manicured bushes, small trees, and flower beds, to a small pavilion covered in matching stone, with iron-wrought chairs, and a table. It was all covered with a white trellis beneath a glass ceiling with iron legs holding it in the air.

Azriel stepped out of the car and said, "If you ask nicely, I'll invite you back to sit over there and have a glass of bourbon with me."

Hernandez chuckled, "I prefer vodka, on the rocks."

He replied, "That can be arranged. My cellar is well-stocked."

She turned from the yard, looked up at him, and said, "Hmph, I have no doubt."

Azriel motioned to the only door in the exterior of the building. "This way, Special Agent Hernandez."

With Hernandez in tow, he made his way to the purple door, covered by a second wrought-iron door. His key opened both, and he ushered her inside. Closing the doors behind him, he flipped on the light switch next to the door and pointed to one of the couches in his living room.

"Make yourself at home while I change." He turned to go, but then stopped and said, "Oh, may I please have my gun and knife back?"

Agent Hernandez looked at his outstretched hand with a quirked eyebrow.

Azriel grinned, smiling wide, and said, "I wasn't the one shooting at you, and we are in my home."

She reached under her burgundy, leather jacket and pulled them out. She tossed him his knife and then his gun. Then, she placed all three of his magazines, and the round that had been in the chamber, on his coffee table.

It did not escape Azriel's notice that while she was tossing him his weapons with her left hand, her right hovered casually near her right hip where her gun hung. A quick glance told him she was carrying a compact Sig Sauer P320.

He nodded toward her gun and said, "I thought the bureau went to Glock 9mm's recently. Why are you carrying a Sig?"

She was looking around his living room and over at his kitchen. He could see her Langley-trained mind cataloguing and assessing.

She continued her mental inventory even as she said, "Well, aren't you perceptive. As a Special Agent in Charge, I have some leeway. Most agents can, if they desire, request to carry a firearm they choose as long as their superiors sign off, and the weapon meets certain criteria. We are still issued the Glock and required to qualify on it. The overwhelming majority carry it. I just prefer my Sig."

Azriel nodded and headed for the stairs. "I'll be right back."

It did not take long for him to find a black tee, pull it on, and return to the living room. When he did, he found Hernandez sitting on the couch facing the door. He had no doubt it was a habit.

He crossed the room and dropped onto the couch on the other side of the coffee table. Once he was comfortable, he produced a small knife he retrieved from his closet.

When he did, he said, "Easy, Special Agent. This is how I explain to you what you saw this evening."

He could see her body shift. On the outside, she appeared calm and relaxed. But he could tell she was ready to move in an instant. He kept the grin off his face and held up the knife with his right hand.

He raised his left hand so that his palm faced her. A slight grimace accompanied the act of drawing the blade across his palm in a straight line. He still felt pain. The feel of the knife cutting into his skin was odd.

Azriel kept his eyes on the woman as her expression changed from puzzled to awe. She watched the wound close up, right before her eyes. Finally, ignoring whatever potential threat she thought he might have posed, she leaped up off the couch, crossed the floor to where he sat, and grabbed his hand.

She ran her finger over the drying blood where the wound had been. Her eyes jumped from his palm to his face and back again.

Her voice was a whisper, as she muttered, "That's not possible." It steadied as she continued, "If I hadn't seen you survive five bullets to the back and chest earlier tonight, I would not believe what I'm seeing right now. Is this a trick? Do you think this is a game!?"

Azriel placed the knife on the coffee table, raised both of his hands and said, "I assure you Special Agent, this is not a game or a parlor trick. You simply stumbled into a world that most mortals live and die never having seen or known about."

He stood up and motioned for her to follow him. First, he stopped at the chessboard sitting next to the window in the living room.

"I was given this chess set by Gerhardt Klausman himself, in 1862, after saving his daughter from what they called an Aushlick. It was a dark thing, set on keeping her in its basement to feed off. It lived on bodily fluid. I killed it and retrieved her. I wouldn't accept his money, so he gifted me one of the five sets he'd made."

Azriel moved on to a stand next to one of the tall bookshelves along the wall. The stand's upper half was a bodice on which hung an old fencing doublet. A sheathed saber leaned against the wall next to it.

He pointed at them both, saying, "These are mementos from my time in the French Army in 1812 under Napoleon." He chuckled. "They came to call me the greatest swordsman in France. I had to prove that on several occasions."

Halfway up one of the other bookcases, he pointed out a six shooter in a glass case. It was a Smith & Wesson, model 3, with a black grip and nickel finish.

His voice dropped a bit as he said, "In 1870, I found my way to Arkansas. I was the first black U.S. Marshal west of the Mississippi. Just like every other time I had moved on to recreate myself and change my identity, before someone realized I wasn't getting any older, I did it in Arkansas. That was one of the times I lost myself in a life. It was hard to leave. I ignore the stories that came out of that time. They are always different from how things really were. In the legend, I'm a white man."

Azriel chuckled to himself again as he moved on to the far wall where a Gustav Klimt painting of black woman in a starry nightgown hung.

"In 1887, when I was in Vienna, I met a young, half-starving art student who'd just finished his studies at the Vienna School of Arts and Crafts known as the *Kunstgewerbeschule*. He was an interesting young man and we talked about art, poetry, and philosophy. Most days I paid for his meal, as he was apt to find me while I ate at a local café." Azriel shook his head at the memory while he stared at the masterpiece and its flaked-gold motif. "Shortly after his death, this arrived with a note from him, thanking me for my friendship, and keeping him from starving."

Hernandez looked at the painting and then over at him and said, "While I'm not an art buff, I've never seen this painting mentioned anywhere. I do know that the last Klimt's that sold at auction went for one hundred and thirty-two million dollars."

Azriel just kept walking without commenting on the worth of the painting. He made his way to a study of sorts at the end of the hallway on the first floor. It was spacious, with more bookshelves, an art deco table-desk with matching leather chair, and high ceilings.

The floor was pale hardwood. A large, Persian rug covered much of the floor and sat under an Eames lounge chair and ottoman set covered in black leather with a walnut, wood shell. He stopped at the katana and matching wakizashi perched on a black stand, covered in purple silk, against the far wall.

They were identical accept in length. The scabbards, called *saya*, were rust-colored with gold medallions painted down their length at equal intervals. The round handguards, or *tsubas,* were golden. The hilts, known as *tsuka*, were wrapped in brown silk revealing the white rayskin covering the hilt beneath the wrap. The cord, called *sageo*, made of heavy silk, like flat rope, was wrapped, intricately, around the upper part of the scabbard. It was white with a pattern of burgundy dots covering it.

"These are from my time in Japan. In 1581, I served under the Hegemon and warlord, Oda Nobunaga. I rose to the rank of samurai. I was the only black man who ever had. As a gift, on the day I attained the title, Lord Nobunaga presented me with this katana and wakizashi. I protected him until the day he died. He was an honorable man. I left Japan and I've never been back."

Azriel turned and directed Hernandez to the set of chairs bracketing a small table in his study.

They sat, and he continued, "I could go on showing you the things I've picked up on my travels or describing the lives I've lived. I keep the mementos because they are the markers of my journey through time. I'm what we call the *Long-lived* – one of the immortals who walk the earth."

Special Agent Hernandez looked at him and then at the Japanese swords.

When she returned her gaze to him, exasperated, she just said, "How?"

Azriel took a deep breath and sighed, before saying, "It's a story of shame. A shame that I've been trying to atone for, for the last two thousand years."

He saw her flinch at the number.

He continued, "Yes, two thousand years, give or take a decade. You see, those of us who are immortal, have come to it in different ways. Vlad was a necromancer. He used dark magic and an agreement with Old Scratch himself to become immortal. More specifically, and this is important – he was made *undead*. Never make a deal with the Scion of hell."

Azriel leaned back in his chair as he warmed to the subject.

"Magnus Salford found an elixir in an ancient cave in Ethiopia while working at an archeological dig. The fool drank it. Galen Verille Du Loc was punished by a Romani Magi after burning the camp she and her traveling tribe set up, in an effort to chase them off his property. He howls at the full moon in regret. And I? My shame is the greatest."

They sat there in silence for a few more heartbeats. Hernandez looked at him like she did not believe a word of it, but then, like she knew it was all true. The sound of glass breaking interrupted them. Azriel was moving before Hernandez knew what was happening.

How had they found him, he wondered?

He stopped halfway to the door of his office and turned around. Hernandez ran right into him. He was running his hands over her before she even realized what was happening. When she opened her mouth, likely to complain about his hands, he showed her the tiny, black tracker – its red dot blinking – he pulled from under the collar of her leather jacket. First, she grimaced, and then she dropped her head forward.

She muttered under her breath, "Are you a rookie?"

The frustrated tone of the question made it clear that it was rhetorical and aimed at herself. She pulled her gun from her holster. Azriel heard the soft click of the safety being removed while he pulled the ancient katana free from its scabbard. Somehow, during whatever scuffle had ensued while he was passed out, one of the acolytes managed to place a tracker on her hoping it would lead them to Azriel. They were right.

He saw the look of disgust on her face. There was no need to rub it in. So, he just shrugged his shoulders at her. Then, with a twirl of the sword in his right hand, he floated down the hallway toward the living room. Azriel knew exactly who he was going to find.

There was no residual smell of an explosive device. There had been no sound prior to the shattering of glass. Given, that his windows were three-and-a-half-inch ballistic glass, it would have taken a tremendous amount of force to break them.

So, when he rounded the corner, with Hernandez covering his left flank, he was not surprised to see Asmodeus sitting in a chair surrounded by glass and twelve of his hulking acolytes. To her credit, Hernandez did not flinch. She just trained her gun on the man in the chair.

Azriel rose from his slight crouch, lowering his sword to his side. He made a show of looking around at the broken glass littering his living room floor.

When he turned back to look at a smug Asmodeus, lounging in the wide, oversized, white, leather chair between the two couches, Azriel simply said, "Really?"

Asmodeus was tall, slim, and wrapped in a black, three-piece suit, tailored to within an inch of its life. A crisp, white, French-cuffed shirt gleamed from under the black wool. A thin, black, silk tie jutted from his neck before curling down under the vest.

Diamonds glittered from the white-gold cufflinks, and the heavy, eighteen-million-dollar Jacob and Company watch on his wrist. He had good taste, even if it was decadent. The watch was known as the billionaire watch and came with two hundred and sixty carats of emerald-cut diamonds. His thin, pale hands boasted manicured fingernails coated with a clear polish that glistened in the soft light.

The black, patent leather oxfords were accented with suede across the uppers where they laced. If he knew Asmodeus, they were Italian—likely Testoni. His black hair was short at the sides, but longer, with a bit of fuss, across the front, and coated with gel. He was old school, so he was clean-shaven.

While he looked like a man of about forty, he was a demon, and one of the oldest of his kind – like a prince in a kingdom of hellspawn. He unbuttoned his jacket, crossed one leg over the other, and smiled a smile that was so full of itself Azriel felt greasy just looking at it.

His voice was twice as slick as his smile.

"Come, come now, my good man. Have a seat. We have so much to discuss."

Azriel looked around at the acolytes. They were Half-men. Men seduced by whatever Asmodues had promised – wealth, power, sex – all the usual enticements – and then given dark power in order to serve their master. Whatever was done to them had changed them, though. They were not demons, but they were not simply men anymore either.

Asmodeus clucked, "Ah, ah, ah. Now, stay calm. I know you're immortal, thanks to that meddlesome freak of nature these glorified monkey's worship. But I don't need to kill you to make you suffer. For example, I could have my acolytes cut you into several pieces and put them in boxes to be buried all over the world. Your head in one place, your arms and legs in another? You get the idea. Now, sit the fuck down!"

Spittle clung to his thin lips as he tried to reign in his temper. Azriel had always had that effect on him.

Azriel said, "Let the woman go, Asmodeus. She's a Special Agent of the FBI. If she goes missing, it will bring all kinds of unwanted attention down on your head. While that might not affect you directly, it will definitely put a crimp in your plans."

Asmodeus looked over at Hernandez as though considering Azriel's request, but before the demon could answer, Hernandez blurted, "I'm not going anywhere. These assholes took a shot at me and planted a tracker on me. You don't do either of those without getting my full attention."

Asmodeus clapped his hands loudly. "Yes, yes! I like her. Well said, Agent Hernandez."

Hernandez barked, "That's Special Agent in Charge, to you."

Asmodeus leaned forward in the chair, cackling with a giddiness Azriel did not like one bit. He replied, "Oh, I really, really like her. You know, Azriel, after you and I settle a few things, I'm going to have a little bit of fun with *Special Agent in Charge* Hernandez." He looked at Hernandez like she was a fresh meal placed on the table in front of him and said, "Te voy a dar una noche que nunca te vas a olvidar, eh chica."

Hernandez blanched, and swallowed hard, but her gun did not waiver. Her only response was to turn up her lip in revulsion. Azriel's jaw clenched, and his hand tightened on the hilt of his sword.

Asmodeus turned back to him and said, "Now, where were we? Oh, yes. We were about to discuss that item you stole from me in Mesopotamia. And how no one steals from me and gets away with it. How long has it been? Three hundred years? You've been a hard man to find. I especially want to know what little totem or trick you've been using to keep yourself hidden from me. I actually had to break down and use the conventional means these walking apes use to find each other. It took forever. And low and behold, you're hiding in Atlanta of all places."

Asmodeus stood up and continued, "Well, let's get to it, shall we? Acolytes, take the woman to the car and restrain Azriel."

Everything in the room slowed down. The air got heavy. It only took a second for Azriel to realize it was not a mental trick borne out of being in a high-pressure situation. It was real. He went to raise his sword, but his hand moved like it weighed a ton.

Three of the acolytes slowly burst into green flames like a movie scene running in slow motion. Three more went flying through the air at what must have been an inch a second. In the middle of it all, a woman came strolling through the broken window behind them.

She was tall, with thick braids of black hair woven close to her scalp and falling down her back to her waist. Her skin was dark brown. She had a small ring of gold medallions strung across her forehead on a chain like a tiara.

Her full lips were painted black. High cheek bones, and a strong chin, complemented big brown eyes, and a medium-sized nose. She was perfect. Her arms and legs were muscular without being bulky.

The gown was sheer, with fitted sleeves, and a plunging neckline. It hugged her body and split up the front so that it revealed her legs up to her thighs as she walked. The split skirt was so long it trailed the ground behind her. The sleeves, chest, bodice, and skirt were covered in red, flowery embroidery.

She was perched on four-inch heels. The shoes had a wide strap around the ankle, and one across the front of her foot, with a gold buckle on the end, showing toes painted with the same black polish as coated her long fingernails. A gold choker encircled her neck, glistening with diamonds and rubies, matching a thick bracelet, and several rings on her fingers.

Her lithe fingers were adorned with long, armor rings, complemented by thinner rings nestled above and below her knuckles. When she reached the center of the room everything sped back up to normal speed. The acolytes on fire dissolved into small heaps of ash. The three that were drifting through the air, slammed into the wall and then dropped to the floor with a loud crack.

Freed from the effects of whatever had slowed them, one of Asmodeus' acolytes rushed the woman. He was large, burly, and a full foot taller than her. But she just reached out and grabbed him by the neck as he reached for her, hoisting him into the air like she was picking up her car keys.

She watched him kick and choke as she held him a few feet off the ground and squeezed. When he stopped moving, she dropped him like he was an empty coffee cup being thrown into a garbage can – his face was purple, his tongue hung out of his mouth. As he hit the ground, she tipped over the broken glass, crossing the room to where Azriel was now standing. It was like watching a model on a Paris Fashion Week runway. She was glorious.

Standing on those heels she was just as tall as he was. When she reached him, she grabbed the sides of his face in her hands and kissed him on the lips like a long, lost lover. When she finished, she leaned back, looked at his face, and rubbed her lipstick off his lips with her right thumb.

Then, she smiled at him with perfect, white teeth, and said, "Hello, darling. How are you? You've been a very naughty boy. You know I've been looking for you. Why did you run away from my men? I know they look pedestrian, but that old saying is still true—good help is hard to find."

She glanced around the room at Asmodeus' acolytes and continued, "Besides, you know I'm not really into henchmen. It's so—'I want to rule the world-ish.' And I have more important things to do with my time."

Azriel cleared his throat before replying, "Hello, Lilith. It's good to see you, especially under these circumstances. But I didn't go with your hired thugs because I haven't changed my mind since the last time we spoke."

Lilith straightened herself. Rising to her full height, she put her hands on her hips, and said, "Hmph."

Then, she waved away what Azriel had just said, like it never happened. Turning to look at Hernandez, she spoke with a strong undercurrent of displeasure in her voice.

"Don't be rude, lover. Introduce me to your friend."

He said, "Lilith, this is Special Agent in Charge, Teresa Hernandez. Agent Hernandez, this is Lilith."

Lilith stepped over to Hernandez and stuck out her hand, with a wicked smile on her face. Hernandez glanced over at Azriel and then back at her. With a half-smile painting her own face, she lowered her gun before reaching out to shake Lilith's hand. When Lilith released the woman's hand after pumping her arm a few times, she said, "And what designs, may I ask, do you have on this handsome immortal?"

Hernandez's mouth fell open. She looked like she was stuck. Lilith said, "Oh, don't be shy, my dear. I understand. He's a lovely piece of yum-yum and he plays hard to get."

Before Hernandez could collect her wits enough to respond, Lilith was already turning to face Asmodeus. "Take a moment to get yourself together Special Agent in Charge, we have other things to deal with in the meantime."

Azriel had never seen Asmodeus look like he wanted to crawl under a rock. The demon looked around as if he was contemplating running, or at least trying too. Instead, he quickly dropped to a knee.

His voice was full of reverence as he said, "My Lady, it is an honor to be in your presence. Please understand that I mean no disrespect, but I have business with the Wanderer."

Hernandez blurted out, "Wait, she's the Lilith from the bible. The first wife of Adam, before Eve?"

The lights dimmed. Lilith moved faster than even Azriel could see. In a blink, she was back in Hernandez' face, but this time she was so close that only a hairsbreadth separated them. Lilith's mouth opened in an inhuman shriek of rage. For the first time, her fangs were visible. Hernandez had closed her eyes as if she was waiting for the end to come at any second. Her hands trembled as they clutched her gun in a tight grip at her waist.

Azriel spoke calmly as Lilith hovered there.

"No, Agent Hernandez. Most everything written about Lilith was written by men interested in the subjugation of women. She became the embodiment of the hysterical, evil woman, the mother of demons, who needed to be controlled. Rather than portray her in her true light, as the equal of men, they painted her as a rebellious spirit – a warning to other women through the ages to stay in their place."

As he spoke, he slowly moved over to where Lilith stood in front of Hernandez.

"The truth is, she was the first creation. A creature of celestial beauty and power. A being of light, meant as a guardian of the creatures that were to come after her. Men rejected that protection. And so, she left them to their downfall and destruction."

Lilith turned her head to look at Azriel and said, "Flatterer."

He smiled at her, took her hand, and twirled her as if they were dancing. The light in the room brightened, and he swayed back and forth with her until she giggled like a little girl.

He looked in her eyes and said, "You are the most beautiful woman I have ever known."

Lilith stopped and pushed him back saying, "Don't worry, I'm not going to hurt your little Special Agent."

Turning her attention back to Asmodeus, who had begun to quietly tip out through the broken window, she clucked her tongue and said, "Ah, ah, ah. Where do you think you're going?"

Asmodeus stopped and turned back to face her. "My Lady, I thought I would leave you to your business."

Lilith waved a hand, and the rest of Asmodeus' acolytes went up in green flames. The howls were blood curdling, and the smell was awful. In seconds, they were ash. Asmodeus' shoulders slumped, but his eyes narrowed.

Lilith said, "Don't worry, I'm not going to interfere with what you came here to do. I'm just making it a fair fight."

Azriel was moving even as Lilith finished. The woman's motives had always been difficult to discern. You could never really know what she was going to do until she did it. He threw the sword at the demon as he leaped over the table. Asmodeus batted it out of the way. But, before he could do anything else, Azriel was on him.

He grabbed him by his neck with both hands and said, "Emesza Ka Procume!"

Asmodeus screamed as his neck burned where Azriel's hands encircled it. He hit Azriel with a backhand blow that sent him flying over the couch. Azriel hit the ground hard and rolled up to his feet in a blink.

As he got to his feet, Asmodeus reached out a hand toward him. A burst of red light engulfed Azriel, but quickly faded. Lilith laughed out loud. Azriel felt his necklace warm as its charm of protection quenched the demon fire. He leaped back over the couch tackling Asmodeus to the floor.

He grabbed the demon's face with his left hand, which held his ring and shouted, "Xai Mos!"

His hand glowed bright white. Asmodeus howled. The ancient thing was strong. Even under the compulsion of a talisman of light, he pushed Azriel's hand, slowly, away from his face. A knee to Azriel's stomach threw him off the demon.

The dark creature was on his feet in an instant. Azriel leaped up to his own. The ring had left the mark of the Eye of Heru on the side of Asmodeus' face. It was red, angry looking, and still had smoke coming off it.

Asmodeus looked from Lilith to Azriel and said, "Another time, Wanderer." With a wave of his arm, Asmodeus disappeared in a thick swirl of black, acrid smoke, leaving the room smelling of sulfur.

Azriel walked over to the broken window and looked out on the night. Everything was suddenly, oddly, quiet. Behind him, Lilith clapped her hands as if she had just finished watching an orchestra perform on an opera stage.

"That was extremely entertaining, darling. If I were you, I'd find that creature and put an end to him before he finds you again. I'd hate to have to stop what I'm doing to try and find all the little boxes he'd buried you in."

Lilith sauntered over to where he was standing. He could not stop his heart from clenching at how stunning she was.

As if she could hear his thoughts, she smiled a long, languid smile and said, "Me too, lover. Me too."

She kissed him, lightly, on his cheek, like a tiny bird alighting on a thin branch.

Whispering in his ear, she said, "Until next time, lover. Since your hands are full at the moment, we can discuss why I'm in Atlanta in a few days. Until then, have fun."

Turning to Hernandez, Lilith said, "You can have him for now, darling. But, in the end, remember, he belongs to me."

With that, she stepped through the window and disappeared into the night, leaving Hernandez sputtering.

"Tell that woman that I … You let her know that we … You need to make it clear to that woman that …."

After a moment, she gave up.

Shoving her gun back into her holster, she said, "I don't even know how to process what just happened. I can't write any of this in a report or I'll lose my badge and end up in some mental facility on heavy drugs."

Azriel just sat on the couch and let her process. After a few minutes, she said, "I'm going to go back to the scene at the Press and Grind and say something about a robbery gone wrong and a missing victim that no one can identify."

She started toward the broken window, stopped, thought better of it and turned toward the door they had entered.

When she got to the door she turned around, looked at Azriel, and said, "So, you really are immortal. And there's a whole world filled with people like you?"

Azriel nodded, raised his eyebrows, and said, "Yes. I was passing through Jerusalem during the holy week of Passover. I stopped on a road where a crowd was gathered. The roman soldiers were busy preparing a man for their butcher's rite, called crucifixion, reserved for criminals, but meant to send a message. It was brutal and often effective. To my everlasting shame, I joined in on the heckling. They were forcing a man to carry his own cross up to the hill where they would complete the horrendous deed. And because I was a small man, swayed by the mob, I joined in. I shouted insults at him. For some reason, he stopped. I shouted again, asking him what was he waiting for? And it was like mine was the only voice he heard through the cacophony all around us. He looked up and stared right into my eyes. And then, he spoke."

Standing at the door, Hernandez crossed herself, starting at her forehead and ending across her chest as if to ward off an evil spirit.

Her voice trembled as she said, "What did he say?"

Azriel continued, "His eyes pierced me like a cold knife to the heart. And he said, *I shall stand and rest, but you will go on until the Last Day.* And when he said it, I knew it was true. He'd cursed me to never die, until the world comes to an end. From then on, they called me the Wanderer."

Teresa Hernandez stood at his door for a moment more, nodding her head almost imperceptibly, before saying, "I need a drink."

She opened the door to leave and stopped. "What if I run into something from your world again?"

Azriel smiled and said, "You know where to find me."

Hernandez left, closing the door behind her. Azriel looked around at the mess that was his living room. There was a number he could call to have it all cleaned up as if it never happened. It was not the first time his world attempted to burst through to the world of mortals. But first, he needed to get his car.

He opened the app on his phone that would route a car to his address to give him a ride back to Virginia street and marveled at how the world had changed in the last two thousand years. Then, he went upstairs to get his other leather jacket.

HUNTER'S FIRST RULE

J amē woke to an incessant banging on her door. The repetitive pounding made her head hurt. Whoever it was didn't know her. Only a stranger would think it was ok to bang on her door like a mannerless fob.

She sat up and ran a hand across her face. Then she tossed the two thick braids of wooly hair dangling across her chest back over her shoulders. She pressed thick lips into a fine line of disgust and sighed.

A quick look at her chronometer confirmed it. Her familiars—you didn't really have friends in the *City*—would know better than to wake her before five *Zulu*. She rolled out of bed and mentally corrected herself. You could have friends in the City. It was just incredibly difficult.

If friends were anything, they were people you trusted—people you could rely on. But the City was all angles and hard edges. It was utterly unforgiving, and it was always watching. It wasn't the kind of place that lent itself to friendship—not real friendship anyway.

Show the City you cared about something, or someone, and you gave it a handle to grab onto—a pressure point. And it knew how to grab hold. It would press until you screamed. Jamē had seen it. It wasn't pretty. Friends would get you killed.

She didn't turn on the lights. Jamē wanted to keep her night-sight. It would still be dark outside. The artificial lights on her level would still be dim, mimicking morning.

Halfway across the room she scooped up her Dha. She pushed up on the *subah* with her thumb, when she reached the door, loosening the blade in its black, partec scabbard, with a soft *click*. Then she uttered a single word.

"Open."

The door slid open with a soft *whoosh*.

Filtch was standing in the doorway, wringing his hands, while trying to look in every direction at once. Jamē was wrong. It wasn't a stranger, just someone stupid. She grabbed a handful of Filtch's shirt, just beneath his neck, with her free hand, and dragged the thin, small man into her quarters.

Jamē slammed Filtch into the wall just as the door *whooshed* closed.

"I'm going to assume you've lost your gilkin mind or taken too much glitch. Because it's barely five-Zulu and you're pounding on my door like your life doesn't mean anything to you."

She jostled Filtch back and forth, roughly, against the wall to drive the point home.

"Give me a reason not to beat the gilk out of you before dumping you down the res-chute. And be quick about it!"

It took Jamē a moment to realize Filtch had been trying to speak the whole time. Her hand around his neck was preventing him from getting a word out.

She released him and realized she'd been holding him a foot off the floor when his feet hit the carpet and he bounced back into the wall with a soft thud. It served the fool right for banging on her door this early in the morning.

She took a step back while Filtch caught his breath. But she didn't put down her blade or relax.

Hunter's Third Rule—Never drop your guard.

Once Filtch caught his breath, he started talking faster than Jamē could fully follow. Something happened the night before, down in the Nine's, across from the Platforms. Some Ret-Cons from the *Subs* snatched Azzura off the street. Filtch tried to help but they took him and disappeared.

Filtch looked all over the Bazz Ward for Jamē but couldn't find her. So, he asked around until he found someone who could tell him where she lived, and he came straight here to tell her. Jamē shoved her Dha blade home in its *sayaddac* with a click and a soft curse.

Jamē tried to tell Azzura about the City. But he was too trusting. It had always been that way, ever since she met him at the Drill next to the Platforms. She couldn't believe he was there by himself. It made her itch to see it.

She knew this was coming. Whenever that Hunter's intuition rose up in her she'd wish it away with—*that's just my own cynicism talking.* But Jamē knew the City. There was nothing soft or benign about it.

Sure, people talked about the *Lush*, but that was a pipedream. The City was always watching. And man, it was patient. The moment you slipped it was there. Not to catch you—to devour you whole, like it hadn't eaten for weeks.

She should've known falling for someone was stupid. You just didn't do that, not in this endless place. Once you showed the City a hint of weakness, you could be sure of one thing. It was coming for you.

So here was Filtch, glitching in her quarters like a hop-fiend twelve days gone, giving Jamē the big bad. They took him last night—snatched him right off the street where everyone could see. The Ret-cons didn't care because who was going into the Subs after them? No one in their right mind. No one who wanted to keep their memories.

They had an enormous head start. She could have killed Filtch right there for taking so long to get word to her. Hadn't he ever heard of a com-channel?

Glikin idiot.

She stood there, wrestling with herself. She should just throw Filtch out of her quarters, headfirst, and go back to bed. It was stupid to think you could take something back from the City. It just wasn't done. When the City took something that was it—done, over, finished.

Whether your pockets were empty, or you had enough credits to live in the Hub, it didn't matter. You could be a Magistrate, or strung out on glitch—the City didn't care. It did not give, but it did take away, and what it took, you never saw again.

Filtch bounced when Jamē threw him out of her quarters. She cleaned up quickly. A hand on the sensor next to her closet opened the door without a sound. Her Meg-suit hung there on its steel trellis. It was black, quantum mesh that took her five jobs to save up enough credits to buy.

The mesh was soft, and pliable as cloth, but effective as heavy plate armor. She liked the look of its cross-weave pattern. It took a single minute to slip into it. Her black, calf-high boots were still leaning against the oversized, leather chair in the corner where she'd left them the night before.

Jamē sat and started to pull them on. She stopped with one boot on. Filtch smelled peculiar. The nascent, half-formed scent lingered in the front room. It was long faded, which made it nearly impossible to identify—like trying to remember a name you knew but couldn't quite put your finger on. She breathed it in again and grimaced.

Filk, she thought.

It eluded her. She shook her head and pulled her other boot on. Finally, she stood and grabbed her black, tech-weave coat. She zipped it up to the top of her neck and clicked the oval, steel buckle of the black, leather belt in place at her waist.

She slid the Dha behind her belt on her left hip, and clipped a long knife, a sleek hand rayser, and three utility cases onto it. She threw the rifle strap over her shoulder, checked that its clip opened and closed properly, and left her quarters with two restive thoughts in the back of her mind. She would deal with them when the time was right. Jamē took the gravilift to the ground level in silence.

The City didn't give back what it took. But that was the entire reason *Hunters* existed. It was how she made her living. Her mother had been a former assassin turned Hunter and earned a reputation for being one of the deadliest to ever ply the trade on the Endless Streets. And she taught Jamē everything she knew—especially the Rules.

Her left hand absently caressed the hilt of the Dha at her waist. The blade had been her mother's. Solange Li Ang loved her but was merciless when it came to teaching her daughter the Rules and Trade of the Hunt.

She versed her in turning the Wave and Tell to her advantage. The only thing she hadn't been able to do was explain to Jamē what the City was and how they got here. She lived to see her daughter become a Hunter with a rep as ruthless as her own. Few things brought a smile to Solange's face, but that had.

If you could find someone with the right skills, and the will to use them, and you could afford it, sometimes—on rare occasions—you could get back what the City had taken. Jamē had retrieved experimental biochips, contraband firearms, and a kidnapped family member or two. Today it was going to be the man she made the mistake of falling for.

It was stupid. She knew better. Cursed herself while it was happening. But she didn't manage to stop it. The heart wanted what it wanted—even in the City. Damn it all to hell. She silently kicked herself and cursed the Endless even as it hummed all around her. Because even though it had taken Azzura, she was going to get him back.

Even as she thought it, *Hunter's Ninth Rule* echoed in her mind. Jamē could hear her mother's voice as she exited the building.

Start at the beginning.

She unlocked the door to her stall on the northern side of the building. She climbed onto her jumpbike and hit the start button. It came to life with a clean, rumbling hum before rising off the ground. She checked to be sure it had a full charge before pulling out onto the Ave.

Jamē didn't bother to look back to make sure the stall door closed. Her mind was already on the Hunt. She needed to be fast and precise if she was going to get Azzura back alive and in one piece. It wasn't a figure of speech. She'd seen the City do worse.

It took about half a cycle to make it to the coordinates where he'd disappeared. The streets were already crowded, even though it was still early. The City didn't sleep.

The artificial lights that mimicked daylight were still dim, but the Ward was lit up with a luminescent glow pouring out of windows, off signs, and transports filling the street. In the City you were always being watched. But today she had an itch between her shoulders that wouldn't relent.

Jamē shook the feeling. She had work to do and needed to be focused. A quick, hard sniff expelled the smell of ion-trails from her nose. Braking hard, she slid her jumpbike into a parking grid in front of Molls Emporium.

She powered down her bike and waited the half-second it took to touch down. She hopped off and retrieved a datapad from one of the storage compartments on the back. It took nearly an entire cycle to discover no one knew anything.

Now, sure—normally people didn't want to see anything, even if they had. You couldn't get anyone to speak in the Heap to save your life. Strangely, it was the same way in the Hub. People didn't want to talk. But this was different, especially down here in the District.

Shopkeepers were notoriously nosy and loose-lipped. Jamē had shown the datapad, with Azzura's image beaming from its screen to everyone from Ilka at the ticket window of Molls, to Paddic hanging from the serving window of his Zonji Food Truck, down on the corner by Lateef Ave. Not only had they not seen him get snatched but they hadn't seen him at all.

She stared at his holo-image for a moment. He had a big smile. His full lips spread into a crooked smile when he flashed those white teeth. His complexion was nearly as dark brown as hers. His thick, black hair was glossy with a light gel used to braid his hair into the complex geometric shapes that adorned his head. He was beautiful. He was also stupid, and no one had seen him.

It didn't add up. The City might decide what it saw and what it didn't, but it wasn't blind. When Jamē came up empty, she flagged down a Runner leaving Paddic's food truck with a container of munda, smothered in gallic sauce.

Swipe was young, as Runner's went, but he was good. If you wanted to send a message off the grid, he was your man. There were occasions when sending a message through the Wave was warranted, but if you wanted it to stay confidential you used a Runner.

He had thick, black locs hanging halfway down his back. His eyes were covered by misty, blue goggles with a heads-up display. He was a plumb little ball, unlike most Runners. There was also Nanji and Hattie Mae—both gorgeously thick as a robby covered in lick-sauce, but they were in a class by themselves.

A brown jumpsuit, with hopboots and a burstpack on his back, meant he didn't need a jump bike or transport. Jamē had no doubt there were other surprises tucked away on his person. Runners weren't helpless. They weren't assassins, but they weren't helpless either. Though most of the time they avoided trouble by knowing the Endless Streets better than you and being too fast for you to put your hands on them.

Swipe had a high voice, which matched his bright disposition. He smiled when he saw Jamē. It took him three seconds to *burst* from the food truck down to where she stood. He landed in a swirl of ion-trail and burst energy.

"Jamē! It's good to see you. On the Hunt? Oh yeah, right! Sorry."

Swipe dropped his voice and looked around like he was being spied on. Jamē tried not to laugh.

The young man continued, "Uh ... so ... uh. What's up?"

She just smiled at him.

Swipe took one look at her smile and said, "You *are* on the Hunt, aren't you?!"

The young Runner grew even more excited, and his whisper rose to a faux whisper loud enough to be heard a block away.

"So, what're we doing? Huh? We tracking assassins? Hunting down Nutters? Stolen Tell Tech? Experimental Biowear? Whatever it is, I'm so IN!"

Jamē held up a hand to get him to stop.

"Swipe, there's no *we*. It's good to see you, though. If you're up to it, I *do* need you for a Run."

His face changed to a full-on pout for half a second until his mind got to the part where Jamē said she wanted him to do a Run. Then his eyes lit up, like a nav-screen, behind his goggles. He flashed her a winning smile and stuck out his hand.

She couldn't help but smile back. The boy's enthusiasm was infectious. She handed Swipe the message and told him where to deliver it. After she gave him the coordinates, she reminded him to stay calm and keep his head down.

Swipe's smile grew even bigger. He shot Jamē a salute before blasting off. The boy left nothing but a fading ion-trail in his wake. She aimed a final smile in Swipe's direction and decided to get a drink while she waited.

The Flez was a quaint little café, two doors down from Molls. They had really good jawa. So Jamē found a quiet table in the back, where she could see all the entrances and exits.

She sat there and sipped on the dark brew in its tiny cup.

Hunter's Twelfth Rule—Always know the way out.

She had no idea where Ollo got the beans to grind, but it was delicious, nutty flavored, and came with a light buzz to the cortex. Jamē was on her second cup and halfway through a piece of sweet bread when it hit her.

She turned up the cup and gulped down the last dregs of the bitter-sweet infusion. She pushed back the chair, stood up, grabbed the remaining half of her sweet bread, and made her way out of the café.

She just stood there on the street and swallowed the last bit of sweetbread. She chewed slowly, exhaling with a grim resolve. Maybe it was the conjunction of place and thought. Maybe the smell of jawa had cleared her nose, triggering some kind of sense memory. It hit her like a biosteel wall.

Jamē made her way back around to the merchants and shopkeepers she questioned earlier. This time she asked them something different. By her second stop, she had her answer, but she kept going. Sure enough, the rest verified her suspicions. By the time she returned to the café, two people were waiting by her jumpbike.

A small patch of anger was beginning to smolder in the back of her mind, but that didn't stop her from smiling warmly at Switch. The small, brown woman was a sight for sore eyes. Her smile matched Jamē's own when she approached.

Switch was a Wave rider—a fractal freak. She had a genius level intellect and knew more about surfing and skewing the Wave than anyone Jamē had ever met. Her thick, wooly hair was pulled up into two enormous puffs. Her brown eyes were a shade lighter than Jamē's own.

She had the face of a beautiful hollow-mod. Her jumpsuit was blue mesh, trimmed in gold, and covered in her own proprietary tech. Bright eyes beamed behind dark blue goggles with a tiny antenna sticking up on the right side of the frame. Jamē towered over her. She swept Switch up in a big sisterly hug.

She put her down and said, "Switch, it's great to see you! Thanks for coming."

Switch straightened the top of her jumpsuit and said, "Well if it isn't the infamous Jamē Li Ang of the Hunter's Guild. It's a pleasure to see you again too, Pan. It's been too long."

Jamē shook her head. Her mother had called her Pan—short for Panda. She could count the number of people who knew that on one hand. You couldn't hide much from a Wave rider like Switch. The small woman made a half-turn, motioning to the man with her, as she said, "You remember Bael, right?"

Jamē had to look up at Bael. He was as tall as a Helium Breather. While Switch surfed the Wave, for the right price, Bael kept her safe. He was a big bad from the Westside—an enhanced warrior with a decent disposition. The man's head was clean-shaven, though he was a few shades darker than Jamē.

Bael had tattoos running up his neck and over one eye. He wore dark, gray, chest armor, blue mesh pants, and black tech boots. Jamē counted four knives, a blaster, and one mean looking rayser rifle. Jamē shook his hand. The large man's grip was firm but not overbearing.

"Nice to see you again, Bael."

Bael nodded in response, with a noncommittal grunt for emphasis, before going back to scanning the area for possible threats. Jamē turned her attention back to Switch.

"Switch, normally I'd invite you into the café for a drink while we caught up, but I'm afraid time is not on our side."

Switch waved off her apology, with an absent hand, as if to say she understood completely.

"Not to worry. How can I help?"

Jamē explained to Switch what had happened and what she needed from her, while Bael watched the street. Her eyes narrowed as she listened. She pressed her lips together in a firm line and nodded.

Her eyes went up and to the left, in that way people's eyes did when they were thinking over a problem.

Jamē waited quietly and watched Bael scan their surroundings.

Finally, Switch snapped her fingers and said, "I've got it. The first thing's easy enough. It'll just take a few minutes riding the Wave. The other is a little more difficult. Hold on."

She tapped the tech band on her arm and a heads-up display glowed to life. Her fingers danced across its holo-keyboard with uncanny speed. Code flitted across its screen faster than Jamē could read it. She wasn't sure she would've understood it even if she could.

Switch's head moved up and down, and side-to-side, as she scrolled through it. Jamē watched as she disappeared into the code of the Wave. It wasn't long before a dot on the screen began to blink.

Switch emitted a squeal of delight and reached into her backpack. She pulled out a small datapad and synced it with her tech band before handing it to Jamē. She took it with a raised eyebrow.

"It's done," she said. "I found them by locating their I.D. in the Wave. Then I backtraced it to their last known. I was able to enter a coded geo-tag linked to their Wave input. Once I tagged their input it was easy enough to attach a data spike to their Tell interface."

Jamē just stood there holding the datapad she had just taken from her and stared at her with a furrowed brow. Switch looked from her, to the datapad, then back at her again. Jamē realized her mouth was hanging open, but she didn't know what to say.

Switch cleared her throat, took a deep breath, and said, "The datapad has a location. This blinking light is the person you're looking for."

Jamē closed her mouth and looked down at the datapad. Sure enough, there was a blinking light with a geo-tag. She knew where he was going. She looked back at Switch with a smile.

"Thank you, Switch. What do I owe you?"

She was already waving her off. "No, Pan. You don't owe me anything. I'm still trying to pay off the debt I owe you."

She unconsciously glanced over at Bael.

When she turned back to Jamē she said, "So, what's next?"

Jamē raised an eyebrow again. She opened her mouth, but Switch cut her off.

"You didn't look close enough at the coordinates of the geo-tag. You're heading for the Tombs. Now, I don't doubt your abilities, Pan. Your reputation is well-deserved. But the Tombs!? You're going to need some help."

Hunter's Eighth Rule—Take help where you can get it.

Jamē smiled and nodded. "Thanks, Switch. I appreciate it."

Switch returned the nod and said, "So, like I said, what's next?"

Jamē took a moment to consider everything she knew. The itch between her shoulders, which had been nothing more than a nuisance earlier, was now a full-blown warning bell going off in her head. They had taken him to the Tombs. It hadn't made sense until now. She let the realization of it wash over her.

The pieces had been floating in the back of her mind as individual, isolated oddities. They were remarkable on their own, but not a cohesive picture.

They took him to the Tombs.

She nearly laughed. But she didn't. Azzura was in real danger—even more danger now, which she wouldn't have thought possible until this very moment.

Hunter's Fifth Rule—Trust your instincts.

She told Switch what she wanted.

"Are you sure?" a surprised Switch replied. "You know what that'll bring down on your head. That's more trouble, not less. It's inescapable trouble."

"You let me worry about that, Switch. Do you have one?"

Switch grimaced, reached into her pack, and passed Jamē a small, metal cube, like it was a cracked egg.

"You be careful with that."

Jamē flashed her grin, shoved it into a pouch on her belt, and fired up her jumpbike. She waved at Switch and sped off, weaving through traffic like the bike was on autopilot, lost in thought, on her way to the Tombs. It took thirty minutes to pass out of the Bazz Ward and into Sector 43.

She could've accessed the Sublevels from her own Ward but no one in their right mind traveled that far in the Tombs. It would be a death sentence. The City went on forever. No one had seen its end, though some claimed to have.

No, the City was unending. Its towers reached so high they disappeared from sight. Its streets stretched so far no one knew how many Sectors there were. But it didn't just go up and out. It also went down. The Sublevels extended so deeply into the ground they were a veritable abyss of dark corridors and systems substratum. They were called the *Subs,* but they'd earned the name *Tombs.*

People who went into the Tombs didn't come back. The City was uncaring, and dangerous. It was also nasty. The Tombs were even more so. The deeper you ventured into the Subs the more dangerous it became.

Rooms and corridors were all that existed down there. Some said there were also vast chambers cloaked in darkness—places where the guts of the City could be found. It was home to Reavers, refugees, Ret-Cons, and discarded, malfunctioning, rogue A.I.'s.

There were gangs down there too. The Scarabs, the Nihils, the 44's, and the Scavengers all ran the lower levels with impunity. The rumor was that every now and then, when the gangs got too big, or too disruptive to be ignored, the Watchers swept the Tombs clean.

Jamē didn't know if that was real or just wishful thinking. What was true? People disappeared. But there were a hundred reasons for that to happen and none of them named Watcher.

She pulled her jumpbike into a hollowed out vacant building, a stone's throw from where the coordinates on the datapad pointed. She was in the 99's.

The 99th Ward was silent. There wasn't a single person in sight. It looked like the rest of the City but for some inexplicable reason was abandoned. No one knew why. If made most people so leery they didn't even drive thought the 99th. Empty buildings were either on the verge of falling down or in such disrepair they were slowly crumbling in on themselves.

She powered down her bike and waited until she felt it touch down before dismounting. The keypad dinged softly as she input the lock code before popping open the storage containers and retrieving extra ammo-cartridges. She grabbed a tactical pack, strapped a tech band onto her wrist, and put on tac-goggles.

The silence was eerie. It made her skin crawl. She made her way over to a grate covering the entrance to the Subs and stared down at its rusted grid-like surface. She glanced around, to be sure she wasn't being watched, let out a deep sigh, and pulled the grate open.

It groaned in protest, shedding rust and dirt as it clanged open. She crouched and stared down into the darkness.

Gilk, she thought, before dropping into the darkness below.

The grate slammed shut over his head with a bang that echoed into the shadows around her. It was dim but not completely dark. The lights still worked on this level. They hummed softly overhead.

The deeper you went into the Tombs the darker it got. The lights rarely functioned on the lower levels. Sometimes it was just disrepair, but other times it was because the people, or things, roaming the Subs broke them. Things down here liked the darkness.

Jamē had synced the datapad Switch gave her with her tech band. She tapped the keypad and engaged its holographic, heads-up display. And there it was.

The geo-tag pulsed softly just above her wrist, indicating a location on the grid of the sub-level. She was going to have to descend several more levels. She sighed, took a deep breath, and steeled herself.

She reached into one of the utility cases on her belt. It held a little treat Switch had provided. She clipped it into place on her belt and pressed the green button on its side. It emitted a low, soft pulse of sound. Every light within thirty paces winked out. She was surrounded by complete and utter darkness.

For most people, the darkness was not a welcome place. But Jamē was raised by an ex-assassin turned Hunter. Her mother trained her to be unafraid, to make fear an intimate friend—to turn it to her own uses. It was an ally, not an enemy, in the hands of a competent Hunter.

While there were things to fear in the Tombs, darkness wasn't one of them. She popped a night shield over her goggles. The goggles allowed her to see in the dark and the shield blocked the light her goggles produced. She moved forward with the darkness wrapped around her like armor.

A dozen steps ahead, a stairwell circled down into the depths. She followed the geo-tag down. There was no resistance, only the sound of her boots on the metal floor. When she reached Sub fourteen, she heard scratching out in the corridor, like claws scraping across steel. But whomever, or whatever, it was didn't enter the stairwell.

Distant echoes of laughter floated down to her as she passed eighteenth. But she continued undiscovered. When she reached the twenty-first Sub the readings on the tech band let her know she'd reached the coordinates. Jamē drew her Dha.

She nudged the door open, slowly, and slid into the corridor. It was empty. The electro-mag pulse knocked out the flickering lights, bathing the entire level in darkness. She flitted from one side of the corridor to the other as she made her way down the hall to the last room on the left. That's where the coordinates pointed.

She eased up to the door and pressed her ear against its cold metal. There was no sound. Jamē eased her hand rayser from its holster and thumbed the safety off. Armed with her rayser in her left hand and her Dha in her right, she kicked the door open and dove into the room with a smooth roll.

Her back hit the wall on the right side of the room as she came up. Her electro-meg pulse beeped, and the lights flared to life. Jamē nearly cut herelf reaching up to snatch her goggles off. The burst of light had nearly blinded her. That's when she heard the laughter.

He was tall and slender. His mech-suit was dark, blue, tech weave with well-placed armor plates. His jacket had tan and black fur around the collar. The tech boots were black, with a buckle at the ankle. His name was Spazz, and he was a Hunter.

His sword hilt stuck up over his shoulder, but he was holding a Ramsir 4gen rayser rifle in his hands, aimed right at Jamē's head. He glared at her with ice-blue eyes and a broad grin spreading wryly above a square jaw. The artificial light of the sublevel washed out the pale skin of his face.

The room was large but had clearly been emptied out recently. Dust marks in the floor showed tracks from furniture legs. A single chair remained in the center of the empty chamber. It sat three paces behind Spazz, with Azzura strapped to it. He was bound and gagged.

When he saw Jamē, he struggled uselessly against his bonds. His muffled shrieks put her teeth on edge. Spazz chuckled softly.

"Well, well, well. If it isn't the great Hunter, Jamē Li Ang. They call you Panda, don't they? Aren't you supposed to be the big bad—the Hunter who always succeeds? I guess the Endless Street will have to revise the story about you, eh?"

Jamē pushed off the wall and slid her Dha back in its scabbard. She looked from Spazz, to Azzura, and then past Azzura to the Reavers crowded together at the back of the room. It was a trap.

She turned back to Spazz and said, "What do you want, *Hunter*."

She made it sound like an indictment as she, slowly, slid her rayser back into its holster on her right hip. Spazz drank in the moment. He licked his lips and glanced from the Reavers to Azzura, savoring it like it was the last bit of savága in the bottom of a wine glass.

"What do I want? Well, let's see. First, I'm going to kill you." He poked his rifle in her direction. "And then I'm going to ransom him to his family for enough credits to move into the Hub. Oh, and I'm going to take your Hunt. It's so large. It has the potential to be so much more profitable than you've made it. I'm going to add it to the other two I've already taken so I'll have the largest Hunt in the City."

Jamē just stood there. Hunters were solitary creatures. But they did know one another. Spazz had always been a disappointment. He was cowardly and wretched. But since Hunters rarely interacted, he'd been allowed to practice the Hunt without interference.

Messing around in another Hunter's domain was taboo. Your Hunt was sacrosanct. You didn't Hunt in another Hunter's territory and you didn't interfere in another Hunter's business. It just didn't happen. There weren't even stories of it having happened.

"I don't believe you," she said.

Spazz's eyes narrowed.

"What do you mean?"

"I mean, I don't believe you. You haven't taken over any Hunter's territory and made it yours. And you aren't going to take mine. I know you're stupid, but you aren't that stupid."

Spazz cackled. He tossed his rifle to one of the Reavers behind him and took a few steps toward Jamē.

"I'm not stupid. You are. You're stupid for having chased this pretty boy blindly down a hole in the ground. And you're

93

stupid for underestimating me. I ambushed Faelin in the Drells and took his Hunt. I threw Tamerelle off the top floor of Anukoo Tower in the 44th Ward and took her Hunt as well. And now I'm going to do the same thing to you! They'll say you went into the Tombs and never came out."

Jamē nodded her head once. Her voice was surprisingly calm. She spoke so softly Spazz almost missed it.

"That's what I thought."

Spazz jerked his head back and sneered, "What do you mean that's what you thought?"

Jamē sniffed softly and said, "Hunter's First Rule, you fool."

Spazz took a step back and she continued.

"I thought it was odd that Filtch would come running to me about something. Then the fool lied about knowing where I live. My quarters aren't a secret. I'm easy to find."

Jamē took a slow half-step forward as she continued.

"Worse than that, the idiot didn't have the sense to wash himself before coming to find me. The scent had faded significantly, which is why it took me a few hours to figure out where I knew it from. And when no one could recall seeing Azzura snatched off the street, I realized something was off. But you know what they did remember seeing? The two of you together. Once I made that connection, the rest of it fell into place."

Her voice was heated now. Jamē had allowed the anger that had been building all morning to start boiling over.

"But you know what the real mistake was, Spazz? You forgot Hunter's First Rule."

She tapped on her tech band again and said, "Did you get that?"

A voice came back through it.

"Yeah, we got it."

Spazz's eyes widened.

He said, "Who ... who was that?!"

Jamē let herself smile now.

She flashed him a grim smile as she said, "Spazz, you ought to be proud of yourself. You've done something today that I've never seen or even heard of. Once I figured out what you were up to, I had Switch search the Wave. She told me about the missing Hunters and the stories surrounding their disappearances. It was easy enough to check if you'd increased your Hunt. You were greedy and stupid. So, I had Switch spread the word among the Hunters in the surrounding Sectors. They rendezvoused with her on the surface, and she let them listen in on our little conversation."

Jamē took another step toward Spazz who was looking around the room like he had nowhere to go.

"You know it's taboo to mess with someone's Hunt, right? You killed two Hunters and been caught trying to kill a third. Guess who's waiting for you on the surface?"

Spazz yelled at the Reavers.

"Kill her! Kill her now!"

Reavers were half-crazed nutters who spent their days roaming the sublevels looking for easy prey. They were unorganized, untrained, poorly equipped brawlers. But there were enough of them to get the job done. They swarmed toward her.

Azzura was still tied to a chair in the middle of the room. She snatched a smoke grenade from her belt, tossed it toward the mass of Reavers, and launched herself toward him. Thick, green smoke filled the room.

She heard hacking and coughing as it repelled them. Their eyes would be tearing up. Their lungs would be burning. It would buy her a few precious moments.

95

She dropped to the metal floor—sliding to the chair—while spraying the room with rayser fire. She couldn't see through the smoke, but she heard at least two three bodies hit the floor.

Jamē gave Azzura a quick hug and there it was—the lilac scent Azzura was fond of wearing filled her nose. What she smelled on Filtch that morning was faded residue—the faint trace of Az's favorite cologne having rubbed off on a man who struggled with him while he was being abducted. If Filtch had taken a shower, the day might have turned out differently.

Hunter's Seventh Rule—Details matter.

The smoke wouldn't stop them for long. She pulled her knife free and cut Azzura's bonds. Then she grabbed a handful of his shirt and dragged him toward the door.

Spittle flew from Spazz's mouth as he yelled, "Don't let her get away!"

The pounding of boots on metal greeted them as they reached the hall. Spazz had stationed Reavers where they could cut off her escape. He wasn't completely incompetent.

Azzura purred in his soft voice.

"We're surrounded Jamē! I'm so sorry. You shouldn't have come for me. This is all my fault."

"Yes, it is, Az. But don't worry. I'm going to get you out of here."

"How, Pan?!"

"Like this."

Jamē reached into the pouch on her belt and pulled out the cube she'd gotten from Switch. A sharp turn on its top produced two metal prongs.

She jammed it into the wall and yelled, "Run, Az!"

It was a logic bomb and a massive one. Switch didn't play around. The device was designed to disrupt the base code of the City. She'd hardly pulled her hand back before it went off.

The thing emitted a shrill, high-pitched screech that quickly passed beyond the range of human hearing. A warping field spread through the walls like a wildfire in dry tinder. It destabilized the structural integrity of the walls, floor, and ceiling.

She pushed Azzura to a full run. When the Reavers ahead of them came into view, Jamē tossed another smoke grenade, covered her mouth, and kept them moving forward.

Azzura yelled, "How is this going to help?"

"Cover your mouth and wait for it," she said.

She shoulder-blocked a Reaver to her left and fired point blank into the chest of one on the right, all the while dragging Az along with her. A disruption of this magnitude was really only good for a few things. One of them arrived even faster than she'd expected. By the time the screams erupted from the smoke cloud behind them, they were already on their way up the stairs. The Watchers had arrived.

Watchers were the only real masters of the Endless Streets. They were extensions of the City. They could form out of any structure—a wall, a floor, or street. They were the hands, eyes, and ears of the City. They were also its enforcers.

The Watchers would contain the damage of the logic bomb in short order, stabilize the warping field, and repair the damage to the City's structure. They'd also eradicate any human being nearby. The screams followed them up the stairwell.

It wasn't long before they reached the grate and exited the sublevels. When they were back on the street level in the 99th, Jamē gave Azzura a quick once-over to be sure he wasn't hurt.

He just stood there looking at the grate. It was only when someone cleared their throat that she stopped fussing over him and looked around.

Jamē glanced over at the woman who had cleared her throat. It was Zamerra. Tall, with skin as dark as night, and as beautiful as any woman had any right to be—Zamerra smiled at Jamē. Six more hardened men and women stood behind Zamerra causally scanning the street.

Erris Stealth nodded at Jamē in appreciation. He was a fraction shorter than Zamerra. The man wore feathers in his halo of black, wooly hair.

"I see your reputation is well-deserved," he said.

Jamē returned the man's a nod of respect with one of her own.

"Thanks for the heads up, Hunter. Did Spazz make it out alive?"

"I think he did. He made a hasty retreat after turning the Reavers on us."

"Well, we'll take care of that filth. Leave him to us. You've done enough."

Zamerra flashed her a big smile.

The other Hunters nodded in agreement.

"He has an accomplice named Filtch who—"

Zamerra cut her off.

"Don't worry, Jamē, we'll deal with all of it. Get this man and yourself to safety and leave the rest with us. Let's not dawdle. We're Hunters, but this is still the 99th."

She was right. They had a victory. But this was still the City. The City knew how to turn a victory into defeat. All you had to do was ask Spazz and Filtch. Jamē took Azzura by the hand.

With one last look at the other Hunters, she said, "Hunter's Thirteenth Rule."

Zamerra nodded, laughed, and said, "Know when to quit."

Jamē led Azzura to her jumpbike and left the Hunt for Spazz and Filtch to the others. She hopped on, waited for Azzura to climb on behind her and hit the ignition.

As the bike roared to life, Azzura said, "Pan, what's Hunter's First Rule?"

She pulled off, heading out of the 99th.

With the wind in her face, and Azzura hanging on to her for dear life, she chuckled and said, "Be sure you aren't the prey."

THE ESCAPE ARTIST

—

The hardest prison to escape is your own mind.
~ unknown

I t took a full month to catch him. On his last attempt, he heard glass shatter, which immediately preceded a free-fall. Asmodeus, one of the kings of the Infernal Order of the Pandemonium, had sent Astaroth to retrieve him. Astaroth was infamously lazy, even for a Duke of hell. It made sense he'd thrown Taum out a window on the fifty-third floor of a skyscraper in Manhattan. Killing a demon in the realm of the Short-lived—what Infernal creatures called the Mundane—was the easiest way to banish them.

One would think killing a demon was a difficult proposition. Generally, it was, unless you were a celestial, one of the fallen, or just higher in the Order of the Pandemonium than the demon in question. But they were also a bit more squishy than normal outside of hell—especially in the Mundane. They'd spent a thousand years convincing the Short-lived otherwise.

Taum landed next to the Lake of Agony, with a mucky splat, in a muddy puddle that smelled of ash and rotten eggs. He shook his fist in the air, aimed metaphorically at the building he'd been tossed out of like a wet ragdoll coming apart at the seams. He'd fretted over his pants as he stood. They were his favorite pair of jeans because they fit his tall, rakish frame perfectly—hard to come by in the realm of the Short-lived.

There hadn't been a demon in sight, which figured. Astaroth was so lazy he hadn't even bothered to make sure Taum was actually back in hell. A gout of flame spewed into the air from the lake like an inopportune belch. At least it was warm. He hated New York in winter.

It was a slog back to his corner of the Pandemonium—what the Short-lived called hell. He'd carved it out for himself and named it Simonean. It wasn't as hard as it sounded, though it had required a few cracked heads, and decorating some of the walls with torn off horns.

His fellows had taken to calling him Taum De Simonean. They thought it was funny. Though few were brave enough to laugh in his face. It reminded them of the Greek for "flat nose" and by extension, *the land of the flat nosed*. But he'd thought of the Hebrew, meaning "listen," as in—*to pay attention to*.

How could he get away with annexing a bit of hell for himself? The Pandemonium was vast—a full four hundred and forty-four levels that seemed unending in length. They laughed at Danté when the occasion arose. Hell was so big, and so full of creatures congenitally predisposed to be narcissists and egomaniacs that it was easy to escape notice.

Short-lived, he thought. *They were all clueless. Philosophers and intellectuals with a grasp of the metaphysical? Don't make me laugh.*

Taum was born Infernal. He was not one of the fallen, like Lucifer and Satan—another confusion among the Short-lived. Nor was he one of them, cast into the Pandemonium after a life of evil and self-indulgence, become infernal by default. He was a true Scarifice—born of flame, sulfur, and what the Short-lived called *Dark Matter.* The problem was he'd never amounted to much as an Infernal. In fact, he'd never even touched a soul, let alone gotten up to the kind of ugliness that passed for duty in this place. Torturing souls turned his stomach.

Taum had spent his entire existence on one thing—escape. He bore the scares to prove it. He hadn't been in the Pandemonium a millennium before his first attempt. The first dozen went entirely unnoticed.

But once you managed to get out it got noticed. When you leave breaches in the fabric of the veil, tears in time and space that look like gaping wounds bleeding through reality, someone notices. The next dozen times he was only out for a few hours. They ended with him cast into the lowest levels of the Infernum, which meant fighting his way back to Simonean. Soon enough, *Taum of Simonean* became a curse uttered by knights, dukes, princes, and kings of the Pandemonium, often followed by spitting on the ground.

He took enough horns, hooves, and teeth to put an end to that and then went back to escaping. It wasn't easy. But there were ways out of hell if you knew where to look.

Early on, he had some limited success by hopping a ride out with demons who were being summoned. The spells were preceded by a high-pitched sound. If he moved fast enough, he could tag along, to the great displeasure of the Infernal whose coattail he rode out on.

It didn't work out well for the Short-lived either. His presence somehow broke the binding of the spell, leaving the demon free to do what they wanted. While they enjoyed themselves with the Short-lived, who'd been audacious enough to try binding them to its will, they weren't grateful enough to forego reporting Taum up the chain of command. He only managed to elude capture for a few days.

After a hundred or so escapes, word reached the Princes. None of them were in a hurry to inform Scratch that a minion was escaping the Infernum, so they took it upon themselves to sort it out. That's when Asmodeus took an interest. He began by sending Knights of the Infernal Order to retrieve him.

It was a week before Furcas caught up to him. He'd stretched the skin of a crotchety old man over himself, sat next to him on a bus stop and began regaling him with the ingredients on his favorite sandwich. Taum had escaped through a thin mortal conundrum about how to deal with catholic priests who were behaving badly. The psychic energy of the decision to sweep it under the rug and transfer the priests to other parishes created an opening on the thirty-third level and found himself in Boston. He hated Boston. The humans were rude. He decided to catch a bus to Providence.

Furcas went on and on about roast beef, sharp cheddar, horseradish—on an onion roll, with the precise number of shallots, and thousand island dressing, while Taum tuned out. The Knight droned on until the bus approached. Then he pushed Taum under it.

He arrived in hell cursing. He hadn't recognized the demon. He thought the aroma was just how people smelled.

Eventually, he found a cracked cistern in an old transgression made from husbands abusing their wives and squeezed his way through. It meant slathering himself in something unmentionable from the Pit of Despair—false apologies and broken promises—which smelled like a clogged sewer on a hot day, but he managed not to gag until he was out. It spewed him out in an alley in a place called Cawker City, Kansas. It them a month to track him down.

The town was home to only a few hundred people, but it had a giant ball of twine as a local attraction. Marchosias was one of the fallen, a Marquis in the Infernal Order. Taum thought he could reason with him. Marchosias had always harbored a desire to return to the Shining City, but having been denied, he'd grown sullen and resentful. Taum tried to run but had the world's largest ball of twine rolled over him.

This time he'd found a Parallelism. When the Short-lived did something truly awful, in the same place, over time, it wore away at the veil between worlds, creating an inflexion point in the Pandemonium—a mirror image. On the third level of hell, he found a reflection of the Huntsville Unit in Texas where they executed people using an electric chair.

The man they were executing was innocent, so the veil ripped wide open for a split second. Taum was through it before it closed and found himself in Huntsville, Texas next to a giant statue of Sam Houston. It was a warm, sunny day with a cool breeze blowing in from the south.

It took Bael a year to find him. If only he hadn't returned to see the statute again. The Short-lived propensity to put up monuments baffled him. Bael was the head of the Infernal Powers and the first demon listed in Wierus' *Pseudomonarchia daemonum*. It was also Taum's misfortune that he taught invisibility. Taum was almost to the road when the statue of Sam Houston squashed him like a bug on a windshield.

He woke up bound to rock on a cliff overlooking the Sea of Affliction. He glanced over the side and saw the roiling souls of Short-lived crying out in horror, clawing at one another in a hopeless struggle to get free.

"Well, look who's awake."

The voice was like a knife scratching across the surface of a plate. Bael had dispensed with his three heads and opted for one, though he kept the crown and the fangs. His skin was like a pale pig, and he smelled like the bathroom at a dilapidated roadside gas station, only filthier.

"Do you have any idea of the trouble you've caused?"

Taum looked around as if to see who Bael was talking to.

"I'm talking to you, shitstain. Why, by all that's cursed and damned, do you keep escaping? You have no idea what you've done. Demons are talking. They're getting ideas. They're starting to think. We don't like that. The Pandemonium has an order. You do what you're told, when you're told, and how you're told. You don't get to decide anything."

Bael had slowly made his way over to where Taum was chained to the rock that was part chair, part rack.

"You've escaped our notice for thousands of years, but I've looked into you. Not a single soul tortured. Not one Short-lived tempted, turned, or puppeted—not one. What, by all that is unholy, have you been thinking?"

His rank breath buffeted Taum's face. A clawed hand grabbed his chin and pushed his head back against the rock.

"Well, the jig is up. Scratch is on his way down. You know what that means."

For the first time in Taum's life he felt odd.

Is this panic?

He forced himself, through sheer will, not to struggle against the chains.

A dark shadow fell over the cliff. Bael dropped to a knee and bowed his head. The sound of leather flapping in the wind was followed by the strongest whiff of sulfur Taum had ever smelled. A deep, resounding bell rang from somewhere in the distance. And then he was there on the cliff, standing over Bael.

Bael intoned, "My Lord, I have returned him as you commanded."

The voice was like nails on a chalkboard but somehow also so low that it made Taum's bones vibrate.

"So, this is our little escape artist, eh?"

"Yes, my Lord. He's escaped the Pandemonium more than a hundred times."

The Morningstar retracted his massive wings and strolled over to Taum. The ground shook with each step. Taum tried to climb under the rock he was chained to.

This is definitely panic, he thought.

"Let me take a look at you."

Lucifer grabbed a handful of Taum's hair and pulled his head back so he could see his face.

"Unremarkable. Though I am impressed that he outwitted every Knight, Duke, Prince, and King of the Infernum."

He released Taum's head with a rough flick of his wrist and returned to where Bael knelt.

"How did he do it? Surely, hell is not some Short-lived convenience store with a flimsy glass door that's open 24 hours a day?"

"No, my Lord. I was just about to begin the interrogation."

Scratch paused for a moment and fingered his chin with a clawed hand.

"I wonder."

"Yes, my Lord?"

"You say he's never once tortured, tempted, turned, or even puppeted a soul?"

"Not one, my Lord. The records are clear."

"And you say he's escaped the Infernum, which should be impossible, more than a hundred times?"

"Yes, my Lord. I don't understand how that was possible."

Scratch paused. Then his wings flared.

"Ah. Yes. Tell me, Bael. If he can get out of hell, can he get into heaven?"

Bael cackled like a villain in a cheap movie.

"Yes, master! What is he can get into heaven!? That would change everything."

"It most certainly would. Let's get some answers from our young, headstrong friend."

Bael rose to his feet. Scratch turned back toward the rock. They both took a single step and froze. The chain lay in the dirt, the rock was empty. Scratch turned back to Bael and howled.

"Again! He's escaped, again!"

Taum was running. Chains were easy enough if you knew the trick. It would take much more than a year to catch him this time.

MANIC PIXIE DREAM GIRL GETS REVENGE

"We should forgive our enemies, but not before they are hanged."
~ Heinrich Heine

Revenge is a prison and time is its Warden. Mads rode in the back of the transport gazing out a reinforced, clear-aluminum window. The skies above Everlearn were too blue. The fluffy, pristinely formed clouds were just the right size and texture to appeal to the eye.

Mads absently rolled the hapicite pendant around in her hand as she watched the clouds drift lazily on their predetermined loop around the facility. The piece of hapicite was chosen with meticulous care so only the tiniest slivers were lasered off to create the small, silver starburst, which held a purple, gleamdream stone set in its center. The long chain securing the pendant around her neck was also made of the rarest mineral in the galaxy—though of a lesser grade. It still glittered in the soft light filtering through the window.

The pilot's rough voice followed a soft chime emitted from the intercom.

"Lieutenant Worth, we'll be landing shortly."

Another chime accompanied a red flashing light in the panel over the entry to the cockpit. Mads clicked her flight harness back into place and prepared for landing. There was no need for the pilot to consider crosswinds, weather conditions, or birds in the air on approach—not in the idyllic atmosphere custom made by Everlearn climate engineers. They were in a high-density Typhoon Class transport. Turbulent weather wouldn't have matter anyway.

She waited for the dull metallic thump of the struts touching down and the momentary howl of the engines back thrust to unbuckle again. She tucked the pendant back inside her jacket and buttoned it the neck. A final chime and a green light told her it was safe to stand.

Mads made her way fore to the exit on the left of the cabin. The pilot exited the cockpit and gave her a sharp salute.

"Lieutenant, I hope you had a pleasant trip?"

The man had decided any low-ranking officer in the Galactic Sovereign Fleet who could afford a private transport to the exclusive facility of Everlearn, on the moon of Empyrean, must be from a family with means and connections. He didn't want to end up on the wrong side of that equation.

"I did, Bondsman. Thank you."

The man self-consciously covered the metal band shackled to his wrist with the end of his sleeve. The bright, green numbers on its liquid glass display lazily ticked away on his wrist. They indicated at least three years left to pay off his debt.

110

Everlearn would be charging him for room, board, clothes, and any other expense he incurred—and all of it deducted from his wages. Even more pernicious? Everlearn owned the buildings they lived in, the stores they shopped in—even the places they paid for entertainment. It was indentured servitude. The counter on their wrists was a clever, if perverse, chimera—a brilliant pacifier meant to keep people like him in line, with the illusion he'd one day be free of it.

No matter how many of them died of old age, with the numbers on their bracelet still slowly turning, it did not provoke rebellion against the practice. The ancient adage about a frog in a slowly boiling pot came to Mads' mind. It was corrupt and predatory. She smiled warmly at the pilot, gave him a standard tip, and exited the shuttle.

A lanky, handsome, young man, with pale golden hair, deep blue eyes, and a soft smile met her at the foot of the ramp.

He inclined his head, looked over his datapad, and said, "Lieutenant Maddie Charl Wyrth?"

His voice rose a fraction, indicating a question, despite her uniform.

"Yes, but since you aren't Corps, you can dispense with the formality. Call me, Mads."

He inclined his head again and said, "Yes, ma'am—I mean, Mads. I'm Ramond Flowers. You may call me, Rammy. I'll be your escort and MPDG."

"MPDG?"

"Oh, yeah," he blushed and continued, "Mindjack Project Direct Guide. It's a mouthful, so we just say MPDG."

She caught him staring. His eyes went from her hips to her breasts, to her bright, purple hair. It was wound into seven, thick, traditional threads, evenly spaced around her head. The finger-thick tendrils fell past her shoulders. One on each side curled back on themselves before casually dropping down, like they felt like wandering on the way. The woven threads of her gloriously wooly hair was a style that was old before humans began colonizing the stars.

Her *mzaa* and *baba* carried the ancient ways with them into the darkness of deep space. She remembered the small bag of okra seeds in her mzaa's bag and a cast iron skillet her baba guarded like it was a member of the family—passed down from brown skinned hand to brown skinned hand for generations.

Mads loved the thick, cake-like bread they made in it and the pot of beans they'd slow-cook to go with it. She wore her hair in threads, knots, braids, and sometimes wildly free in a large, messy halo in honor of that ancient culture.

Flowers blushed when he realized she'd caught him staring.

He straightened the white coat of his suit, with a quick tug, and squeaked, "How was your trip?"

"Pleasant enough," she replied. "The Port on Caliban was busy, but the flight up from the planet was quiet."

The young man nodded.

"That's nice to hear. Caliban can be a lot to take in. The Bonded live down there and overcrowding in the city can be a bit much to endure. Thankfully, private shuttles are available for our most discerning clients." By which he meant, wealthy.

He had enough self-possession not to smirk. Mads' soft grunt was her entire statement on the matter.

"Did you receive my payment?"

He grinned and ducked his head in that way people did when they thought they were in the company of the wealthy. It was like a litmus test for character. Some groveled, others sucked up, more sought favor.

"Yes, ma'am—uh, Mads." His voice got progressively oily as continued. "It's not often we're paid in hapicite, especially not the purest grade. Rest assured your entire stay with us is fully covered."

Bile rose in her throat. She told herself to focus.

"Good. My quarters?"

The young man bowed and motioned toward the facility with an exaggerated flourish of an extended arm.

"Right this way, Mads."

Flowers turned, tucked his datapad under his arm, and started off toward the main entrance. The Everlearn facility, as white as his uniform, was a feat of architectural elegance. Its thin, megaplex—like huddled fingers pointing toward the sky—glistened in the afternoon sun.

They walked on white concrete without a seam or crack. The grounds were covered in immaculately groomed flora. The visage of its unending sea of precisely manicured grass was only broken by patches of orange begonias, purple irises, and pink lotus flowers, bunched together in overflowing explosions of color. The facility was surrounded by a hedge as tall as a tree.

Security was ostentatious and comprehensive. She passed through brain, eye, and body scans. It wasn't enough to project a blank mind devoid of thought. The brain scan was calibrated to catch that kind of deception. Mads thought back through her flight from the surface of Caliban—its trajectories, flight path, and her assessment of the shuttle and its pilot.

The scan would also pick up heightened activity in the section of her brain that would give her away as a hacker. It's why she chose her cover with care. A logistics officer in the Corps, used to running high end military ops computers, would have very similar brain markers—not identical, but close.

She'd also included heavily redacted files in her application to hint at questions Everlearn wouldn't be cleared to ask or expect

113

answers. Well placed bribes got her background checks answered by someone in the appropriate department of the Corps. The Galactic Corps sprawling administration, and inevitable corruption, was the only thing that made that possible.

It had taken months to find the right officer in the right billet, with the right moral flexibility. Everlearn security was conscientious enough to have included all of it in her file. She forced herself to breathe slowly.

Nothing to see here, boys, she thought.

A superior looked over the shoulder of the guard checking her scans. The young man pointed at the screen and the older guard leaned over and whispered to him. He immediately nodded to Flowers who smiled and gave Mads a thumbs up.

The interior of Everlearn was as study in customer manipulation. Mads was greeted by gray walls, smooth, gray, marble floors, and an ambient lavender scent. The smell was meant to foster good emotions. The lighting was dim—known to foster indulgence in purchases. A soft, unobtrusive, classical composition played in the background. It was intended to say we are sophisticated.

The art on the walls was sparse but colorful. She noted impressionistic work by Dal, abstracts by Verilan, and photo realism by Merr. It whispered—*be at ease, we're a successful company*—in corporate speak.

Then, there was the décor. The furniture, as sparsely arranged as the art on the walls, was rich, verdant green, vibrant, clear, sea blue, and deep, lush purple. It screamed—reliability, quality, and luxury. *Trust us. Let us spoil you.*

Most people never noticed all the little ways a corporation sought to manipulate them. Everlearn wanted you primed to spend lots and lots of money—and to feel happy about it. Mads simply smiled at Flowers as he led her through the thick web of manipulation meant to foster conspicuous consumption.

The other quiet bit of subconscious manipulation was how the Bonded wore gray. It made them blend into the background of the walls. They could clean, do repairs, and perform all the menial tasks needed to keep a facility of this magnitude running smoothly without ever being noticed.

You had to want to see them, or they were invisible. But how do you ignore all the tiny green numbers ticking away on wrists all around you? It was perverse. Mads kept her eyes forward and her expression neutral. There were facial recog scans happening at regular intervals throughout the facility—an additional layer of internal security, which doubled as a way of monitoring the Bonded.

She'd seen the schematics. The scans functioned by using algorithms that captured and analyzed micro-expressions to predict behavior. A flash of disdain on the face, even for a millisecond, would trigger an alert that sent a guard to have a discussion with the culprit.

Soon enough, they arrived at the rooms reserved for her stay. She leaned against the wall and smiled at him as he typed a code into a small keypad. Flowers blushed as he fumbled the code. The keypad barked a rude tone and red light at him, forcing him to enter it again. She glanced at the back of his shiny datapad. Finally, door opened with the softest *whush*.

It was more of the same inside. There was a bed, a large, soft chair, and a desk, all situated so you could look out on a lovely garden view from the massive window that doubled as a wall. The art, smell, and colors were more of the same.

"Here is the control pad for your quarters. An executive chef is on standby anytime, day or night. They are prepared to make anything you'd like. Hit the call button and a concierge can have just about anything brought to your room—anything at all."

Mads didn't like the ending inflection in his voice. She shuddered to think what kinds of things, or people, were fed to Everlearn clients. The moon Empyrean and its contingent planet Caliban sat conveniently outside the jurisdiction of the Galactic Charter of 3782.

If you were a planet of means, or one armed to the teeth, gills, or other evolutionary appendage, you were likely a founding member of the Galactic Union of Worlds and on its Security Council. The seven Planetary members of the Security Council were the real power of the Union. They drew the lines on the star charts.

Everlearn's corporate charter was registered on Ethereal. Ethereal just happened to be a Permanent member on the GUW Security Council. Mads grit her teeth when she thought about it. It was corruption on a cosmic scale. It was so big no one believed it and if they did, they didn't think they could do anything about it.

But Mads knew something most didn't. Bureaucracies that big were easily fooled. They were also monumentally arrogant. They didn't think anyone could do anything about it either.

"Get some rest, Mads. Your Mindjacks are scheduled to begin in the morning."

Mads walked Flowers back to the door and said, "Thank you, Ramond. I'll see you in the morning."

She brushed something nonexistent off his shoulder and his face flushed bright red as he backed out. She waved at him as the door slid closed and then her smile vanished. It was time to get ready.

Mads searched every inch of the quarters. She ruled out the presence of listening devices and cameras. Then, she moved all the furniture against the walls. Her breathing slowed as she sat in the center of the room. It wasn't long before she was sitting with her legs folded up into her lap and drifting in her mindspace. It had taken years to learn the mental discipline necessary for what she was going to attempt. She had to be calm and focused. She would only get one shot.

Her eyes snapped open. She could feel his footsteps coming down the hall. Mads quickly moved the furniture back in place. A soft chime indicated he was at the door.

She pushed the button next to the door and it slid open to reveal Flowers in a fresh white uniform and a bright smile.

"Good morning, Mads. Oh, forgive me. I should've shown you where your clothes are stored."

He entered the room and made his way to a tall, slim wardrobe in the corner.

He pulled open the door and motioned to a set of folded clothes.

"The shower is through that door. I'll wait outside until you're ready."

"Thank you, Ramond. What would I do without you?"

He ducked his head and grinned. He was pleased with himself.

Good, she thought.

"I'll just be a moment."

He stepped outside and she grabbed the clothes she'd discovered when she searched the room the night before. After a quick shower, she threw on the white pants and top, before sliding on the soft white shoes. She stood next to the door for an extra few minutes before hitting the button again.

"I'm so sorry to keep you waiting, Ramond. I think I'm ready. I'd forget my head if it wasn't attached."

He shook his head and said, "No, no, Mads. No problem at all. I'm here to serve. If you're ready?"

"Yes, please. Lead on, Macduff!"

Flowers quirked an eyebrow.

"Oh, sorry, Ramond. Just an old literary reference. My mother loved to read. She was especially fond of ancient Terran literature. *I know why the caged bird sings? The fire next time?*"

Flowers pursed his lips, shrugged almost imperceptibly, and nodded politely.

"Ah. I see. Anyway, it's this way."

Lead on, Macduff, she thought. *A vapid cog in an arrogant machine.*

A young woman in gray approached with folded towels and a basket full of cleaning supplies in her arms. Flowers made a show of stopping her just outside Mads' room.

"Lieutenant Wyrth is an honored guest. Be sure her room is spotless."

The young Bondswoman bent at the knees and bowed her head.

"Yes, sir."

Flowers started off down the hall and Mads whispered, "It's probably a mess in there. I'm not a morning person."

The young woman flinched, her eyes darted toward Flowers' back, and then landed on Mads. She dipped her body again and nodded.

Mads watched her scurry into the room. Flowers hadn't noticed. He was too busy strutting down the hallway. It wouldn't even have occurred to him that Mads would've spoken to the Bondswoman. A soft derisive snort of air left her nose.

She kept her eyes aimed at the door the bondswoman had disappeared behind. The facial recog tech would chalk her derision up to displeasure with the servant rather than its intended target. She turned and followed him.

His shoulders were straight. His head was held high. His stride was long, and he was a little too conscious of it all. He was an MPDG of one of the most powerful corporations in the galaxy and he was feeling himself. He thought she was impressed.

He led her through a maze of nearly identical hallways—gray marble floors, white walls, the occasional expensive piece of art on the wall. Mads ignored it all and kept count. Right, right, left, left, left, right, left, left, right—she memorized it as they went.

RIGHT, by the stream where Othood died. RIGHT, past the hill where his mother cried. LEFT, at the willow Maxim saved. LEFT, by the buildings that they razed.

"What's that tune," Flowers asked? "It sounds ominous."

"Oh, just something that calms my nerves. I like how the low notes feel in my throat."

She added a nervous chuckle and Flowers said, "Not to worry. I'll be with you the entire time. I won't let anything happen to you."

"That's very kind of you, Ramond." *Very kind.*

The last hallway ended in an enormously oversized door. Ramond entered his code and the thing slowly swept inward. It was three feet thick and opened like a vault. Everlearn's most prized technology was on the other side.

The chamber was big enough to be a starship hangar. Cool air hit her face as she entered. Thin, white columns filled the chamber at precise intervals. They were covered in blinking, blue lights.

Mainframe, she thought.

"If I remember correctly, according to your application, this is your first Mindjack?"

"Yes, it is. It's not what I was imagining. How does it work?"

"Don't worry. I'll walk you through it."

119

Mads made an exaggerated twist of her head as she took in the entire lab.

"Is it just us? No cameras?

"Yes. Everlearn takes your privacy, protecting your data, and Mindjack experience seriously. I will be the only person who sees it or has access to what goes on here."

"Huh. I guess that's reassuring. But what if there's a problem or an emergency?"

"I'll be monitoring you the entire time from my station and there's an Intervention Team in the next room with a full suite of highly trained, medical technicians. Problems are incredibly rare. But rest assured, we're ready for any eventuality."

Mads looked away and smirked. *Any eventuality?*

"Ok. I guess I'm ready."

"Very good. Followed me."

Flowers led her to the far side of the chamber. They walked through another door into a small room with a bench and a set of cabinets on the wall. He reached into one and produced a set of small patches.

He placed them on her temples and the back of her neck

He cleared his throat and said, "If you'll turn around and pull up your shirt?"

He proceeded to place more of them down her spine to the small of her back.

"These will allow me to monitor your jack."

Mads pulled her shirt down and turned back around.

"So, where's the chair? Or sphere? Or whatever you use for the Mindjack?"

Flowers grinned.

"Ah. Yes. Those are how our competitors facilitate a Mindjack, but thankfully you've come to Everlearn. Follow me."

He walked to the door at the other side of the small room, looked back at her, and said, "Take a deep breath. It can be a bit disorientating."

He entered his code again and the door slid open to reveal a doorway filled with blue light. He winked at her and disappeared through it. Mads followed.

It was like stepping into a cold shower. She shivered. Tiny bumps rose on the back of her neck. The hair on her forearms stood on its end. She wrapped her arms around herself and thought she'd never be warm again.

Then, suddenly, the sensation was gone. She was standing in what she could only describe as a blank space. It was white for as far as the eye could see. A nothingness that had no end. The only surface she could see was the white floor beneath her feet.

Flowers spread his arms wide and said, "This is what we call the Oasis." He paused. His entire demeanor could only be described as gloating—the self-satisfied, smug smile, the congratulatory nod of the head, and the insufferable tone of his voice. "I know. Spectacular isn't it."

Mads blew a low, long, soft whistle.

"It looks like it goes on forever."

Flowers nodded appreciatively, as if he'd built it himself.

"It kinda does. Rather than strap you to a table and wire you to an interface feeding your brain electrical impulses, which it reads as reality, Everlearn created this."

"What is it? How does it work?"

"Most of it is proprietary information I'm not supposed to divulge." He leaned in conspiratorially and continued, "But for you, Mads, I'll make an exception."

She ducked her head, looked up at him from underneath her brows, and feigned a blush.

"I appreciate that, Ramond. It would make me a little less afraid of this whole experience."

She saw his chest poke out a bit. He pointed at the doorway they'd come through.

"The doorway is a threshold to a pocket universe we've artificially created."

His fingers ran nimbly across his datapad and suddenly, the blank expanse changed. They were standing next to a small, trickling stream running through a lush valley. The sky was pristine blue, and mountains loomed in the distance.

"It's programmable space, wrapped inside a time-dilation field. For very hours that passes in here, minutes pass outside the field. The longer you stay inside the slower time passes outside. Think of it this way, and this is just an estimate—a day in here is like an hour out there, a month is like a day. The engineering that makes it possible is actually fascinating. Maybe after your Mindjack is over we can discuss it more, say over a drink?"

She feigned another blush and said, "Maybe." Her gaze rose to the mountains in the distance. "So, this is why Everlearn is so much more expensive than places like Mindcore?"

"Exactly," Flowers said as he jabbed a finger in her direction. "Only the best for customers like you."

Mads took a deep breath. "Ok. Should we get started?"

A flurry of Flowers' fingers on his datapad changed the environment again. This time they were on top of a mountain, standing in the center of a large ring of hardened earth. A tall man in black stood across from her.

"We've programmed your instructors with the best martial skills in existence, according to your specs. And because you paid for the platinum package, they come with a complete personality. Remember, I'll be monitoring your progress from my station in the antechamber. Good luck on your training! When you're ready to exit, just say *door.*"

Flowers walked to the edge of the ring, through the glowing, blue doorway and was gone. Then the door vanished and Mads was left alone with her programmed instructor.

"So, you want to learn how to fight."

The tall man had skin as black as obsidian. He was draped in black silk. It was an ancient Terran style. She could see a kimono covered by a *kamishimo*—a kind of sleeveless jacket with exaggerated shoulders, and wide flowing pants called *hakama*. He wore a belt around his waist that Mads knew was an *obi*, with two swords tucked into it.

His words were a statement of fact rather than a question.

Mads said, "Hai," and bowed her head. "I want to learn the sword."

His voice was deep, but he had a pleasant expression on his face.

"I see. Very well. You may call me, Yasuke. And this," he motioned to his left as the air warped like the distortion caused by extreme heat, "is Joseph Bologne and Jean-Louis Michel."

Mads smiled. Joseph Bologne, also known as Le Chevalier De Saint-Georges, was the greatest swordsman in Europe in the 18th century on Old Earth. Born into enslavement on a plantation on the island of Guadalupe, he was the son of a rich plantation owner and an enslaved black woman.

The circumstances of it narrowed her eyes and made her grit her teeth. She knew the history of it. He inherited his black skin and good looks from his mother. His father took him and his mother to France where he had the kind of upbringing afforded to the wealthy, white, French upper class.

At school he studied math and history in the morning and in the afternoon he fenced. He came under the tutelage of the master swordsman Nicolas Texier de la Boëssière, and by all accounts grew to be the greatest swordsman of his age. He wore a fussy, white shirt, with billowing sleeves, a green vest, blue pantaloons, with white stockings, and brown leather boots.

Standing next to him was Jean-Louis Michel. Michel was light skinned like Joseph. Unlike Yasuke and Joseph, Jean-Louis was short and slender. He was barely over five feet tall. He was born in the 19th century in a place called Saint-Domingue, which later became known as Haiti on Old Earth. His father was a French fencing coach.

He served in the French army under the conqueror Napoleon and was most famous for a series of duels outside Madrid, Spain. In a quarrel between soldiers of his regiment and an Italian regiment, it was said he killed three Italian sword masters and wounded another ten in less than forty minutes.

He wore a green double-breasted coat with tails and a large collar, white pants, and black boots. A thick, cream, dotted scarf was tied around his neck and tucked into his collar. He wore a pleasant smile, like the other two. These were to be her teachers. The greatest swordsmen of their eras. She liked the idea that they looked like her. Who better to prepare her for what was to come.

Yasuke tossed her a katana. Jean-Louis and Joseph took up positions on the edge of the ring. They began with how to hold the sword and how to stand. She was nearly giddy with joy when the program had Jean-Louis speak words he'd made famous.

"A sword should be held as one holds a little bird; not so tightly as to crush it, but just enough to prevent it escaping from the hand."

All three held sticks as thick as a finger and long as an arm. They used them to tap and arm or leg that was out of place, or to slash in like a sword strike. They were unrelenting.

It wasn't long before she was drenched in sweat. Her arms and legs ached. But it was exhilarating. Their mastery of the art was undeniable and remarkable. And she was learning.

It wasn't just that mere minutes had passed on the outside giving her all the time in the world to learn. She knew the patches on her body were storing electrical impulses and imprinting them in her brain. Muscle memory was being stored. What would take her years to encode in her mind and body under normal circumstances would be accumulated in days in this environment. You could learn anything you wanted with Mindjack tech if you could afford it.

"Door."

Her teachers vanished as the glowing doorway appeared. For her it had been hours. Outside, only minutes had passed. When she stepped out of the small room into the large chamber, Flowers was waiting with a towel and table covered in food.

She wiped herself off and ate while he checked the calibration of the patches and the status of her Mindjack.

"You're doing great, Mads."

She nodded and shoved a forkful of baked fish into her mouth. The mixed vegetables were delicious and complemented the redfish, which was cooked in a chutney.

Flowers said, "If you sleep in the Oasis this will go even faster. Or you can return to your quarters, and we'll pick up tomorrow."

Mads washed everything down with a sweet red wine.

"That's a great idea, Ramond."

She dropped her towel on the table and headed back in. There was a small house a few feet from the ring when she re-entered the Oasis. It was stylish, well-appointed, and equipped with the most comfortable bed she'd ever been in. She showered, changed, and slept. Yasuke woke her by shaking her leg.

It wasn't long before she was back in the ring and training. It all became a blur. She trained, exited for food, and returned to the Oasis for more training and sleep. By the time a month had passed inside, the day outside had been spent. The only pause in the cycle was giving Flowers a night to sleep himself and they were back at it again.

It didn't stop him from taking every opportunity he could get to ply her with small talk. He wasn't *really happy*, not sure what he wanted to do with his life, and sure he was waiting for something or *someone* to come along and inspire him. She caught him staring often enough. While it was simple enough to turn his questions away like parrying a sword thrust, it was still exhausting and irritating.

Two months passed in the Oasis—which translated to two full days outside the time dilation field—before Yasuke, Jean-Michel, and Joseph told her there was nothing more they could teach her. The *tinging* sound vibrating in the air was an indication they'd switched to real metal blades. Yet, in more than two dozen passes with katana, foil, and saber, not one of her teachers managed a single touch on her. The men bowed before they vanished. She wasn't even breathing hard.

She glanced at a readout as she exited the Oasis and entered the large chamber that housed the mainframe. It was the morning of the third day since she'd arrived.

Impeccable timing, she thought.

A young man was wheeling in a cart of food meant for her breakfast. He stopped next to the small, cloth-covered table that had been set up for her meals. She could sleep in the Oasis, but any food constructed in it wouldn't be real.

He went to place one of the trays on the table. His wristband beeped, the green numbers zeroed out, and it clicked open. He just stood there staring at it with his mouth hanging open. He raised his wrist and the metal band fell off and clattered to the floor.

The young man looked over at Mads and said, "Most of us didn't believe it. I'm sorry I doubted, ma'am." And then he turned and ran.

An alarm began blaring loudly. Flowers jumped up from behind his workstation where he'd been napping.

"What, what's happening!?"

Mads flashed him the first genuine smile she'd smiled since entering Everlearn.

"I am."

She hit him in the temple, and he dropped to floor like one of the bags of dross leftover from mining on her home planet. By the time he came around she had him strapped to a chair.

He shook his head and mumbled, "What, what—what are you doing?"

"Oh, me? I've used your security code to gain access to the subroutines in the mainframe." Her fingers danced across the screen. "I'm inputting a nasty little virus I created after learning to code at Mindcore last year."

Flowers strained against the bonds she'd made by tearing the tablecloth into strips and weaving them into makeshift ropes.

"Wait, this wasn't your first Mindjack? Are you insane? Do you know how dangerous it is to double-jack so close together? You're supposed to wait at least three years between Jacks to prevent seepage, lesions, and even an aneurism. It could've killed you."

Mads grabbed the sandwich off the plate she'd brought over to the workstation and took a large bite. She chewed and talked at the same time.

"Excuse me for talking with my mouth full. You're right. But my sources thought that since Everlearn's Mindjack was so

127

different from the standard process the risk of serious complications was less than 40%."

Flowers strained to see what Mads was doing.

"Why would you risk it, even if that was true?"

She finished inputting the code and grabbed the other half of her sandwich. She took a bite and pointed the sandwich at him.

"Oh, I needed access to the Oasis mainframe. And try as I might, I couldn't figure out any other way to get access. I have to hand it to you. Your security is top notch."

Mads wiped her sleeve across her mouth and took another bite.

Flowers slumped into the chair and frowned.

"But, why, Mads. Why?"

"That's always the question, isn't it. Why."

She finished off the sandwich, glanced at the screen on the workstation, and nodded to herself. Three steps took her to the edge of the workstation where she leaned against it and looked down at Flowers.

"About a decade ago, Everlearn discovered that my colony was sitting on one of the riches deposits of hapicite in the quadrant. And do you know what they did?"

Flowers opened his mouth but Mads shook her head.

"No, no, that's a rhetorical question. Did they negotiate with the colony and enter into an agreement to mine the hapicite for a fair price? Because that would've made us some of the riches people in the galaxy. No. They had their cronies on the Security Council of the Galactic Union redraw a line on the star charts that put my planet Shango outside Union jurisdiction."

The alarm stopped blaring. She leaned back, looked at the screen, glanced at the time, and nodded again, before turning back to Flowers.

"You should be able to guess what happened next. They eradicated my entire colony. My family, friends, and neighbors, all gone in the blink of an eye. They did it from orbit. We never stood a chance."

Her eyes narrowed and her lips pressed into a firm line. Flowers' eyes widened. But she took a deep breath, crossed her arms, and continued.

"I was lucky. I used to love to collect odd, or pretty rocks in the hills around our settlement. I'd bring them home and show my mzaa and baba what I'd found. That day my pockets were bulging with rocks and my hands were full."

She looked off at the ceiling—her mind going back to that day.

"Mr. Shadza happened to be in the hills looking for gudba— a kind of tuber native to Shango. It's delicious when cut up, seasoned, and fried. We watched Everlearn ships turn our colony into a hole in the ground. We hid for days until he was able to get us off planet."

She reached down and twirled the starburst pendant hanging from her neck.

"Here's where things get interesting, Flowers."

Her tone made him push the chair back. It made a short screeching sound as the legs dug into the floor.

"The rocks in my hands, pockets, and littering the hillside? Almost all of them were raw hapicite ore. Turned out to be a fortune. It didn't make me rich. It made me wildly wealthy. Do you know the difference, Flowers?"

She chuckled darkly.

"I set Mr. Shadza up on a planet of his choice. And one day, while bankers buzzed around me in an office, genuflecting and treating me like royalty, while we discussed my assets and did some complicated financial planning, a different kind of plan began forming in my mind."

She took two quick steps over to Flowers, grabbed his knees, and knelt in front of him.

"You see, Flowers, when you've got that kind of money, you can do almost anything you want. And what I wanted was revenge. And let me be clear—I didn't give a drec about justice. No, I wanted pure, simple, distilled revenge. Do you know what Shango means, Flowers? It's the name of an ancient Old Earth god. It means the *Bringer of Thunder.*"

She loosened her grip on his knees and stood.

Flowers yelped, "But, what you're talking about, it's impossible."

Mads cackled.

"You're almost right, Flowers. Not impossible. Improbable? Definitely. A thing like that would take years of planning, preparation, training, and, most importantly, a whole lot of money."

She leaned in until she was nose to nose with him and said, "Don't ever drec with someone who has all the time in the universe and more money than a god."

The soft hum of the mainframe went quiet as it died. It was almost anti-climactic.

Mads straightened and said, "That's it. Your mainframe is dead. Your backups are fried. The message I sent while uploading the virus took care of your off-site storage facility. There'll be nothing more than a crater left where it used to stand. The pirates I hired had instructions to give the technicians enough time to evacuate before they began their bombardment."

She patted him on the head.

"I know you had this vision of me being your salvation. That I'd fall for you and help lift you out of your doldrums and mediocrity. But this isn't your story, Flowers. It's mine."

She turned her back on him and headed for the doorway.

"You won't make it out of here! Security will stop you!"

Mads left him whining and straining ineffectually against her makeshift bonds. His code opened the massive door. Under normal circumstances a contingent of guards would have been waiting on the other side, but they were busy dealing with the Bonded. She'd paid off every bond in the facility and timed the payments to hit their accounts this morning. Every Bonded bracelet had deactivated and fallen off at the exact same moment. Chaos ensued.

She followed the twists and turns of the hallways she'd memorized back to her quarters. A few taps of the buttons next to her door opened it. Inside she found the clothes she'd paid the woman servicing her room to smuggle in, and a sword.

Even the servants couldn't smuggle in an energy weapon. But a length of metal? That was doable. Telling her she *wasn't a morning person* when she first saw her was the agreed upon code to set things in motion.

Mads dressed quickly. The interior of the facility was a madhouse but getting out was still going to be a challenge. The building shook beneath her feet and the alarms began blaring again.

Good, she thought.

Pay enough and the Bonded working in and around the power plant would make things explode. Her *clothes* were made from tactical fiber. Her blue top was a reinforced jacket with a chest plate made from hundreds of tiny, silver, flexible pins.

The pants and hooded cape were also blue, trimmed with the same silver pins Her brown boots were heavy leather with reinforced toes. She pulled the hood up over her head and unsheathed the sword. It was time to go.

She'd used the same memory trick that got her to her quarters as she ran through the hallways backtracking to the entrance. A squad of guards were holding it against Bonded trying to leave. Just as Mads rounded the corner, a second squad showed up to reinforce them. The floor shook again. It nearly took her off her feet.

A third squad appeared behind her. The sound of her mzaa's voice echoed in Mads mind. It was from an Old Earth book by one of her favorite writers—a long-dead author named Zora—called, *Dust Tracks on a Road.*

I have been in Sorrow's kitchen and licked out all the pots. Then I have stood on the peaky mountain wrapped in rainbows, with a harp and sword in my hands.

Mads screamed and charged. The next few minutes were a blur of long-simmering rage. Destroying Everlearn's tech and their ability to keep functioning was one thing but taking her rage out on them physically was a whole other kind of catharsis.

Her programmable teachers had done their job well. The guards had blasters and shock sticks, but she had a sword. She moved in and around them like a dancer. The cutting-edge, tactical fiber and plate shielding woven into her clothes diffused the effects of the handful of bolts and shocks that would have rendered her unconscious. The guards' ballistic uniforms did not save them from her alloy blade.

At some point the Bonded picked up dropped blasters and shock sticks. They joined in with the robust enthusiasm of years of built-up enmity coursing through their hot blood. It was a rout. When her eyes cleared and her rage died down, she was standing outside under a perfectly programmed blue sky, bathed in golden sunlight.

The freed Bondsmen and Bondswomen passed her with pure glee written on their faces. She felt their hands patting her on the shoulder and back. The shuttles Mads hired on Caliban, for this very moment, were landing and taking off—filled with the freed. Behind her, Everlearn burned.

She pulled a com-device, snuck in with her clothes, from her pocket, entered a code, and watched the ship she'd hidden in orbit on the other side of Caliban come streaking through the sky. It descended into the atmosphere on autopilot.

It was a high-end, intrepid class, cruiser—sleek, fast, and armed to the teeth. If the facility hadn't been offline, it would've been blown out of the sky on approach. She was already walking toward it as it set down on the manicured grass.

It wasn't until she was back in orbit that she realized she had no idea where she was going. Taking out Everlearn had consumed her entire life. It was all she'd thought about every single day for years.

Even her dreams were about the destruction of the company that had taken so much from her. Now that it was over, she was stunned, a bit confused, and overcome.

The ship's com chirped. Mads opened the channel without even thinking about it.

"Uh, ma'am. This is Chanda on the shuttle Ozymandias. We all just wanted to thank you for paying off our bonds. You'll never know how much this means to us."

Mads cleared her throat and said, "It was my pleasure, Chanda. Thank everyone for me. I couldn't have done this without your help."

"Yes, ma'am. You're welcome."

"What are you going to do with your freedom, Chanda?"

The com channel fell silent. The soft buzz of static was the only sound filling the air.

Then Chanda said, "I've got a brother Bonded to the mining company, Broken Earth Proprietary Group. They mine all over the Galactic Union. If he's still alive, I'm going to find him."

Mads quickly pulled up BEP's records on her computer. It took all of ten seconds to see how predatory the company was—the environmental devastation it left in its wake. A few more seconds and the list of complaints filed with the GU by Bonded working its mine fields filled her screen. She leaned back and stared out the front port of her ship at the shuttle moving slowly out of orbit.

"Hey, Chanda." Mads tilted her head from side to side. Her neck made a soft cracking sound.

"How would you like some company?"

PERIL☉US FALLS

Water gives life. Steel protects it.
~The Old Woman in the Mountain

Neither of the twin planets, orbiting in the habitable zone of an abandoned star system, had a name. She'd scoured the star charts on the way, but to no avail. She discovered the archeological find of a lifetime on the first desolate rock—a high-density super planet—and it was tucked away in her jump-pack.

Who would she tell first?

She had no idea. Discovering it was going to be a lot easier than safely announcing its existence.

The second planet was quarantined. It was called *Infernal.* The only reason she knew its name was the warning being broadcast on a loop from the beacon in orbit:

> *This is the planet Infernal. It is quarantined. Landing is prohibited, by the authority of the Enduring.*
> *This is the planet Infernal. It is quarantined. Landing is prohibited, by the authority of the Enduring.*

The message continued transmitting into space unabated. It lit up her com-board with warning lights. The monotone, male voice, with its crisp pronunciation, echoed from her com-system.

A normal person would have logged the warning in their nav-chart, marked the planet off-limits, and moved on. But Wilhemina Periwinkle Akinawa had earned her nickname.

Her given name was an homage to her *Utata*, Will Akinawa, and her *Umama* Amy's favorite color—Periwinkle. It was a simple, if elegant, purple-blue hue, named for a plant of the same appellation. But after witnessing her incessant penchant for getting into trouble—from the time she could walk—her father, who was in the habit of calling her Peri, began calling her *Perilous.*

Perilous should've logged Infernal in her computer and moved on. She had her prize. But the message was ancient.

She scanned the beacon, and it was even older—the oldest piece of tech she'd ever come across.

What was an antique beacon doing beaming an ancient quarantine message into space, around a desolate planet, in an abandoned sector of space?

That tantalizing question was the reason they caught her in orbit—that and having her sensors aimed at the beacon. She never saw them coming.

Her ship fell from the sky like a comet that's drifted too far from the gravitational forces propelling it through space. The squadron of Hornets that fired on her had emerged from their hiding place in the debris field of Infernal's massive rings. Their old line, Deep Space, Destroyer Class Cruiser must have been somewhere in the small system.

Her ship, the *Zanzibar,* took heavy fire. Perilous turned him sharply, into the atmosphere, as she tried to execute evasive maneuvers. The ship was plunging through the exosphere into the ionosphere, but she managed to rock him left and right while trying to regain control of the blazing descent.

Shockwaves, from heavy canon fire, exploded all around the hull. The Zanzibar shook violently. She rubbed the console gently like it was the furry head of a pet, while whispering to the god of fools and rogues that he'd hold together.

He can take it, she told herself.

The Zanzibar had never let her down. He was the fastest ship in the Forgotten Sector. This wasn't her first run-in with ships from the Enduring's renegade fleet. Perilous had managed to stay a step ahead of them for days while excavating sites on the handful of planets in this system.

The Zanzibar screamed into Infernal's stratosphere. He probably looked like a streak of flame, being drawn by an invisible celestial finger across the sky, from the planet's surface. She had no idea what was down there.

She'd barely gotten readings indicating the surface had a breathable atmosphere before she found herself under attack. Though the Enduring hadn't attempted to restart the abandoned terraforming process on any of the nearby planets, they still didn't like unregistered ships passing through the star system.

Perilous couldn't even hazard a guess as to why they cared about a lone ship, with an archaeologist on board, on the edge of the Known. They couldn't possibly know what she'd found.

There was no time to think about it. She had precious cargo on board and a promise to keep—which was becoming a more tenuous proposition by the moment. The Zanzibar shuddered, followed by flashing, red lights blinking wildly across the entire navigation console. Her ship dropped precipitously through the troposphere and her stomach tried to climb up into her throat.

The Hornet squadron swarmed behind her, in and out of her ship's flaming wake. The entire bridge shook as if the Zanzibar was about to fly apart, making it nearly impossible to input commands. The engineering and life support consoles exploded, sending hot, gold sparks flying.

Smoke began to fill the bridge. Behind her, a fire sprang to life along a secondary console and up a wall. The Zanz was designed to be piloted by five people, but she'd rigged his systems to be flown by a single person. All those bypasses were rapidly failing.

He was sleek and fast. He looked like a wide knife-blade with large, circular, Inter-Sol engines on either side, connected by short, curved wings. There were three decks, guns fore and aft, heavy hull plating, luminous, multi-frequency shields, and a Starlight drive capable of jumping into the slipstream. But right now, he was just a crashing ship falling from the sky.

Perilous pulled herself from her seat, fighting the terminal g-forces created by the runaway descent. She clawed her way along the wall to the life support controls and activated the fire suppression system.

Somehow, she managed to enter the activation code while the console dodged her finger. The system burst to life with the sound of rushing air. The gray mist flooded the compartment from nozzles in the ceiling.

As vapor filled the bridge, suppressing the fire, Perilous half-bounced, half-fell, back into her seat. She tried to get control of the engines. If she didn't fire them in time, she was going to be bits of charred debris strewn across miles of dark landscape.

A flashing, green panel told her the spill port on the starboard engine was fused. She shunted the plasma to the secondary bypass and rerouted it to the pre-stage intercooler. After re-initializing the stabilizers, she primed the Inter-Sol engines for re-ignition and waited.

It was going to be close. If she fired them too soon, the ship would be too high, and the engines would stall. If she waited too long, she wouldn't have time to pull out of the uncontrolled descent.

The Zanzibar went into a flat spin, slamming her back into her seat, and holding her there. Perilous closed her eyes—straining to keep her finger near the ignition button—and ran the numbers in her head, while she tried not to throw up. Her eyes flicked back and forth rapidly, as if she was in REM sleep, while she calculated ship weight, speed, thrust capacity, spin, gravity and—

"Now!" she screamed, as if someone was there to hear her. Her eyes snapped opened as she hit the button.

The Inter-Sol engines fired. The force of it slammed her forward into the console. She threw her arms up to cover her face. She hit hard but landed on her elbows and forearms.

She shoved herself off the panel and furiously imputed navigational commands, while disengaging the main screen's blast shield. Infernal's surface flew toward her, though she could barely see through the darkness shrouding the tidal-locked planet. She fired a series of flares, which lit up the dark sky, showering the ground below in bright light.

Perilous pushed the engines to one hundred and fifteen percent with the kind of unorthodox programming an engineer would run from with their arms covering their head. A high-pitched whine filled the bridge as the engines redlined.

Right before the Zanzibar crashed headlong into the rocky surface and exploded into a thousand pieces of fiery metal, the ground slowed. The hull groaned under the strain. Her shoulders scrunched up around her head and she closed her eyes.

There was a hard *thud*. The ship shook beneath her so hard it rattled her teeth. A loud hiss accompanied the engines powering down. Perilous leaned back in her seat and sighed. The ship was down.

She slouched down in her seat. Alarms blared. The lights flickered. Sparks flew from consoles like they were spitting in protest at the ship's rough usage. Perilous coughed.

The air was contaminated. She covered her mouth with her left hand and input several more commands in the console in front of her. The loud wail of the alarms stopped. The warning lights winked out and she initiated a purge of the conduits for the life support system.

It was unclear how much time she had before her pursuers landed. There wasn't time to assess the damage to the Zanzibar— though it was likely critical. He wouldn't be able to fly anytime soon, if at all.

She couldn't run. Fighting would be suicide. Her only alternative was to hide.

If she could hide long enough, maybe they would give up looking and leave. Though the idea of being stranded on a dead planet made her nauseous.

One problem at a time, Wil, she thought.

She was certainly earning her nickname today. She could almost see her Utata's face. He'd be shaking his head. Her Umama would've thrown her hands up and left the room to prepare her lecture on safe archeological praxis. She'd be quietly proud of her daughter's fearlessness—though the lecture would include a footnote on having children before you got yourself killed and ended the family line.

Perilous raced to the lower deck. She was already wearing her terra-suit. The outer layer was made of a large-mesh neoprene covered in black, aluminized mylar. The pattern always made her think of a honeycomb.

Just beneath the outer layer was a bodysuit made of gray, striated bio-weave. When she reached the rear hatch, she threw on her black larsik-skin jacket and gloves. She threw her holstered rayser on around her waist as she ran, closing the steel buckle of the black belt with a loud *click*.

She slid her father's sheathed knife behind her belt, in the small of her back, and threw on her jump-pack. Thankfully, she hadn't taken the time to remove her precious find from her pack. It was the most important discovery of her entire career and leaving it behind would've made all this *sturm und drang* a dreadful waste.

Her parents spent their entire lives searching the stars for it. Will and Amy Akinawa believed it could bring peace to the *Known* if it ended up in the right hands. When she went out on excavation sites, she usually corralled her thick, black hair together in loose braids, knots, or threads, but there wasn't any time for hairdressing.

Perilous punched the red button next to the hatch with her gloved fist. She watched it slide open with a soft hiss revealing the dark landscape outside. At least the hatch was still working.

Infernal orbited a red dwarf. It hung very close to its mother star causing it to be tidal-locked. It meant half of Infernal was incredibly hot and bathed in red-tinged light, while the other half was cold and perpetually cloaked in darkness.

Perilous had managed to crash just across the dividing line on the dark side of the planet. This close to starside meant it wasn't

141

shrouded in complete darkness. The sky was lit up with stars and the residual glow from the light side of the planet.

She hadn't taken more than ten steps off her ship before her terrestrial suit began compensating for the cold. She pulled a black scarf from her pack and wrapped it so it covered her nose and mouth.

She also retrieved a scanner and raised it to her eyes to sweep the horizon. It cycled through the visual spectrums until she could make out the landscape.

It was all dark gray and flat for as far as she could see. There were rocks strewn across the ground like a god had been playing a game of skip, but that was the only characteristic of the surrounding area—save for the singular, surprising presence of a half-buried structure a few hundred feet in front of her.

Ships circled above her, in the night sky, like floating dots trailing thin lines of ion gas. They were descending slowly and would be on top of the Zanzibar in minutes. She adjusted the pack on her back and started for the structure at a full run.

Her black boots made a soft, crunching sound on the surface as she darted across the rocky ground. She was standing in front of it in less than a minute. It had appeared asymmetrical from several hundred feet away. But standing in front of it, she could tell it was the top of a massive head. Even the exposed head stretched hundreds of feet into the sky.

The entire structure must have once stood so high, it might have appeared to reach up to the stars. She wove her way through the large rocks surrounding it. When she was close enough, she reached out and placed her hand on its cool surface. It was like obsidian—a black stone with gray striations.

She moved along it, feeling her way down its side, until her hand found a doorway. There was no actual door. It was just an opening, which disappeared into darkness.

A breeze, emanating from within the structure, hit her in the face. It carried the smell of an old tomb, or a library with moldy books, to her nose. She glanced back at the Zanzibar, in the distance, and saw the squadron of Hornets setting down around it. She had no choice. There was nowhere else to hide.

Perilous opened a pouch on the outside of her jump-pack and pulled out a pair of black goggles. She pulled them on over her head, down onto her eyes, and dialed up the infrared spectrum with the small dial on the side. Then, with nothing left to lose, she stepped inside.

Here goes nothing.

Ten paces in, Perilous stumbled forward, nearly missing the first step. A staircase stretched down into the darkness. Smooth, black walls crowded in on her from both sides of a narrow passageway. She pulled her rayser from its holster with the soft scrape of metal on leather and kept going.

The scuffing sound of her boots on stone echoed all around her. It was frightening loud in the still silence. She climbed down the steps for what seemed like an eternity. Her knees buckled when she finally tried to place her foot on another non-existent step. She'd hit bottom.

Her goggles cycled through to a viewable spectrum, though it was still incredibly dim. It would have been preferable to use a flashlight, but that would have been like shooting off a flare pointing directly to her.

A large chamber stretched out in front of her. It was approximately forty feet high and another fifty across. Parts of the ceiling had caved in, covering the floor with rubble. The walls were covered in some ancient form of carving accented by a system of symbology that was utterly foreign to her. Though, it appeared, that some of the shapes were human-like.

A large, black, rectangular, stone block sat to her right. It was covered in more stone symbols. Perilous realized her mouth was dry. Was it the atmosphere? Or was it the stale air? Or maybe it was fear.

She pulled off her jump-pack, laid it on the stone block, and pulled out a thermos. The hair on the back of her neck stood on end. She jerked her head left and right. Her hand, with a mind of its own, yanked her rayser up to eye-level, as she tried to aim it everywhere at once. But she saw nothing.

Stay calm, Wil, she told herself.

Her heart was trying to run out of her chest. She raised her free hand to the side of her goggles, clicked through the various spectrums again, but there was nothing to be seen. Slowly, she slid her rayser back into its holster.

Her father's knife was poking her in the back, so she pulled it out and laid it on the stone block. Once her heart slowed down, and she was satisfied she was alone, she grabbed the thermos, unscrewed the top, and took a long swig of water.

She wiped her mouth with the back of her hand and sat the thermos on the stone block next to the knife, even as she tried to keep an eye on the entire chamber. She must have found an uneven part of the carvings on the stone because the thermos tipped over, spilling some of her water across its surface. She steadied the thermos, screwed the top back on, and prepared to continue exploring the structure.

Blaster fire rang out from behind her. She ducked down behind the black, stone slab. The squad had followed her into the structure.

Perilous snatched up her pack and made a mad dash deeper into the chamber with blaster fire following close behind her. She fired her rayser, blindly, behind her as she ran. She heard the whirring of their scanners tripping through the light spectrum trying to find the right setting so they could see better.

When she reached the far wall, she saw another doorway. She had no idea what was in front of her, but she ducked through it, and throwing caution to the wind, ran.

The passage curved like a snake, taking her deeper into the structure. It was only after she had her jump-pack on her back again that she realized she'd left her knife and thermos on the stone block. She cursed.

The thermos wasn't a great loss, but she loved that knife. It was one of the only things she still had that belonged to her father. Still, she didn't stop running. As much as she wanted to go back for the knife, she knew she couldn't. If it was a choice between her father's knife and escaping her pursuers, it wasn't a debate. She could be perilous, but she wasn't stupid.

She could almost see her father's face in her mind as she ran headlong into the dark, shaking his head at the thought she'd even briefly entertain the notion of going back for a knife.

The passage wound around until it slanted downward. It ended in another doorway. This one opened onto another chamber. A quick scan told her it had three levels, with staircases on either side, and hundreds of shelves lined up in rows. And wonder of wonders, they were filled with books.

It was like finding buried treasure. She looked around in awe. What might she find if she had the time to scour these shelves? An ancient library, on a derelict planet, in the Forgotten Sector? It was glorious. But the sound of metal boots on stone, behind her, told her she wouldn't get to indulge that fantasy. She kept running.

She sprinted across the chamber, down the spiraling staircase, descending all three levels at a run, until she found an exit. She darted through it, slid around a curved corner, and stumbled out into what appeared to be a vast hangar.

She raced across the hangar, her footfalls echoing in the open space, as she searched for a way out. The floor around her exploded with more blaster fire before she could reach the other side. She leaped over a console, landing hard, and rolled over, pulling herself up to a crouch. She was trapped.

The other side of the hangar was at least fifty paces away. There was no door or exit she could see. Even if there was one, there was no way for her to reach it before the men chasing her could get a bead on her.

Perilous listened to the sound of boots landing on the hanger floor as the men filled the entrance. There must have been twelve of them. She tracked the soft *thump* of those boots on the metal floor. They were fanning out in a semi-circle around her position.

Soon they would cross to where she was crouched and either capture her or kill her. Perilous held her rayser in both hands, with its sights pressed against her forehead. She was not going out without a fight. She steeled herself.

I guess this is it.

She took a deep breath, whispered a hushed apology to her parents, and prepared to launch herself at her pursuers. A scream echoed across the chamber. Blaster fire seemed to explode everywhere at once.

It took a moment to realize they weren't firing at her. The sound of metal ringing on metal, mixed with the screams of men, and more blaster fire, reverberated across the dark hangar. Perilous crouched down as low as she could get without actually laying on the floor.

The sound of men dying in terror, and explosions from wildly spraying blasters filled her ears. Perilous looked frantically for an exit. She didn't want to leave her cover without a direction in mind, but there just wasn't anywhere to go. And then, it all went silent.

The only thing she could hear was the pounding of her own heart in her ears. She wasn't used to being afraid. It was a rare thing for her. But fear crept up from inside her and grabbed hold with a death grip.

She'd long since learned how to take care of herself. Perilous was proud of her reputation for being fearless among her Guild colleagues. She'd go anywhere and do almost anything to get the job done. But, right now, she couldn't even make herself move.

The silence stretched on and on, until it became interminable—unbearable. She looked down and noticed the rayser in her hand was shaking. Her pulse raced. She could hear herself breathing in the darkness.

Finally, whispered to herself, "Get up, Periwinkle. Get. Up."

She still didn't move. She clenched her empty hand into a fist to try and stop it from shaking. She clamped her other hand down hard on her rayser's grip trying to accomplish the same end. She spoke to herself, again. This time, she spoke in a stern voice.

"Dammit, Wilhemina Periwinkle Akinawa. Get. Up. Now!"

This time she didn't think about it. She just jumped up from behind the console and fired her rayser in every direction all at once. It shook in her hand as the bright, green, pulses of energy burst from the rayser's emitter. But there was nothing to hit.

Finally, she forced herself to stop. It was only then that she saw the entrance to the hanger was littered with unmoving bodies dressed in mechsuits. Blasters, with wisps of smoke drifting up from their emitters, lay in unmoving hands. Perilous could smell the ionization still hanging in the stale air.

Pools of blood spread out from them. They were all dead. It should have been a relief, but it wasn't. What could have done such a thing? What could have massacred twelve heavily armed members of an Enduring fighter squadron?

Perilous had no idea how long she stood there. She just did, with her rayser pointed in the direction of the motionless bodies. Finally, she forced herself to move. She would retrace her steps to the surface, try to repair her ship, and get off Infernal as fast as she could. And she would never look back. She had no desire to meet whatever had done this.

She crossed the hangar in a crouch, with both hands on her rayser, trying to keep it steady. She moved so slow it must have taken five whole minutes to make it to the doorway. She gave the bodies a wide birth.

She tried not to look at them, but she couldn't help noticing the missing limbs. She heard a soft moan and nearly jumped out of her skin. She glanced in the direction the sound emanated from and saw one of the pilots looking up at her.

His arm was missing. He was nearly dead. He reached toward her with his other arm. His mouth moved as he tried to speak. Perilous just crouched there, by the doorway, watching him. Finally, he spoke in a ragged whisper.

"You released it? Are you insane?"

His hand dropped to his chest as his breathing became shallow.

He licked his lips and gasped, "What have you done?"

Perilous saw the horror in his eyes. His head slumped back onto the floor, and he was gone. She crouched there for a moment more. What did he mean? He blamed her for whatever killed him? But why would that have been her fault?

Perilous forced herself to keep moving. When she finally made it through the doorway, she ran. She raced up the passageway into the ancient library. She took the steps two and three at a time as she ascended its three levels. She careened through the top level into the other passage, without thought for a shelf or a book.

Up and around, she slid, until she was running back into the first the chamber where she had left her knife and thermos. It took everything she had in her to stop at the rectangular stone block to retrieve the knife. But when she looked over the stone block, she could not find it or the thermos.

What she did find was the top of the stone block slid back, revealing an empty interior. It no longer looked like a solid stone block at all. It looked like a coffin or a sarcophagus—an empty one.

The cylinder bounced on the floor, twice, with a metallic *clang* before skidding to a stop near her feet. Perilous looked down just in time to watch the stun grenade explode. A wave of energy washed over her, and darkness swallowed her whole. She was unconscious before her body hit the floor.

Perilous raised her chin off her chest with an involuntary groan. Her head throbbed as she looked around. Metal constraint-bands held her ankles and wrists in place.

The room was about twenty feet square, and she was sitting—bound—in the very center. The chair was the only furniture in a room with all the character of a prison cell. The walls were metal. The ceiling was low. It was a metal box. That told her everything she needed to know.

When the only door slid open with a soft *whosh* and a man in a gray and white uniform strolled in, Perilous knew where she was. The door closed behind him.

He was just shy of about six feet tall. His dark brown complexion was just a shade darker than her own. His hair was finger-length but twirled into tiny twists. His jawline was chiseled

149

and angled to a narrow chin. A wide nose stuck out over thick lips. The sneer is what made him unattractive—as did the nasal tone of his voice.

"I am Commander Nussu Kaldar, of the Enduring Cruiser Valiant. My captain ordered you locked away. You will be taken to our starbase in a nearby sector where you will stand trial for this madness. But, before you are dropped into a deep, dark hole and forgotten, I had to see you for myself. I wanted to know if you were insane, stupid, or both."

He pranced around the small cell like a preening bird putting its feathers on display. He looked her up and down like he was inspecting a dishevel soldier in a review line. Perilous picked a spot on the wall and stared at it. She wasn't going to give him the satisfaction of a response.

She ignored him and, instead, turned her mind to more important matters. The first order of business was escaping this room—this wasn't the first tight spot she'd been in. Then, she needed to find her jump-pack. After that, she'd worry about finding a way off this ship—likely the battle cruiser and home to the Hornets that shot her down.

There was always a way off a ship like this. She wasn't proud of how frightened she'd been on the surface of Infernal, but her head was back in the game now. There were still a few tricks up her sleeve.

Nussu Kaldar was standing to her right and still starring.

Ew, she thought.

She was about to insult him, just for fun, when the lights went out. An alarm blared. A red emergency light switched on overhead.

Kaldar ran to the door and entered his code in the access pad. The door slid open. He stepped into the hall and was struck by something, which sent him flying back into the room. He barely missed Perilous as he flew by.

He hit the floor hard. Perilous craned her neck to look over at where he was crumpled on the deck. He wasn't moving. He just lay there. Was he dead, or just unconscious?

She watched the figure stroll into the cell. It felt like a chill ran through her. The thing loomed at nearly seven feet tall.

It approached the chair and stood over her. Then it produced her lost knife from somewhere in the flowing black robes it wore.

It brandished it in front of her face, while a cool voice said, "Is this your knife?"

It turned out to be a *her*. Perilous was not a short woman, but even if she hadn't been sitting this woman would've towered over her.

Her black robe was closed with a black sash around her waist. A black underrobe, with a high collar, peeked out from the top of the outer robe. Her head was covered by black cloth wrapped several times around it, forming a kind of hat with a matching veil.

The curled toes of her black boots stuck out from under the hem of the flowing robes. Her fingers were covered with silver rings of varying sizes and shapes. Her wrists were stacked with silver bracelets.

Perilous could only see her dark eyes peeking out above the black veil. Her skin was as black as her clothing. The only other adornment Perilous could see was a sword stuck in her sash, and Perilous' knife in her hand. The slightly curved sword hilt was covered in silver gilt. The scabbard was black with silver accents.

Perilous yelled, "Help! Help! Someone, help!"

She strained against the constraint-bands, to no avail. She was going to die here. Her heart raced in her chest.

A small, palm-sized, gray disk floated into the cell from the corridor. It drifted over to Perilous and stopped to hover a few feet overhead. A green light emanated from it.

The light cascaded over her, from head to toe. When it winked out, a high-pitched, computerized voice emanated from it.

"Why are you yelling for help?"

Perilous looked from the disk to the tall, slender woman in black.

She stopped her futile struggle against the constraints and said, "Uh ... I ... I'm sorry. I thought you were going to kill me like you did those other men. That was you down on the surface of Infernal, wasn't it?"

The floating disk pulled back from Perilous and circled the tall woman.

She spoke in that chilling voice again and said, "Light, Inceku."

At her command, the disk glowed with a low intensity blue light. Slowly, it grew brighter until Perilous was able to see clearly. The disk rose higher, flooding the entire room with light. Perilous nearly caught her breath as she gazed fully on the woman in front of her.

The woman said, "I will ask again. Is this your knife?"

Perilous cleared her throat and said, "Yes, it's my knife."

The woman nodded curtly and leaned down closer to Perilous' face. Her voice was a little deeper than might be expected. It was also hard, like metal. But it had a melody to it, that made it almost pleasant to hear.

She continued, "And was that your water poured onto my resting place?"

She must have meant where Perilous had spilled her water on top of what she now knew was a black, stone sarcophagus. So, she nodded.

The woman nodded her own head in response and continued, "Good. I am grateful I did not make a mistake. Inceku scanned the sarcophagus, detected your DNA, and traced you to the hanger—

but he has been known to make mistakes. He is in sore need of an update. I am sorry I left you there, but there were other intruders in the Temple who had to be dealt with."

The disk floating overhead sputtered as if it was insulted that the woman thought it had made a mistake identifying Perilous.

"You have presented water and steel as the traditional Offering. I accept. Are you ready to make the Bond? We do not have much time."

The woman looked around the room as if just noticing how empty it was. Her comment about time suddenly brought the reality of the alarm still blaring back to Perilous' attention.

I need to get off this ship!

Perilous stared at the woman, with narrowed eyes and a crinkled nose, as if she was speaking an unknown language. But the woman just gazed back at her, twirling the knife in her hand.

Perilous said, "I'm not sure what you mean?"

The disk, still floating overhead, hummed and spoke, "You have given the Nazzareem the customary Offering of water and steel. She will now serve as your *Okun*."

Perilous opened her mouth but did not know what to say.

She looked up at the disk and said, "What if I don't want an Okun? Whatever that is."

"According to custom, after being given the ritual offerings, Acacia of the Nazzareem, Daughter of the Night, Servant of the Way, having then been rejected, would be forced to take your life. Honor must be satisfied."

The woman, apparently named Acacia, responded as though it was a phrase uttered a thousand times.

"Honor must be satisfied."

Perilous' eyes went wide, and her mouth dropped open. Acacia had saved her not once but twice. But now she would kill her?

Perilous shook her head, still stunned, and said, "Well then, Acacia, Daughter of the Night, Servant of the Way, I accept."

The disk floated down to hover in the air between them. It bathed the chair in a beam of green light. The constraint-bands around her wrists and ankles fell off with a soft click. Perilous stood and rubbed her wrists.

She looked down at Nussu Kaldar, who was still unconscious, and said, "Ok, we have to go."

But the disk, which clearly housed some kind of artificial intelligence, said, "We may not leave just yet. Please, repeat after me: I, speak your name, will never aim you unjustly, use you unwisely, or cause you to be dishonored. This is my bond."

Perilous looked up at the taller woman and said, "I, Wilhemina Periwinkle Akinawa, will never aim you unjustly, use you unwisely, or cause you to be dishonored. This is my bond."

Acacia replied, "I, Acacia, Daughter of the Night, born of the Mountain, Servant of the Way, will serve your cause, keep you from harm, and lay down my life for you if necessary. This is my bond."

The AI said, "Hold out your hand."

She held out her hand as requested. Acacia held out her own. A bright, blue light emanated from the floating disk. The beam flashed onto their hands and focused into a tight beam. Perilous yelped.

When the light cleared, the backs of both their hands had a small, blue sword emblazoned on them. Perilous lifted her hand to look at it. It was like a tattoo but made of light.

It faded away as she stared at it, until she moved her hand, and then it lit up again. While Perilous gazed in awe at the back of her hand, Acacia pulled the black veil down revealing the rest of her face. The woman was stunning.

She looked other worldly—not in the way some of her male colleagues would see her, an exotic example of otherness, but unique—an ancient example of something distinct from the current biological hegemony of the Known. She smiled at Perilous with bright, white teeth and pronounced canines.

They were sharp like fangs, and longer than normal. She had high cheekbones, full lips, and a small but broad nose with a silver ring hanging from her septum.

Acacia tucked Perilous' knife into its sheath and then in her sash. She waved off Inceku like you would an insect buzzing around your head, she said, "What now, Mistress?"

Perilous looked around the cell and then out toward the corridor.

"We need a way off this ship. But first, I need to find my jump-pack. I can't leave without it."

Acacia waved off the suggestion saying, "I found the pack you left behind in the sarcophagus chamber. It is on board the ship."

Perilous quirked an eyebrow and said, "What ship?"

The towering woman said, "I believe it was the ship that brought you to Infernal? Inceku said the name in the ship's registry is the Zanzibar."

Perilous said, "You got him to fly?"

Her voice was thick with incredulity.

"Yes, Mistress. Inceku was able to get the ship operational, but he will need more time to bring the Starlight drive online."

Perilous blinked and stared at Acacia for a moment, allowing it to sink in.

"Well, where is he?"

Acacia's voice was still cool and unperturbed.

"The ship is mag-locked to the hull of this Cruiser, near its auxiliary hatch."

"Uh, Ok. Well, let's get to the Zanzibar."

Acacia nodded, "Yes, Mistress. Follow me."

She fell in behind Acacia as they entered the corridor. What followed, baffled her. The woman trotted ahead, with Inceku floating above them. Armed guards swarmed through the decks of the Cruiser. But, Acacia, with only a sword in her hand, swept through them like a comet burning a trail through a star system.

She moved faster than Perilous thought possible. One moment, she was in front of Perilous, and somehow, in the time it took her to blink, she was behind a detachment of guards, dismembering them.

At one point, Perilous thought she saw the woman vanish as she turned the corner ahead of her. But that could not possibly be what she had seen. Blaster fire left black burn marks on the spot where Acacia had been standing and the wall behind it.

By the time Perilous turned the corner, all she found was another pile of dead men, slumped near one another in the corridor, with Acacia motioning for her to catch up. Soon enough, the woman was escorting her into an auxiliary hatch, which led onto the Zanzibar.

As soon as Perilous mounted the ramp, Acacia turned back toward the interior of the Cruiser.

"Acacia, where are you going?"

She smiled, barring her perfect teeth with their fang-like canines.

"I am going to buy you some time, Mistress. Inceku will plug back into the Zanzibar and get the Starlight drive functioning. He will need time to complete the repairs. I will ensure that the crew of this Enduring ship learns you are protected. Go, I will return shortly."

The woman—a towering apparition wrapped in black—disappeared into the dark of the corridor. The crew of the Cruiser had not managed to restore power yet. Perilous almost felt sorry for them.

She turned, entered the Zanzibar as the hatch closed, and quickly made her way to the bridge. Once there, Perilous dropped into her seat and began checking the ship's systems. Inceku floated across the bridge and attached itself to the main console.

One by one, panels glowed to life. Perilous watched as system after system came online. She stood up and walked around the bridge, checking everything from navigation to the readout on the engines. Slowly, Inceku was bypassing damaged systems, rerouting power, and priming the engines.

She returned to her seat and ran a diagnostic on the Starlight drive. Sure enough, while the Inter-Sol engines were functioning, the Starlight drive was still offline.

"Inceku, how long until we can jump into Slipstream?"

"Twenty minutes, Mistress."

She cursed. Twenty minutes was an eternity in a fight or an escape.

"Why can't the Cruiser detect us? We are, after all, attached to its hull."

"I have cloaked the energy signature of the ship so the Cruiser's sensors cannot detect us. If we were in range of a viewport, anyone looking out one could see us. But we will not appear on any of their instruments."

"Cloaked, huh?"

She raised an eyebrow at the idea a ship could be cloaked, even the type of cloaking Inceku was describing.

"Ok. It's a good thing they don't know where we are, but what's next? They'll eventually launch more Hornets to search for us once they realize we aren't on board. And one of them will discover us. We can't stay here indefinitely."

Inceku chimed.

"Not to worry, Mistress. They will be too busy."

The AI clearly meant too busy with Acacia.

"What is she going to do?"

"Mistress, she is going to rid you of your problem."

Perilous sat there for a moment before she asked, "Why are the Enduring so afraid of Acacia? I mean, aside from her astounding facility for violence. They act as if she's some kind of monster."

Inceku beeped and chirped as if he was cycling through a set of computations before finally saying, "Because of what happened between the Enduring and the Nazzareem."

Perilous could not stop herself from wondering what was happening over on the Cruiser.

"Can you patch us into the com-system of the Valiant so I can hear what's happening over there?"

"Yes, Mistress. I will follow Acacia's progress for you, from deck to deck."

The connection to the Valiant's com-system opened with a series of beeps, and Perilous heard a scream punch through the open channel. Somehow, she knew it was not Acacia. She glanced down at the glowing tattoo on the back of her hand.

While Acacia made her way through the other ship, she sat on the bridge of the Zanzibar and listened. She continued her conversation with only the morbid sounds of Acacia's rampage in the background.

"Tell me what happened between the Enduring and the Nazzareem, Inceku."

The AI buzzed, chimed, and chirped as if it were calling up the memory, before saying, "Thousands of years ago, when the first expeditions from the member planets of the Known reached the edge of Known space to what is now called the Forgotten Sector, they discovered an ancient civilization of warriors known as the Nazzareem. The tidal-locked planet seemed uninhabitable at first. But they discovered a thriving, technologically advanced civilization, which had adapted to the planet's peculiarities. On the edge of the dark side of the planet they found a single mountain, worshipped like a temple. Inside that mountain lived a woman of indeterminate age, known only as the *Old Woman in the Mountain*."

A bloodcurdling scream echoed though the com-channel along with yelling and the sound of boots thumping on deckplates. Inceku continued unperturbed.

"The explorers sent word to their planets and some of them sent emissaries. One planet, Valeria, discovered that the members of the ancient civilization wanted nothing more than to practice their skills as warriors in the service of others. So, Valeria entered into a pact with the Nazzareem. They took the Bond."

Someone was howling into the Valiant's com for help on deck eleven. Inceku whirred, chirped, and continued.

"For a thousand years, Valeria prospered. Their ships, their cities, and expeditions were guarded by the warriors of the Nazzareem. The Nazzareem became the most feared beings in this distant sector of the galaxy. They were loyal, fearless, and skilled beyond compare. They would even fight each other in ritual combat, if their Bond-Holders came to an impasse among themselves. Many a grievance between ships, merchants, and colonies were resolved by two Okun doing battle. It was a sight to behold. In an age of blasters and Slipstream starships, there were still beings who fought with swords. The Nazzareem had the technological wherewithal to build advanced weaponry, but they only ever carried a sword stuck in the black sashes wrapped around their waists."

Perilous listened to the story Inceku spun with one ear and the screams, mixed with blaster fire, coming from the Valiant through the open com-channel with the other.

"So, what happened?"

"The Valerians got into a trade dispute with a planet from a nearby system called Luxor. When the negotiations broke down, the Senate on Valeria sent word to the Nazzareem that the people of Luxor had stolen from them, dishonoring them in the process. They sent the Nazzareem to Luxor to punish them for it and to restore their honor. And the Nazzareem did just that. A horde of the greatest warriors the galaxy had ever seen descended from the night sky on an unsuspecting Luxor like avenging spirits. They burned the planet to the ground. The people of Luxor had blasters, metal bio-suits, slipstream capable starships, defense grids, and other advanced technology, but none of it matter. When it was over, and the Nazzareem strolled into what was left of the central archive on Luxor, they learned the truth. The data they retrieved revealed the Valerians had lied. It was the people of Luxor who had been cheated in the deal not the Valerians. And the Valerians had used the Nazzareem to cover up their crime. An inconceivable rage rippled through the Nazzareem like a wave. But the Valerians were monitoring the activity on the ground—particularly the Luxorian Central Archive. They had hoped to be able to wipe the data once the archive's firewall had fallen. But they were too late. They watched as the First Warrior, and commander, of the Nazzareem discovered their treachery. And in a panic, the Valerians did the unthinkable. They launched Desecrators from orbit. The antimatter torpedoes were also known as planet killers. In one fell swoop, the Valerians destroyed Luxor and most of the Nazzareem, who were still planet-side—all in a matter of minutes. Then, they turned their attention to the Nazzareem homeworld. Before anyone knew what was happening, they destroyed it too. They had seen the wrath of the Nazzareem fall on people for more than a thousand years. The Valerians knew if they left even one alive they were courting doom. They thought they eradicated every single one on that awful day. And when they were done, they placed a beacon in orbit around the dead planet to keep anyone from ever discovering their sin. They should have searched the planet afterward. But their terror kept them on their starships. Acacia only survived because she was in a healing chamber, in the temple of Abassa, on the dark side of the planet. The Tower of Akral was buried in the destruction, but the sarcophagus kept her safe, and asleep. She was in suspended animation until you stumbled upon her. And now she is free, and with a Bond. And you have set her loose on her ancient enemies."

"But if she was in suspended animation, how did she know what happened to her people?"

Inceku said, "I shared the transmission sent by the First Warrior from Luxor, and an account of what happened once she was awake."

Perilous stared at Inceku and shook her head almost imperceptibly. The sounds of fighting and people dying echoed across her bridge, through the open com-channel. She should have stopped Acacia. She should have called her back to the Zanzibar. But her mouth would not open—her hand would not move. She just sat there and listened.

Acacia made her way through the Cruiser, deck by deck. Alarms continued to sound on the Valiant. Perilous listened as the crew tried everything in their power to survive the rampage. They decompressed entire decks. They turned off life-support. They manually jammed doors and rerouted power to security fields. It was all to no avail.

Somehow, with just a sword in her hand, the woman managed to eradicate everyone who crossed her path, like she was hunting vermin that had infested a building. It was insanity. It should not have been possible. She was like an avenging force from some ancient myth or fairytale. Perilous must have listened to the carnage for nearly a half hour. And then, suddenly, there was only silence.

She sat up straight when she realized several minutes had passed with no sounds save for the blaring alarms reverberating through the Cruiser's decks. And then even those stopped with a sharp chirp. All that remained was a soft buzz coming through the com-channel, like empty static.

Perilous checked her instruments, but they were working fine. The channel was still open. There just wasn't anything to transmit. And then she saw the red light flash on her panel, indicting a hatch to the Zanzibar opening. She stood and slowly made her way to the lower deck. She only made it halfway.

One deck down, she met Acacia on her way up to the bridge. The woman had blood on her face and hands. Her black robes were wet in spots, with what Perilous assumed was more blood. It dripped from her sword blade onto the deck like raindrops.

Perilous took an involuntary step back. She wasn't sure if it was from fear or surprise. But Acacia saw it. She wiped her sword blade on her sleeve, slid it back in its scabbard at her waist, and knelt down, placing her right hand flat on the deck.

She looked up from where she crouched and said, "Mistress, you have nothing to fear from me. The Bond is all. If you keep your part, I will always be faithful to mine. Thank you for allowing me to deal with your enemies and the ancient adversaries of my people."

Perilous looked down at Acacia for a moment, swallowed hard, and said, "You're welcome, Acacia. Go get cleaned up. If Inceku was right when he estimated repair time, we should be able to jump into Slipstream now."

Acacia stood and said, "Yes, Mistress."

Perilous pointed back down the length of the deck from the direction Acacia had come and said, "Back down to the end of the deck, turn right, and you will find quarters. Choose one. They each have particle showers. There is a clothing rezmat in the wall between the last two quarters. It will clean your clothing."

Acacia nodded and turned back in the direction Perilous had indicated. She watched her go. When she disappeared around the corner, Perilous turned and made her way back to the bridge.

When she arrived, she dropped back into her seat and said, "Inceku, is the Starlight drive operational?"

"Yes, Mistress. We can jump into Slipstream once we clear the star's gravity well."

"Very well. Detach us from the Valiant and set a course out of the system."

"Yes, Mistress."

Perilous sat back in the chair and watched Inceku detach the Zanzibar from the hull of the Valiant. She felt the ship swing beneath her, as maneuvering thrusters turned the Zanizbar until the Inter-Sol engines kicked in, blasting the ship on course out of the star system.

She watched the Valiant through the main viewport as it shrunk from view. It was dark, and adrift in space like a floating tomb. She let the AI pilot the Zanzibar while she disappeared into her own thoughts.

She lost track of time. It was only when Acacia dropped down onto the deck next to her chair, folding her long legs up into her lap, that Perilous realized nearly an hour had passed.

The woman's veil hung loosely around her neck as she smiled up at her. Perilous grimaced. It was not long before she was back to being lost in thought, even with Acacia nearby. After letting her ruminate, uninterrupted, for a while, Acacia spoke up.

"What has a grip on your mind, Mistress?"

Perilous looked down at her. At some point she was going to have to have a discussion with the woman about calling her

Mistress. She starred down at Acacia for a moment. But it was clear she was looking right through her.

Acacia tilted her head and narrowed her eyes as if she were trying to read Perilous.

Finally, Perilous shook herself out of her reverie and said, "Yes. I have something important on my mind. I guess I should tell you about it, since our trouble with the Enduring is not going to be the last problem we face. Come with me."

Perilous rose from her chair. Acacia flowed up from the floor in a single movement. Perilous left the bridge with her Okun in tow. She had to look over her shoulder to make sure Acacia was behind her. The woman did not make a sound as she followed. It was creepy.

She tried to ignore it and continued on until she reached the main cargo hold. Inceku had informed her that Acacia had placed her jump-pack in the hold. And there it was, against the wall, to the right of the door. She lifted the pack off the deck and found a nearby crate to set it on. She unbuckled the straps, pulled open the flap, and reached inside to pull out her find.

She laid it gently on the crate. It was a platinum sleeve about a foot and a half in diameter. It opened like a book. When she popped it open, Acacia inhaled with awe. Her eyes widened and she leaned in for a closer look.

It was a large, circular, gold-plated, copper disk. There were nine diagrams engraved on the face. Perilous described them to the woman. In the upper left section, there was a circle that looked like the disk, with a binary code around its circumference.

Below that was a profile view of the same image with a similar binary code indicating how to *play* the disk and at what speed. There were seven other images with other coding, including a wave form, frame references, time scans, and an illustration of the two states of a hydrogen atom with spin measurements for their protons and electrons, which gave a fundamental clock reference for all the other diagrams on the disk.

Acacia nodded and said, "It's beautiful. But why is it so important to you."

Perilous pointed to the last diagram, in the bottom left section. It looked like a starburst with a dot at the center and thin lines bursting outward.

"This is the most significant part of this disk. It's a pulsar map. It defines the location of a certain star using the location of fourteen pulsars in the galaxy. Each of the lines are made with binary codes defining the frequencies of each of the pulses. It's a map."

Perilous couldn't contain her excitement. Acacia looked more closely at the diagram.

"I see, Mistress. That is ingenious. But a map to where?"

Perilous continued, "That's just it. The case containing the disk had a cartridge and needle. The diagrams on the face showed me how to play the disk. And when I did, I heard music, and languages, and sounds of creatures. The messages made it clear. The disk is from Earth. The pulsar map is a map to the location of Earth's sun, and by extension Earth itself. Now, that may not mean much to you. But, while you've been asleep, many planets in the Known have fought over whether they could lay claim to being the Original Earth. Wars have been fought over it. For nearly three thousand years no one has been able to find any fossil records or evidence to point to its definitive location. That knowledge was thought lost to the ages. This golden disk, launched from Earth tens of thousands of years ago, is likely the greatest archaeological find in the Known."

Acacia seemed impressed, but not overly excited by it all. She simply said, "Mistress, it seems to me that if this find is as important as you say, then it's fortunate we have found one another. You will need my sword before this is all said and done. But don't worry, I will keep you safe."

With that, Acacia turned and left the cargo hold. Perilous watched her go. She chuckled to herself at Acacia's lack of excitement. The woman was non-plus about it all. But, as Perilous gazed down at the gold-plated copper disk in her hands, she had the suspicion that this woman, who had likely been asleep for two thousand years or more, was right.

Some would see the disk she had pried loose from the charred remains of an ancient probe crashed on a distant planet, as a sacred piece of history to be venerated. Others would see it as a talisman capable of bestowing power. The truly dangerous, however, would be those who saw a definitive map to the Original Earth as a threat.

They would want to destroy it and anyone who had seen it or come in contact with it. Perilous would have to be extremely careful. A misstep could have deadly consequences.

She knew all about finding things. She knew her way around star charts, historical clues, and archaeological techniques for unearthing artifacts and preserving them. But, when it came to politics and negotiating the treacherous waters of power and influence, Perilous was lost.

She gently placed the disk back in its platinum sleeve before sliding it back into her jump-pack. She carried the pack with her as she left the cargo hold. As she made her way back to the bridge, she decided Acacia was right. She didn't know what power in the universe had crash-landed her on Infernal or caused her to inadvertently offer up water and steel to an ancient goddess—demon? And while she knew, under normal circumstances, Acacia should not frighten her—what the woman could do did.

At the moment, all Perilous could do was thank the gods of the Known that she found her. It was all risky. Taking the disk to the heart of the Known and announcing its existence, with an ancient creature by her side—all very risky. But that was why she walked the last few feet toward the bridge with a broad grin on her face. Her father hadn't called her Perilous for nothing.

Now, all she had to do was figure out how to tell Acacia she was part Valerian.

PLANET 113

~

Our sin shackles us to our fate.
~ Inscription above the Temple of Purification
in the Shining City

[8] *Then the earth shook and trembled; the foundations of heaven moved and shook, because he was wroth.* [9] *There went up a smoke out of his nostrils, and fire out of his mouth devoured: coals were kindled by it.* [10] *He bowed the heavens also, and came down; and darkness was under his feet.* [11] *And he rode upon a cherub, and did fly: and he was seen upon the wings of the wind.* [12] *And he made darkness pavilions round about him, dark waters, and thick clouds of the skies.* [13] *Through the brightness before him were coals of fire kindled.*

~ 2 Samuel 22:8-16

T he *A'ku* alerted them when it dropped out of *Ethereal Space*. The Builder rocked in their seat as the ship shuttered. Passing into *Corporeal Space* could sometimes be rocky. They checked their instruments. The A'ku had detected a Category One and changed course. Pah sent a coded message to the Shining City containing the preliminary scans.

The A'ku skimmed the exosphere. Massive super storms raged over half the planet. Magnetic readings indicated reversed poles. Seventy percent of the landmasses were beneath acidic water. Coral reefs, plankton, and nearly all marine life was gone. By the time A'ku was setting down, they had received a provisional reply, contingent upon a final assessment.

Pah waited for the soft *chunk*, combined with a single shudder of the ship, which told them the A'ku had landed. They made their way to the hatch as A'ku went into temporary hibernation. When they arrived, the hatch slid silently open. A slim beam of blue light extended to the ground below. They walked down the beam onto blackened, lifeless dirt. Three steps from A'ku, the beam dissipated, and the hatch closed.

They stood on a small rise overlooking a flat stretch of land near a tepid lake. Pah pushed some of the blackened earth around with the toe of their black boot. They knelt, hovering a large brown hand over the soil. The soft glow of green light eradiated from their palm. Large lips pressed into a thin line. There was sand, silt, and clay, but no nitrogen, phosphorus, sulfur, or micronutrients. They crouched, scooping up a handful, and letting it run through their dark brown fingers.

They gazed up into what should have been a clear blue sky. But it was shrouded by gray particulates of carbon monoxide, ozone, nitrogen oxides, and volatile organic compounds blocking out the rays of the system's main sequence star. According to

170

where this continent sat and where the planet's rotation was in its current cycle, the star should be fully visible, and flooding the ground with light.

They touched the sigil embedded in their forehead, placing the tips of two fingers on the golden starburst, and whispered, "Our sin shackles us to our fate."

They stood and made their way down to the lake. As they walked, they looked for anything green – any indication of even the possibility of flora. But all the way to the dark horizon there was nothing but the blackened skeletons of trees. Where the ground was not barren black earth, it was covered in tan lifeless grass like an ossified sea of death. Their sadness deepened with each step.

When they reached the lake, they were not surprised by what they found. It was fouled. The rancid smell rose to greet them. Parts of it were covered in thick gray slug. Nothing lived in its waters. They gazed into it and saw their reflection looking back.

Their robe was blue, as the water should have been. Shimmering gold brocade ran up the arms and across the bodice. Their shaved brown head, and face, glistened lightly. Even in the dimness of the toxic shroud covering the sky, the golden sigil on their forehead shone with a soft light.

Pah reached up to touch their face and the golden bracelets around their wrist jangled softly. The golden rings on their fingers sparkled. The sadness is their eyes could still be seen in the putrid reflection.

It was a heartbreaking cycle they were an eternal witness to. Planet after planet, begun in abundance, with life overflowing, found to be fouled and toxic. They would land, assess the damage, and call for a cleansing. And the cycle would begin again – hope, but then carelessness and greed, followed by destruction, heralding

171

rebirth. According to the *Eternal Record of Creation*, this would be Planet 113's ninth.

Pah had seen enough.

With a wave of their hand, they conjured a blue globe of pulsating light. They touched it lightly. Their fingertips flowed over the bright surface, inputting their final assessment. They had no doubt it would mean an implementation of the Holy Directive. An *Architect* would arrive shortly, and the cleansing would begin.

A scream jerked them away from their reverie. The globe vanished. They looked off to the right, across the sea of dead grass, past the skeletons of trees and saw them. A female terrestrial, dragging a small male child behind her, was running from a small group of large males. They were closing the distance between them fast.

Pah calculated the rate of speed in their mind and determined that it would be another one hundred and twenty-three seconds before they caught up to her. As Pah watched them close the gap, they told themself, *It is not your concern. You are prohibited. Stay out of it, Builder. Stay out of it.*

They watched the group overtake the female and child. She screamed and tried to fight but was knocked to the ground. The small boy stood by watching helplessly and crying. Pah turned and began walking toward the A'ku. The planet was definitely a Category One.

In the *Umzi,* back in the Shining City, they would argue the *Right and Good* of the Precepts and that nothing was gained by focusing on the circumstances of individual terrestrials. That was neither their charge nor *Calling.* They were supposed to carry out the Holy Directive once a planet was designated a Category One.

Pah reached down to touch the inside of their left wrist with their right finger so they could *Step* across the landscape to where the woman lay. But before they could they saw a flash of golden light. The men fell back from the woman, throwing up their hands to cover their eyes. When the light faded a small woman was standing between them and their prey.

Pah touched the inside of their wrist and *Stepped*. In a blink they were standing near the woman. But they remained *Unseen* so they could watch.

She was only a girl. Her skin was a darker brown than Pah's. Her hair was a lustrous mane of thick black hair covering her head like a large wooly crown. She wore a simple brown tunic that tied at her shoulder with a bit of brown cloth tied around her waist. Matching brown pants tucked into soft brown slip-on boots. It was all covered in leaves and vines embroidered in bright green thread.

She did not speak. She simply stood there waiting.

The men were thin, dirty, and haggard. Their clothes hung on their gaunt limbs like laundry on a clothesline. Their eyes were sunken, and their hair clumped with dirt. Pah covered their nose to block the smell.

Once the men realized it was a small girl between them and their prey they attacked. But the girl did not move. Instead, she spread her arms wide and closed her eyes.

Pah could see what they could not. Golden light flowed out of her, washing over them like waves of emotional energy. It did not hurt them, but it did stop them in their tracks.

Pah watched in rapt attention as the men fell to their knees and cried out. It wasn't pain. It was something else. Soul crushing lament painted their faces.

They prostrated themselves, covering up like they naked before her gaze. They shuddered from tears their bodies could not produce. Their stomachs heaved, attempting to throw up food from empty stomachs.

Pah could not tear their eyes away. They realized their mouth was hanging open and closed it.

The girl turned away from the torment and anguish. She took a few steps toward the woman and helped her up. She followed her a few more feet to where the small boy stood shaking.

A few calming words and a touch for each soothed their fear. Then the girl told them to wait.

When she turned from them, she said, "Were you just going to watch?"

It took Pah a moment to register that she was talking to them.

"Yes, Holy One. I am speaking to you. Will you reveal yourself?"

It was against the Precepts of the Right and Good. But Pah's curiosity got the better of them. They touched the inside of their wrist again and made themselves *Seen*.

Pah looked down on them. Even the largest terrestrials were like tiny children next to the Builders.

The men took one look at them and scattered. The woman pulled at her child as she slowly backed away.

The girl turned to the woman and said, "Don't be afraid. The Holy One will not harm you."

She turned back to Pah and gazed up at them.

"So, were you really going to just watch?"

"It is against—"

The girl, the woman, and child clamped their hands over their ears and cried out. Pah had never spoken with terrestrials and so had forgotten what their voice would do them.

They *changed* their voice and tried again.

"I apologize. I am unused to speaking with terrestrials." They placed their hand over their heart and continued, "Forgive me."

The girl removed her hands from her ears and nodded. The woman cautiously moved her hands from her ears to the boy's, even as she held him close to body.

"I'm Aja. I've been waiting for you, Holy One."

174

"Is that so?"

"Yes, Great One. The inevitability of your arrival has been passed down from generation to generation."

"I see. And why have you been waiting for me?"

Aja made a sweeping gesture with her hand that took in their surroundings.

Pah smirked and nodded.

"Yes, we took notice. But I am not sure you understand the ramifications of my arrival."

The girl dropped her hand to her side and stared up at Pah for a moment before saying, "Are you not here to save us?"

"In a word, no. I am not."

"Then, why are you here?"

"The Holy Directive. This world is to be sanitized and reconditioned."

Aja looked to the horizon, over to the woman and child, and back to Pah.

"Why?"

This time it was Pah who made a sweeping gesture with his hand at their surroundings.

Aja said, "Ah, I see."

She crossed her arms over her chest and tapped her finger against pursed lips.

After a moment of thought she continued, "May I show you something before you sanitize and recondition us?"

It was all a violation – that they almost intervened, that they revealed themselves to a terrestrial, that they were even having this conversation. Their final assessment was complete. Pah had no doubt that the Architect would arrive soon. But they could not help themselves.

"Lead the way."

With a curt nod, the girl reached out for the woman who took her hand while still clutching tightly to the boy. Aja reached up her other hand and Pah bent down so that she could grab theirs. Her tiny hand was barely able to hold their smallest finger.

They were all engulfed in golden light and in a blink they moved.

Pah felt the transition. It wasn't quite Stepping but it was something similar. When they looked up from the girl, they saw that they stood at the entrance to a valley. Pah reached out and felt A'ku off to the north and east.

They followed Aja into the valley. The woman and her child ran ahead. They did not feel the barrier they passed through, but Pah did. It was like stepping onto a different planet.

The grass was thick and green. Fully leaved, verdant trees sprawled along the valley floor. A crystal-clear stream of water wound its way among multi-colored foliage. The air was bright and clean.

Soon, they arrived at a small collection of wooden houses surrounded by neatly tended gardens. A blue bird darted overhead, chirping, as if to say, hello. Chickens roamed freely and cows grazed behind the houses.

A small crowd of a dozen people gathered to meet them. They tried to greet the woman and child but mostly stared at Pah who stood back and watched.

Aja spoke a few soft words to the group. They gathered up the woman and child taking them into one of the larger houses. Once they were alone Aja made her way back to where Pah waited.

"What should I call you?"

"You may call me, Builder."

She nodded slowly.

"What do you think of our sanctuary?"

They gazed around the small settlement, taking it all in.

176

"It is a wonder."

Aja smiled. "I think so, too."

Pah tilted their head and said, "I think I know the answer, but humor me. How and why?"

She did not hesitate but motioned for Pah to kneel. "Please, I will show you."

Pah knelt and bent down so she could reach their head. Aja placed her tiny hands on either side of their face and the world vanished in a flood of golden light.

Her voice echoed in their mind as a vision of the world materialized before Pah's eyes. The world was young again and full of life.

"My particular convergence of DNA has coalesced nine times in the history of my world. Each time that human being came to lead people to a better world."

As she spoke the world changed as if they were watching the flow of time itself.

"Sometimes they were met with skepticism, sometimes with acceptance, but almost always with violence. The world struggled to accept the truth of what they presented."

The images slowed to show a woman crying for joy, a man leaving behind his belongings, and a small group of people sitting in a circle singing. The vision blurred, spun, and stopped again. This time it solidified into a jeering crowd throwing rocks and building burning to the ground as they cheered."

"And yet, my particular DNA coalesced into being again and again. Each time it was not me, but it was a kind of me. But no matter how many times it occurred the world never fully accepted what was offered. By the time I was born the world was in ruin."

Pah felt her hands leave their face and the world came back into focus.

They stood and looked around at the small settlement again.

177

"If you understand all of that, why did you create all of this? Why are you still trying to save them?"

Aja also looked around as she pursed her lips again and thought about Pah's questions. Her gaze swept one way and then another. As she turned to look back up at them, her eye caught something a few paces away in the undergrowth beneath a weeping tree. She took five steps and bent down, reaching into the grass. Pah watched as she grabbed a small tortoise that had somehow managed to end up on its back flailing its tiny legs in futility. She scooped it up, turned it over, placed it on its feet, and watched it amble off into the brush.

She stood, turned back to Pah, shrugged, and said, "Its who I am."

Her smile was big and bright. It made Pah warm inside. They realized they were smiling too. They opened their mouth, but before they could speak, thunder sounded high overhead.

Pah looked up and saw black clouds of smoke, gouts of flame, and blue flashing lights. The clouds parted and an immense gray vessel descended into the sky.

They heard Aja whisper, "A wheel within a wheel."

All Pah could say was, "The Architect."

They watched as the vessel descended until it stopped and hovered above the valley.

Pah looked down at Aja and said, "Your efforts have been laudable, but a waste, I'm afraid. The Architect is here. That means the Holy Directive has been approved and the cleansing of this world is about to commence. I'm sorry, I wish there was something to be done."

Aja swallowed hard, looked from Pah to the large building where the small group of people had come out to see what was happening, and said, "I have come nine times to this world. At first, I came with knowledge. Then, I came with wisdom. But this time, I came with power."

She vanished in a burst of golden light.

Pah felt her go. They knew immediately where she had gone. They touched the inside of their wrist and Stepped.

When they arrived in the Chamber of Making, Pah saw Aja standing in its center gazing up. To her it must have felt like being inside a mountain. The smooth gray floor disappeared into darkness on every side, as did the top of the chamber. Several Builders stood around looking at the small girl like they were seeing a lost child and wondering where her parents were. The only structure was the Seat of the Most High. Even Pah had to stretch their neck to look up to see where the Architect sat, perched just below the darkness.

The Architects robes were black like the unending space of a galaxy, sparkling with shimmering stars spinning around one another like spiraling solar systems, flowing down onto the top of structure like tail of a comet. Their skin was a darker brown than Pah's own. A floating circle of cosmic particles, like the rings of planets, crowned their head. Their voice came from everywhere and nowhere.

Pah, what have you brought into the Sanctum?

Pah cleared their throat and said, "I did not bring them, Architect. They brought themselves."

Three of the Builders moved toward Aja as if they were preparing to shoo her away. But as they got close, she bawled her hands into fists and a golden glow surrounded her.

"I am Aja. This planet is under my protection."

Pah watched in a fascinated horror. Nothing like this had ever happened in the history of the Shining City. They could not turn their eyes away from what they were seeing.

Undeterred, the Builders reached for the small girl. When they did the golden glow pulsed, expanded, and bounced off their hands. It could not repel them, but neither could they break through to touch her.

They looked at their hands, reached for the glowing nimbus again, and looked at their hands once more. It was fascination more than anything. They had come across something new and they were intrigued. When they realized they could not get through they looked up at the Architect.

Then something happened that Pah had never seen before.

The Architect rose from their seat and drifted down to the floor. Pah bowed his head along with the other Builders but not so low that he could not see what was happening.

Aja remained defiant. The look on her face made Pah smirk. The Shining City would be abuzz with this for the next ten thousand years. A terrestrial had entered an Architect's ship and defied the Holy Directive.

The Architect approached her, and the Builders backed away, making room. When the Architect reached for her, her radiance increased. This time the hand passed through her defense. But the Architect stopped short of touching her.

They waved their hand in and out of her luminescence and considered the tiny girl with a face even Pah could not read.

After a few more moments, they said, *Interesting. Who are you child, and why have you entered the Sanctum without invitation or right?*

Aja darted a glance at Pah and then back at the Architect.

Pah cannot help you, child.

Aja straightened her back and said, "I don't need the Builder's help. And it's you who are here without invitation or right. I know you're here to destroy my planet. I will not allow it."

The Architect looked over at Pah before returning their attention to Aja.

I see that today is full of surprises. I am afraid you are mistaken child. We are the Caretakers of Life. You exist because we made you and this planet. You have squandered that gift, again, and it is our duty to rectify the matter. There is nothing you can do to stop it.

With a wave of the Architect's hand, Aja's light vanished.

Pah, return her to the planet so that we may commence the cleansing.

As the Architect turned away from Aja, Pah quickly crossed to where she stood.

Aja looked up at Pah with such a plaintive look that their heart broke.

Without thought they said, "What about the Arbitration, Architect?"

The Architect stopped and turned.

You would invoke Ajudication?

Pah looked at Aja again, swallowed, and said, "Yes, Architect."

You understand the consequence if she is found wanting?

Pah thought for a moment. They had been in attendance as one hundred and thirteen planets were cleansed. Aeon after aeon, it had all been the same. This was the first time they had cared about the outcome. Maybe that was why there was a prohibition against speaking with terrestrials. They weren't supposed to get attached or involved. But Pah could not help themselves.

"Yes, Architect."

Then so be it.

The Builders formed a ring around Pah and Aja.

Aja said, "What have you done?"

"It is your only chance. I am linked to your fate now, little one."

"Thank you, Great One."

"Do not thank me yet."

When the ring of Builders parted, the Architect approached them with a scale in their hand.

When they stopped in front of Aja they said, *Are you ready to be judged, child?*

With a quick look at Pah, who stood silently by, she said, "I am."

Pah could tell by the look on her face that she did not know what to expect. It was not complicated or involved though. The Architect produced a feather from within their shimmering robes. It was made of pure black light that glistened with tiny white stars sparkling inside. They placed it on one side of the scales.

Then the Architect reached into Aja's chest. She exhaled sharply. Her heart came out in the Architect's palm. It wasn't, actually, her heart. It was golden and pulsing with light. It was what terrestials on her planet would call a soul. Pah knew it was all that she was, all that she had lived – every act, thought, word, and choice. It was the whole of her life and being.

The Architect placed it on the other side of the scale.

All the Builders leaned in to watch. If Pah breathed like a terrestrial, they would have been holding their breath. They watched, unable to tear their eyes away, forgetting, in that moment, that their own fate was tied to the outcome. They had never seen an Adjudication before. They were not even sure one had ever been performed. It was an archaic ritual taught in their preparing along with all of the other Precepts of the Right and Good. But Pah had never known it to be anything other than academic.

The scale tilted, weighed, and finally balanced.

A soft murmer ran through the Builders. The Architect looked closely at the scale and waited. It felt like a thousand years passed in the Sanctum as they watched. But the balance did not change.

Time moved again as the Architect took up Aja's being and placed it back in her chest. The scale disappeared into the Architect robes as they drifted back up to their seat.

Pah touched the inside of their wrist and Aja's shoulder. They Stepped back to the valley.

"What happened?" Aja squeaked.

But Pah simply watched as the Architect's vessel ascended back into the heavens and vanished.

"Great One, what happened?"

"You passed, child. You were judged and found Right and Good."

"Does that mean we are safe?"

"Yes, for now."

Aja breathed a deep sigh.

"I must tell the others the good news."

She took three quick steps toward the group of people still huddled by the large building. But then she stopped and turned back to Pah.

"I guess that means you are leaving now?"

Pah watched the spot where the Architects ship had disappeared for a while longer. Then, they turned to where Aja stood watching them.

"No. The price of your having passed judgement is that I must stay and shepherd this world back to health. I am bound here now. And cannot return to the Shining City until it has been accomplished."

Aja looked around at the valley and up into the sky.

"But that will take thousands of years."

"Yes, it will."

Aja opened her mouth, but Pah held up a hand to stop her.

"It is ok, child. I understood the cost. Now go, tell your people what has occurred."

183

Aja stared at Pah for a moment longer and said, "Thank you, Great One. We will talk later."

She flashed a big grin at them and dashed off toward the building.

Pah was gone before she reached them.

In a blink, they were back inside A'ku ascending into the skies. They located the highest mountain on the planet and set A'ku down. With a wave of their hand, they hid A'ku from sight. They were so high that they were above the clouds. They made their way to an observation deck and took up their watch. There were thousands of years of work to do. And the terrestrials could never know that they were there.

"No, child, I'm afraid we will never talk again."

LOOKING FOR GODEAU

"Good millet is known at the harvest."
~ farmer's proverb

Gorgamund *the Destroyer* was rampaging through the midwestern territories headed east. Tannin, carrying a tiny daughter in her arms, with a taller, skinny daughter hiding in her shadow stood outside Danyelle's settlement shaking with the aftermath of what she had seen let it spill from her like a punctured water skin.

She told the elders that she hadn't seen him. But his men shouted his name above the din of the death and destruction they wrought. Tannin's settlement was gone. It had been eradicated from the face of the world. Those who did not escape into the night were conscripted. Its men were pressed into service. Its women and children were fed to horde for its entertainment.

Danyelle's stomach ached from how she squeezed her insides into a knot at the horror of it all. Even worse, though they took the woman and her girls in, the elders decided they could reason with this Destroyer. They thought the ammunition factory at the heart of the settlement, which had survived the Fall, would be their advantage.

That and the *knowing* of how to make the ammunition, passed down by the settlement's ancestors to its present inhabitants was to be their ultimate bargaining chit. Danyelle thought it was madness. They were lambs awaiting a slaughter.

Once, they might have rallied – might have prepared to man the makeshift walls with rifles, handguns, and all the ammunition they could shoot. But after the sickness ravaged the settlement two winters gone, it had not only taken her parents, and a third of the settlement, but also their fight.

They were shadows of their former selves. It would take another twenty years to build the community back to where it had been. It was also why they hadn't turned the woman and her daughters away. They would be needed to rebuild. But that wouldn't happen if they didn't find a way to repel this jumped-up warlord and his horde.

Danyelle added another mark to the small square of parchment in her hand. With the reins clenched between her teeth, she counted the jots with the tip a broken pencil hovering above them. *Thirty.* It was hard to believe. She rolled the piece of pencil up in the bit of parchment before tucking them both in her coat pocket. She had started home twice.

The second time, she made it half a day on the road home before gritting her teeth, uttering a curse, and turning back to the search. She couldn't shake the stories. The elders whispered them over late-night fires. The same elders who usually told fanciful tales about handheld devices, which contained the accumulated knowledge of humanity.

It was all impossible to believe. But she and the others young people would sit in rapt attention with the light from the fires making them look like wraiths in the night. They claimed that all you had to do was tap on a glass screen to communicate with people on the other side of the world, or to call up any information you could possibly want. *Could such a thing be true? Of course not.*

The few elders who talked about the *Before,* in haunted whispers, appeared to believe it without question. Their eyes hardened and their lips pressed together into a firm line as they held out their hands pantomiming how the device worked. Soon enough, the ecstatic light of memory would fade from their eyes leaving only disgust at what had been lost. Danyelle heard words like *waste*, *greed*, and *apathy* among their mumblings, dropped like an ear of corn from a bundled arm full headed for a cart, as they walked away.

She first heard the word *waliyi* in those whispers. It took months to convince one of the elders to even repeat it. Chiku said it was a myth, a fairytale, best left to the pages of an artifact that might as well be as mythic - a book.

Danyelle tried not to think about all the *knowing* that had been lost—what wonders were gone forever. If you got lucky, you could find an elder drinking *urdun* at twilight. If they drank enough, they would stare into the fire and talk about the *Before*—machines that could carry you across the sky, being able to talk to someone on the other side of the world, or a large box that transmitted moving images of people. It was on a night like that when Danyelle heard about the waliyi.

Danyelle's mouth hung open as Chiku described someone who could be called to help if you were in trouble. *Help*. Help? It hung in her mind like a vision brought on by exposure to burning herbs. The myth said the waliyi could rid a settlement of a single rabid altered, an entire nest, or marauding group of raiders—if they could be convinced.

But, as Chiku gazed into the dwindling fire, she shrugged and said it was a story her mother told her. When her husband came to take her home, he told Danyelle it was a fanciful myth created by desperate people clinging to the delusion that someone would come to help them. He waved her off saying she should forget what Chiku has said.

It's just a story.

He flung the words over his shoulder, like spilled salt, as he led Chiku away. As he disappeared into the darkness with Chiku leaning heavily on his arm his grim words gripped her like the echoes of a nightmare that held on to you even after you woke – *no one helps in the After.*

Chiku fended off every attempt to get her to talk about the waliyi after that night, but her eyes sparkled whenever Danyelle spoke the word. Danyelle almost let it die. But the threat of Gorgamund hung over every breath she took and every thought that ran through her mind. She wanted to scream as the rest of the community just carried on as if nothing had changed. The whispers faded into the darkness of untended memory. Until the first day of winter.

Her butt was sore from long days in the saddle. She tightened the black and brown scarf wrapped around her neck as the cold wind blew a small flurry of snowflakes in her face. If her skin hadn't been dark brown, her nose would have been bright red like Kazashi's the day Danyelle snuck out just before dawn.

Her thick, brown coat, with layers of clothes underneath, kept the cold at bay. Its brown, shearling collar tickled her earlobes. Brown, wool gloves kept her hands warm, though they were fingerless at the tips, and frayed around the edges. Danyelle did not like anything between her finger and a trigger.

She ran a gloved hand through her long, thick, black hair, shaking out snowflakes before they accumulated. She adjusted her rifle in her lap with her right hand and guided her horse along the trail with the reins back in her left.

The hill wasn't steep, but it was covered in trees. She led her mount through, weaving left and right, until she came to a large, silver bell hanging from a thick branch.

The old townie, with his scraggly, salt and pepper beard, peered over the top of a rusted barricade made from sheet-metal and piled-up metal debris, and said when she found the bell to ring it. He was explicit that under no circumstances was she to go any farther up the hill.

The old man wouldn't open what he laughingly thought of as a gate even after she showed him her eyes and teeth. She was forced to roll up her sleeves and bare her arms as he watched through his scope. Even after he didn't let her in, but he did lower his rifle.

Danyelle's stomach growled so loudly that it startled her. She looked around as if there was someone to politely tell, *excuse me*. But she was alone – as alone as she had been the entire journey. There were certainly brushes with the changed. You couldn't traverse the outland without that reality intervening. She'd managed to outrun the changed, who sniffed the air like wild animals. They were terrifyingly fast but weren't able to catch a healthy horse running flat-out.

189

Danyelle only fired her rifle once. She could hazard a guess as to what they wanted. But she had plenty of ammunition in her pack and the blessing of having seen them coming from her perch on a hill.

After she put three of them down, with a single shot each, from a few hundred yards, the rest got the message. Instead of staying in her campsite, she rode through the night to put as much distance between her and them as possible. It was dangerous.

You couldn't see anyone coming and your horse could end up lame. But she thought it was still a better risk than staying where someone knew she was encamped. It was maddening that you had to worry about other people as much as you did the dead. The Fall changed people. At least that's what her parents taught her. People were decent once. But when food was scarce and the world had ended, savagery won out.

Danyelle ran out of food the next day—at least the food she could eat. That was three days ago. What had been left in her saddlebags was a traditional offering. That morning, her stomach groaning loud enough to point anything in the outlands directly to her, she prepared a large bowl of fried catfish, baked yams, and acaçá.

It was a ritual offering to Ogun. At least it was according to the elder, Baba Balogun. The aroma wafting up from the bowl, covered with cheesecloth, made her mouth water. Her stomach growled again, as if in pointed protest. She prepared the dish at the foot of the hill so that it would be fresh. But it reminded her of her own ravenous hunger.

When she climbed into the saddle to head uphill, a young girl wandered out of the trees. Danyelle was not sure if the girl being alone or wearing tattered clothes with a dirty face and nothing on her feet startled her more. She submitted to water from Danyelle's canteen to wash her face, and a blanket to keep her warm.

Once she guzzled the last of the water, she was willing to talk in a ragged voice. Her mother was dead, and she had been wandering the woods for days. The girl was starved with a half-vacant look in her eyes. It pulled at Danyelle.

The traditional offering was meant to help convince the wayili to come help her settlement against Gorgamund but the girl was in trouble. It wasn't a real choice. She fed the girl and took her back to the rusted, shabby, makeshift gate of the small settlement at the foot of the hill.

To her amazement, scraggily beard dragged it open. The rusty tines along the bottom threw up dust as they dug into the ground. A loud creak, followed by an incessant squeal of metal crying out for attention filled the aired. He kept his rifle half-trained on her with one hand causing his aim to wander like a butterfly fluttering in the wind.

An older woman scurried out from behind junked metal horses doubling as a wall to take the girl in hand. Danyelle wouldn't loosen her grip on the girl's arm until she'd extracted a vow from the woman regarding the girl's safety. A vow in the *After* was rare and sacred.

A *Vowbreaker* could expect to be visited by misfortune. Both she and the woman clasped hands and spit on the ground. Only then did Danyelle release her grip on the girl's arm even as she gave the woman a hardened glare.

So, there she sat, staring at the large, polished, silver bell hanging from the tree. She had no sacred meal to offer and no idea if she would even be able to make it back to her settlement with the help, she knew they desperately needed. Her stomach announced her position again.

"Sounds like you need a meal."

Danyelle flinched. She swung her rifle up to her shoulder and twisted in the direction of the voice. A woman stood there, draped

191

in soft dappled moonlight, with her thumbs tucked behind her belt. A wry smile adorned her dark-brown face. Danyelle just stared at her through her scope.

She was just over six feet tall judging by where her head was in relation to the horse's shoulder. The grin was broad revealing bright white teeth. Her hair was long and thick with a texture that matched Danyelle's own.

Instead of black it was silver. Danyelle could see the fine lines around her eyes and mouth in the shimmering glow of moonlight, though the rest of her face was smooth and unblemished.

Her boots were brown leather with a heavy heel, rounded toe, and silver buckles around the calf. Her close-fitting pants were dark blue with a double knee sewn into them. She wore a matching vest over a deep green shirt with a large collar covered in a leaf pattern.

A blue and green scarf was wrapped around her neck and tucked into the top of her shirt. Danyelle did not fail to notice the stacked birch-handled knife and black handgun strapped to the brown leather belt, or the scoped rifle slung over her shoulder.

Before Danyelle could respond to her, a loud siren blared from the bottom of the hill. She jerked her head around to gaze down the slope in its direction. It was coming from scraggily beard's settlement. Danyelle sat there, frozen to the spot.

Her horse canted a few steps sideways. *It's not your problem*, she told herself as she tightened her grip on the reigns. Scraggily beard was less than welcoming and whatever was happening did not involve her. It was the unspoken rule in the After – mind your own business.

A telltale orange nimbus bloomed above the trees like a warm glow. *Fire*. With a curse, she turned her mount toward the bottom of the hill, sparing a brief glance toward the woman. She was gone. She had probably headed back to her home to do what Danyelle should be doing—minding her own business. Instead, she snapped the reigns and dug in her heels. She pulled hard on the reins at the edge of the treeline.

Hidden from sight, among the trees, Danyelle gazed out on a group of ravengers trying to take down the make-shift gate to the small settlement. It was already on fire. They were hurling flaming bottles that exploded against the gate and walls.

Howls rose from the small pack of men and mutants, as they pranced back and forth like animals baying at the swelling moon in the sky. Danyelle counted two dozen at least. A quick look though her scope revealed the red claw scrawled across their coats, vests, and chests in paint. It was a contingent from Gorgamund's horde.

She watched as the inhabitants of the small settlement mustered an anemic respond consisting of badly placed random shots and cowering behind rusted metal. The reports told her they were small caliber hunting rifles and an assortment of handguns. It still could have been effective if the persons firing were decent shots. As it was, the ravengers carried on with their attack unperturbed.

The growing flames danced before her eyes. Danyelle argued with herself as the ravengers banged at the gate and walls. Each time the gate or section of a wall shuddered it was punctuated by piercing screams from behind the gate. Danyelle could recognize the sound of unbridled fear even from a distance. She also knew the unique sound of women and children.

Danyelle wasn't usually one to curse but she gritted her teeth and muttered, "Fuck."

Her shoulders slumped as she exhaled a heavily. She raised her rifle, shaking her head in exasperation at herself. Kazashi's voice rang in her mind as if her friend was standing next to her in the trees.

We don't get involved.

193

Mind your own business. The refrain was drummed into them from the time they could walk. Danyelle had tried to live up to it, but it had never set right with her.

She pulled back the charging handle on her rifle. When she released it, it made a satisfying clack shoving a round into the chamber. She took aim at the head of one of the leaders of the small horde through her scope.

"So, you're going to help?"

Danyelle cursed again. This time it was a string of several choice words. But she did not flinch. She lowered her rifle and looked to her left to see the same woman standing in the treeline looking out on the ravengers.

The flames lit up her brown face and silver hair. They also reflected off the blade of the sword she was holding in her right hand. Danyelle opened her mouth to ask about the blade. But the woman flashed a big, broad grin at her and dashed out into the open.

She was stunned.

What was she doing!

Danyelle turned her head and watched as the woman moved through the ravengers like they were dolls made of straw. Her form was flawless. Danyelle knew knife fighting. This was like watching a dance.

Fighting was always messy. It never looked like this. But the woman was fast, efficient, and artful. It was like watching a painter applying swirls of color to a canvas. One by one the ravengers fell under her blade.

She darted in and among them making it difficult for any single ravenger to open fire without taking the chance they would hit one of their own. Limbs and heads hit the ground like ripe fruit dropping from a tree limb. And just like that the raiding party dwindled to a few raging loners.

One of them, standing thirty paces off to the right, was taking aim at the woman. Without thinking, Danyelle raised her rifle to her shoulder in one fluid motion and sent a round down range. The sharp crack of her rifle reverberated through the trees.

The man dropped before the sound of the report faded. Three of the remaining ravengers turned in the direction of the sound and saw her in the treeline. They took one look at their fallen friend and came howling toward her. Two began firing their handguns as they ran.

Shots whizzed past her head. Her horse bucked and tossed her from the saddle. Danyelle hit the ground hard. The wind raced out of her lungs like it had somewhere else to be. Her rifle tumbled across the ground. Bullets crashed into the dirt around her and all she could do was gasp for air.

Her mouth opened and closed, begging for air. A wry thought crossed her mind as she lay there gasping.

This is why you mind your own business.

She was about to die because she always had to help.

Danyelle rolled over on her stomach and clawed at the ground toward her rifle. A bullet grazed her shoulder and she tried to scream but nothing came out. She frantically pushed at the ground with her boots, digging her hands in the dirt, while trying desperately to suck in air.

Just as she clutched frantically at the butt of her rifle a pair of hands grabbed her roughly and tossed her through the air. She landed a few feet away with a soft thud and a grunt.

Your knife! she thought. *Slow down,* she told herself as she remembered her training.

In situations like these, slow is fast and fast is slow. Danyelle forced herself to slow down and reach for her knife.

One of the ravengers leaped on her. His breath was fetid. His body odor made her gag. But she blocked his grasping hands with

195

her arm and pulled her knife free. If he had just shot her, she would be dead, but he wanted something else.

So, she gave it to him—a knife shoved through the soft tissue under his chin, up into his brain. He slumped over with a gurgle. With his head out of the way Danyelle was able to see his partner standing a few feet away with his mouth hanging open, frozen to the spot.

She snatched the dead ravengers handgun out of his pants and fired two shots into the gaping one's head. He dropped to his knees, his mouth open, his eyes wide, before falling face first into the dirt.

Danyelle scanned the immediate area with the front sight of the handgun moving left to right and back again. The third ravenger had disappeared. She laid her head back and stared up into the sky.

Breathe, girl. Just breathe, she told herself.

She was not sure how long she laid there but after an indeterminate number of heartbeats she heard someone approaching. She rolled up on her forearm and aimed the handgun at them.

The woman said, "That's the second time you've aimed a gun at me today. Let's stop doing that."

Danyelle smiled weakly and nodded before slumping back over onto her back and mumbling, "Fuck me."

The woman made her way over to where Danyelle lay. She grabbed the dead ravenger's body and dragged him off into the darkness. A short while later she returned for the other one.

When Danyelle raised her head again, she could see that the woman was dragging them down to a pile of bodies already being engulfed by orange flames.

As Danyelle laid back, she thought, *right, if you don't burn them, they come back.*

She was content to lay there and breathe. Laying in the dark, time became an indiscriminate blur of wind in the trees and the crackling of a bonfire. When the woman returned, she was leading Danyelle's horse. They both came over and stared down at her. The moon above them outlined their forms in soft white light.

The woman smiled down at Danyelle and said, "So, helping again, huh? You just don't care about the rules of surviving the outlands. Interesting. Are you ready to get up?"

Danyelle nodded and the woman reached a hand down to her. Her grip was firm. She pulled Danyelle up off the ground like she was a small doll.

Once Danyelle was on her feet, the woman said, "Let's go take a look at that shoulder."

Danyelle had almost forgotten she was bleeding.

The woman helped her back into the saddle and led the horse by its reins up the hill. By the time Danyelle was breathing normally again, they were approaching a small log cabin in a clearing at the top of the hill.

It was a simple affair, but it appeared sturdy. The logs were evenly cut and shaped. There were no gaps or holes in the walls or where each log met. The windows were glass and framed with wooden shutters. The steps were symmetrical. The porch was level. But the shingles covering the roof were black and made of a material she was unfamiliar with.

The woman hitched Danyelle's horse to a nearby tree and helped her out of the saddle. Danyelle steadied herself and held a hand up to the woman with a short nod. The woman smiled, pulled her hands back, and turned toward the cabin. She motioned over her shoulder for Danyelle to follow.

Once they were inside the woman set about getting Danyelle out of her coat and shirt so she could clean and bandage the wound. It was superficial but an infection would be deadly. As the woman worked on her shoulder, Danyelle looked around.

It was a lot larger than she expected given what she saw out front. Though it was only about thirty paces wide, it must have been fifty long. She counted four rooms and a set of stairs leading to a second floor. The fireplace crackled with split logs burning beneath a black pot suspended over the flames.

Whatever was bubbling in the pot filled the room with a smell that made her mouth water. The floor was covered with animal hides in brown, white, and black. Danyelle's mouth fell open when she saw the shelves holding books. There were also weapons and tools, but it was hard to tear her eyes away from the books.

A large couch, a few chairs, a table, and work bench filled out the front room. On the front wall to her right, next to the window, was another shelf filled with plants.

She recognized plump purple, yellow, and red tomatoes along with several types of herb—*basil?* she thought.

Her nose caught the scent of mint, and her eyes the telltale leaves of rosemary. By the time her shoulder was clean and dressed, Danyelle had thought up a thousand questions. But they would have to wait. She had come here for a reason.

"Honored elder, I apologize for not having the traditional sacred meal as an offering –"

The woman cut her off by saying, "Hmmm, why not? I know who you think I am?"

Danyelle swallowed hard.

"I came across a young girl who was starved and in desperate need of help. I had no food of my own left and so I gave her your meal."

The woman sat in a chair across from Danyelle, folded her feet up onto her thighs, cupped her hands in lap, one on top of the other, and said, "Ah, I see. There's that word again. Help."

She waved her left hand as if dismissing something invisible before placing in back into her lap and continued, " Don't worry. I'm not who you think I am anyway."

Danyelle tilted her head and pursed her lips, "You're not the wayili?"

The woman said, "My name is Godeau. And while I'm as old as these hills and I've been known to help those in distress over the intervening millennia, I am not a god – Ogun, Anansi, Odin, Shiva, or otherwise."

Godeau stared like she was looking straight through her.

Danyelle could not erase the perplexed look on her face, as the woman continued, "The meal you brought is from an ancient tradition of offering to the gods of a lost continent that was once called Africa. The briefest glance at you tells me they were your ancestors. Sometimes, I get visitors whose elders have equipped them with bits and pieces of knowledge from their past even though it's useless now. So, let's end the suspense. Why are you here?"

Danyelle cleared her throat and said, "Our settlement needs your help, Waliyi. A warlord has risen east of here. He's managed to assemble a large force, including the changed. He is gobbling up settlement after settlement, leaving nothing but burned ruins in his wake, and he will be on our doorstep soon. We need your help."

She listened to Danyelle, nodding as she talked.

The woman chuckled. "You can't escape that word to save your life can you? What are your elders planning on doing? I'm assuming they don't know you are here and don't approve of your plan, if they even know about it, or else they would be here themselves."

Danyelle blushed, looked down at her hands, and said, "You're right, Waliyi. They don't know I'm here. I'm here because they think they can negotiate with him."

Godeau said, "With what?"

She reached into her coat pocket and produced a small burlap bag, tossing it across the room to the woman. Godeau snatched it from the air with a practiced ease and untied the string so she could look in. When she did, she nodded, reached in the bag and produced a handful of bullets.

"Our settlement was built around a factory that was once used to manufacture bullets in the *Before*. The people who worked there passed the knowledge of the making down to their descendants. We don't have the capacity we once did because keeping all the machines running has been difficult. But we are capable of producing enough for our usage and for trade. The elders think they can strike a deal with the warlord."

Godeau pointed a her.

"But you know this warlord won't spare your settlement. And you know your people will be killed or made slaves to make bullets for him."

Danyelle nodded quietly. *How does she see right through me?*

She exhaled sharply, and said, "Will you help us?"

Godeau shook her head and said, "I wonder if it's even possible to stop you from using that word?"

Then she sat there for a moment, with her eyes gazing at Danyelle intently, before saying, "I think I will. But, first, it's time for you to wake up."

And then, she clapped her hands.

———

Danyelle's eyes blinked open slowly. Everything was fuzzy and muffled, like she had cotton in her ears and a sack over her head. The room was white and empty. A woman who stood over her. She was gazing down at Danyelle with a warm smile. Her voice was just as warm.

"Take it easy. The *Process* can be hard on the body. Take slow, deep breaths. You'll adjust in a few seconds."

Danyelle drew in breath like she was sipping too hot tea. Her vison cleared as she sat up on a narrow bed. Her head still felt like it was full of round hay bales, but the woman's voice was somehow calming.

"That's it. Easy now. It'll all start coming back to you in a moment. Just breathe."

Danyelle looked at her and then realized she recognized her.

Her voice sounded like a frog croaking when she said, "I know you."

The woman replied with a nod. "Yes, you do. We met as you were making camp, three days ago. We shared a meal together. It was the last of your food. You were very kind."

Danyelle said, "What happened?"

The woman pressed her lips together as her mouth twisted into a bashful grin and she said, "You were so kind, I decided to test you."

She frowned and said, "Test me for what?"

The woman motioned to a small stack of folded clothes on the only other piece of furniture in the room and said, "Get dressed and I'll show you."

Danyelle looked under the sheet covering her and realized she was naked. She blushed.

The woman waved it off with a smirk and said, "Don't worry. You've been perfectly safe and treated very respectfully."

The smirk became a broad smile as the woman pointed toward the small table behind Danyelle. Then she turned and opened the only door.

On her way out she said, "Come on out when you're ready. There's no rush."

Danyelle waited for her to close the door before she leaped off the table. She regretted it immediately as the room started to spin. She clutched at the edge of the narrow bed and leaned there until it stopped.

When it did, she crossed the room, slowly, until she reached the table. It took a while for her to dress. Her clothes had been cleaned and pressed. Her boots looked better than they had in months. A bright layer of polish gleamed on their surface in the room's soft light. Even her belt and silver buckle had been given the same treatment.

By the time she was fully dressed, her head was better. The world no longer seemed covered by a large blanket. She tried to look calm as she opened the door and stepped out into a long, narrow hall that was just as white and empty as the room.

Her boots made a soft clacking sound on the shiny, white floor. It took another thirty paces for her to reach the end of the hallway. She had noticed a small incline as she crossed the length of the hall. When she opened the door, she was met by bright moonlight.

The woman was sitting on a wide stump surrounded by chopped wood. She stood when Danyelle exited the hall and closed the door behind her. When Danyelle looked around it turned out to be the same cabin she remembered. The room and the hall were clearly underneath it. When she looked back at the woman, she finally realized she was the same woman, silvery hair and all.

The woman nodded and said, "Good, you're starting to remember. When we first began doing this, we would wake people up in completely different surroundings. Over the years we started to realize that the acclimation process would be easier if we matched the construct with an existing structure. That way the subject woke to familiar surroundings. Once we began doing that the *saved* suffered very few schisms."

Danyelle only understood half of what the woman was saying. *Saved?*

The woman saw the look in her eyes and said, "Right, right, I'm sorry, sometimes I forget how much you all have lost to the ravages of time, and this nightmare you've created."

She motioned at her surroundings, with an upturned hand, when she said *nightmare.*

Danyelle spoke slowly. "Your name is, Godeau?"

The woman indicated a wood chair a few paces from where she was sitting as she said, "Good."

They stared at each other for another moment before Danyelle realized the woman was waiting. She crossed the grassy knoll between them and sat in the proffered chair. Somewhere in the distance a bird whistled. Nothing but silence answered it.

The woman said, "Yes. That's the name I've taken here. It's from an old play I like. Sort of. Anyway, the important thing is that I'm here to offer you a gift."

"A gift? What kind of gift?"

"Why, salvation of course."

With the wave of her hand a brilliant, bluish, beam of light settled on a gray, circular stone marker a dozen paces away. Danyelle hadn't noticed it until that moment. It was three strides across and covered in symbols chiseled into the surface. Tiny, sparkling, flashes of white light exploded inside the blue beam like stars in the night sky.

Danyelle realized her mouth was hanging open, so she said, "What is that?"

Godeau gazed over at the beam of light and said, "If you step inside it will take you away from here to a better place."

Danyelle, still mesmerized by what she was seeing, muttered, "A better place?"

Godeau said, "Yes, a better place. A place where there will be no more sorrow or sadness. It's a place of pure beauty. A world without the changed, the dead rising, or unevolved humans."

Danyelle blinked, scrunched her forehead, and said, "Is that even possible?"

Godeau motioned to the beam of light again and said, "Yes."

Danyelle whispered, "How?"

Godeau sighed heavily. "It's always the same with you lot. I guess I shouldn't expect you to be any different."

The woman leaned forward, resting her forearms on her thighs, took another deep breath and said, "This will be difficult for you to understand, but please, wait until I'm finished. We—well, I'm from another world."

Godeau pointed to the night sky as she continued, "Some of those tiny lights are stars like the one you see rise every morning. And around them are worlds just like this one. And some of those worlds have people on them like this one. I belong to a people older than them all. We very nearly destroyed ourselves and our world as our civilization grew. But, somehow, we managed to survive long enough to grow wise enough to save ourselves and our world from the mistakes of our past. Soon we were venturing out among those lights on ships that could carry us to other worlds like yours. At first, we found world after world in utter ruins. They had faced the same challenges we had and failed to save themselves. The numbers were so vast and unrelenting that we nearly turned around and went back home. You see, Danyelle, our people have a sensitivity to suffering built into our very being. It was overwhelming. We mourned with each desolate world we landed on - the empty structures, the wastelands, the remains of the inhabitants, it brought us to tears. We were overwhelmed by a deep, abiding sadness that we couldn't shake."

Godeau paused for a moment.

She rubbed at her eyes and cleared her throat before continuing. "So, the elders of our people met and deliberated. Our greatest minds determined that there was a kind of hurdle every civilization on every planet had to overcome in order to survive. They called it the *Paralaxsis*. People in your distant past called it the *Great Filter*. The elders determined that if we didn't help, most of the civilizations on most worlds would destroy themselves. So, they instituted the First Commandment. If we could help a civilization cross the threshold of paralaxsis we would."

She sat there for a moment. And without thinking, Danyelle blurted, "But what if you couldn't help a world cross over?"

Godeau perked up and nodded as a new smile spread across her face.

"Ah. Very good, Danyelle, very good. It has dawned on you that your world did not make it past the Great Filter. Hence this nightmare all around us. So, in the event we couldn't save a world from a nightmare like this, they instituted the Second Commandment."

Godeau pointed to the blue beam of light again.

Danyelle whispered, "Salvation?"

She nodded and said, "Yes, salvation. We find the beings on the dying planet who deserve to be saved and we relocate them to a new world where they have a chance. You see, Danyelle—and let me put this in a way that is specific to your world—we have discovered that, in many civilizations, aside from the ones that share a singular consciousness, a single person can be a bright, noble thing, but a group of you are, all too often, savage, short-sighted, and brutish."

Godeau stood up and looked down at Danyelle. Her soft smile was tinged with something Danyelle could not quite put her finger on. Was it sadness?

She stood slowly and spoke as she stared at the beam of light. "But what about my settlement?"

Godeau's voice was back to its warm and comforting tone.

"Don't worry. We'll send someone to deal with the warlord. There are still some things we can do to help. And one of them is to keep the truly awful monsters at bay while we do our work."

Danyelle walked slowly toward the light. Godeau walked alongside her like a guardian protecting the way. When they reached the light, something occurred to Danyelle, and she turned back to face Godeau.

She moved her hand up and down in front of Godeau and said, "Is this what you really look like?"

Godeau chuckled and muttered, "Again, it never fails." Raising her voice, she continued, "No, it's not."

Danyelle stood there for a moment and said, "Well, can I see what you really look like?"

She grinned and said, "If you decide to be saved, and you step onto the platform I will show you my true form. But understand, once you step into the light there is no going back. So be very sure that this is what you want."

Danyelle stood there for a while. She looked at the beam of light and then looked up into the night sky. She could not tell where the beam was coming from.

She looked back at Godeau. A world without the dead? No more changed or hunger or dangerous outlands. No more warlords or dangerous men who only know how to take. It was all so tempting.

"Thank you, Godeau. But I can't leave."

Godeau sighed.

"I hoped you would. You're too good for this place."

Danyelle said, "I'm not sure that's true. But even if it is, what happens to a world where everyone who is good just leaves?"

She looked around for her horse.

"I have to stay and fight."

Godeau looked at her for a moment and said, "It's a shame. But if you are determined to stay in this nightmare and help. And of course, you are—I still want to give you a gift."

Before Danyelle could say anything, the woman crossed the space between them and touched her forehead. Her entire body began to tingle. It was like she floating in a sea of light.

It only lasted a moment, but she felt like it took an age. When Godeau stepped back, Danyelle looked at her hands. She felt strong. She felt like she could pull a tree up out the ground and run for week without stopping. Godeau just smiled as she watched.

The woman said, "Come with me."

Danyelle followed her around the side of the cabin to something covered in a gray cloth. Godeau pulled it off to reveal a large iron-horse.

She pointed to panels along the roof and said, "These take the light from sun and run the vehicle."

It had giant nobby wheels and metal grates on all the windows.

She said, "It'll get you where you're going in a few hours. There's ammunition in the back for your rifle, along with water and food."

Godeau reached down and removed her knife and its sheath from her belt. "And take this. It will help keep you safe."

Danyelle climbed into the iron-horse and Godeau showed her how to start it. It roared to life like a ravenous beast, ready to chew up the ground beneath it.

Godeau said, "I'd offer you a blessing but I'm not a god. Besides, I don't think you'll need it. Stay safe and try not to let helping get you killed."

She smiled at the woman and pulled off.

Het-Heru strolled out of the Processing unit and crossed over to Godeau.

"She decided to stay?"

"Yes. It's a pity. But I admire her character."

"Are we going to help her?"

"We'll do what we can without being discovered. This world is enough of a nightmare without warlords. Pack up. We're moving to the Alpha site."

As Het-Heru headed back inside a bright light engulf Godeau. When it faded, she was herself again. She was taller than she had been. Her limbs were thinner. Her hair was still thick like wool, but it was black and curly, flowing down across her shoulders and down her back.

A white spark like a tiny star somehow floated in front of her forehead as if it was attached there. Her skin was even darker now, a brown so deep it was almost black. She had six eyes and they glowed with green light.

Black light, like a gossamer gown, flowed around her body. It too, sparkled with tiny bits of light making it look like she was draped in the night sky. Black wings extended from her back with spans as long as she was tall.

She watched the all-terrain vehicle disappear in the distance and whispered, "A blessing on you, child."

And then she turned and followed Het-Heru inside. There was work to do.

CONSECRATED

Never was there a clearer case of 'stealing the livery of the court of heaven to serve the devil in.'
        ~ *Frederick Douglass*

Y es, it was partly the bourbon. But mostly, it was that it was two in the morning and early autumn. The night was cool. The air smelled like cut grass and discarded charcoal briquets.

It was so late on a Thursday night, or early on a Friday morning depending on your philosophy of telling time, that the street outside the coffee shop was empty. That was part of it too—fully lit streets, stoplights turned to flashing, but no one in sight.

He loved it. Maybe it was also that fall always reminded him of the first week of a new college semester, which meant old friends and new acquaintances—and now he was self-aware enough to know that feeling was really about new possibility.

Jeff tossed the butt of his cigar in the cigarette pail next to the door. The windows were long since darkened but the employees didn't care if you sat at the stone tables out front after they were gone.

The parking lot in the front was the size of a deck of cards so he parked down the street. A crescent moon, that hung so low in the night sky that it was like a tree branch you could reach up to and pluck an apple from, cast a glow so luminescent the hundred tinier lights around it strained to be seen.

It was as if they were jealous of how much sky the moon took up. The soft clap of the leather soles of his boots on the sidewalk was only interrupted by the jarring infrequency of a car rolling by. It was so quiet. It was like that moment between when the orchestra finished a piece and the audience decided to applaud. It felt like the whole world belonged to him.

He saw a flicker of movement from the corner of his eye and froze. The rear parking lot, nestled behind the shops like a backpack between the shoulders, was only open to deliveries and employees unless you wanted a three-hundred-dollar tow bill.

Had he really seen something or was it just really late?

He shrugged it off and started walking again. Jeff made it three more steps before he heard a muffled cry.

His mother had raised him to stick his nose in. He eventually learned it was also naturally in him. When you're on the mat or in the ring, and you get hit, you learn something about yourself. Your instinct is either to step back or step in.

Jeff was also, always, incredibly aware of being a large Black man. Any time he forgot, even for a moment, someone would remind him by moving their purse to the other side of their body, locking their door at a stop light, or refusing to get on an elevator with him. So, he made sure to stay in the light and move slowly. He put his hands up as he rounded the corner.

The other thing was to mentally dial for a light tone and raise his voice from its more naturally deep one. God forbid it was a white woman doing some crazy shit. He did not need to have to explain to cops why he was in the back lot after midnight with a scared white woman.

"Hey, no need to be afraid. I just heard something as I was walking by and I'm just checking to make sure everything is ok."

Did that sound friendly enough? Was it unthreatening? Ease inducing? This shit was exhausting.

He moved to his right so he would round the corner from the middle of the lot and be in plain sight. Hopefully they would be able to see him clearly.

"I have my hands up. Let me know you're ok and I'll move on. I was just heading to my car. Hello?"

Nothing. Fuck, he thought.

If this was going to be a thing he was going to be pissed. This was America though. One moment you're living your Black joyful life and the next you're carrying the weight of all of America's bullshit. In the back of his mind a small voice was saying move the fuck on.

But the louder one was saying someone might be in trouble. He quickly considered and then tossed the idea of pulling out his phone and recording. Darkness, the late hour, and something in his hand, would be a pretext for some scared white person. And they'd get away with it. The last thing he wanted was to be a hashtag or have his name on a fucking tee shirt.

Jeff stepped around the corner and stopped dead. The smell of sulphur hit him like a cloud of joy-smoke at a house party. The

211

first thing he saw was the black cap-toe brogues. They were glossy with polish.

The suit was sharper than a thumb tack. It was slim-cut, royal blue, and chalk striped. The white guy wearing it was average height with close-cropped black hair. He was holding a white guy in jeans, a checkered shirt, and work boots with well-worn soles like he was a limp ragdoll. And his chest was torn open.

"Hey!"

It was instinct more than anything else. Jeff had barely processed what he was seeing. He took three quick steps toward them. The guy in the perfectly pressed suit dropped the dead guy. The body made a soft thudding sound when it hit the pavement. Then, suit-guy turned toward him.

When Jeff got a good look at him, he instinctively threw his hands up, covering his face and chest. It was suit-guy's face. It summoned something primordial in him, a defense mechanism that was deeply biological.

The rest of suit-guy should have matched his face—like claws, fangs, or a misshapen body. But it didn't. He looked like a wealthy businessman with a five-hundred-dollar haircut and a three-thousand-dollar suit. The incongruity was blood dripping from his lips onto his chin and the heart he was holding in his hand, which was still beating. And then there were the eyes. His eyes were completely black.

Jeff was frozen to the spot. He could not move. It felt like something was holding him there. A small voice, in the back of his mind, screamed. It said, *run*! But he couldn't move. He wasn't even sure if he was breathing. What the fuck was he looking at?

Suit-guy went from standing twenty feet away to right in front of him in a weird jump-cut, like a scene out of a Jordan Peele horror flick. But Jeff still could not move. His nose filled with the smell of sulfur. His mouth tasted like copper.

In an odd moment of clarity, the kind where you feel like you're standing outside yourself watching, he realized he was going to die. It was a calm, clear, rational assessment. This was how it ended. The man reached out a manicured hand to grab him.

Jeff watched the world slow to a crawl. His mind raced. His mom wouldn't know what had happened to him. He would miss the next Black Panther movie. He would never get to find out what might have happened between him and Olive. And then creepy suit-guy howled.

The sound of it made Jeff's heart beat faster and his head pound. Suit-guy shrieked and pulled his hand away. Suddenly, he could move. Before he could run, a jagged slit of red light appeared a few feet away and creepy suit-guy stepped through it. In a flash, he was gone.

Jeff stared at the spot where he disappeared for a moment.

What the fuck just happened?

Then he looked down at the dead white guy, glanced around the parking lot, and said, "Oh shit."

He should run, he thought. No, he should slowly, but quickly, walk away. If he was found with this dead white guy, they would put him on death row. No one would believe that he didn't kill him.

"Interesting."

Jeff nearly jumped out of his skin. He spun around to see another Black guy leaning against a pole, a few feet away, under the building's covered walkway.

"Yeah, you should be as dead as that white dude."

—

His skin was dark brown, and he was nearly as tall as Jeff. While Jeff sported a thickly curled afro with a close-cut beard and mustache, the man was clean shaven—head and face. Right away he noticed the short-sleeved, black, polo sweater with waist band, slim black jeans, and black, Italian, dress boots. Jeff had an eye for fashion.

It was casual but he still looked like he'd stepped out of a page of Gentleman's Quarterly. Jeff also clocked the black Rolex, large gold ring, and Zulugrass bead bracelets stacked on his wrist. The beads were black with green, red, and gold interspersed in the stringed circles.

But it took him a few moments to register the black 1911 handgun, covered in strange scrollwork, and the knife with the curved hilt tucked in his belt. It was also covered in decorative scrollwork accompanied by glittering blue and green gemstones.

"You can put your hands down."

His voice was even deeper than Jeff's.

"Uh, are you sure?" he said, indicating the gun with a nod of his head.

The man glanced down at his hand and said, "Oh, yeah, sorry. This isn't for you. It was meant for the Infernal."

Jeff cocked his head to the right and said, "Infernal?"

The man slid the gun into a leather holster, tucked inside his jeans, on the back of his right hip.

Then he smiled, extended his hand, and said, "I'm Azriel."

His hand shot out before he could stop it. It was such a socially ingrained habit that the man was already holding his hand before Jeff could decide if having him in his personal space was wise. He had a strong grip.

"Uh, I'm Jeff. Jeff Jarvis."

The moment where a normal handshake would end passed but Azriel did not let go of his hand.

Instead, the man stared at his hand and said, "Hmm. I see."

"You see? What does that mean? And what's an Infernal?"

Azriel released Jeff's hand, pulled out his phone, and held up a finger while he dialed.

"Hey, this is Azriel. We've got another one. I'm pinging the location. Get some Cleaners over here immediately."

He lowered his finger, hung up the phone, and said, "Look, you've got a lot to catch up on and very little time to do it. Come with me and I'll explain what I can. Unless you'd rather stay here and hope nobody catches you with that poor guy's body?"

Jeff glanced over at the guy lying prone on the ground and tried to avoid staring at the gaping wound in his chest.

"Oh, hell no. Do you know what kind of shitstorm would follow being caught with a white boy's mutilated corpse? As long as you've got someone coming to deal with it, I'm good. Someone should call the cops – but long after I'm gone. You know those assholes. A slight breeze and they're gunning you down in the street. Frightened bitches. You'd think if they were that scared, they'd find another job."

Azriel nodded and said, "Yeah. Facts. But don't worry. After the Cleaners are done, I'll call a new friend of mine. She's an F.B.I. Agent. And this won't be her first time dealing with something like this."

———

Jeff rode in silence all the way to what he assumed was Azriel's house. He thought about the car to keep his mind from spinning out of control. It was a classi—a nineteen sixty-six mustang Fastback. But it was custom. Jeff loved a beautiful car and this one was choice.

215

The paint job was a unique blue-gray with a black hood, roof, and grill. Bits of red ran through the detailing as highlights. Large wheels with satin-black rims, red brake calipers, and matching red rotors, finished the look. It roared. Whoever worked on it dropped it, giving it a lower aggressive profile. He guessed there was an Edelbrock crate engine under the hood making his seat rumble beneath him.

The house was as beautiful as the car. It was spartan grays and creams. The furniture was contemporary, like the stuff you saw in the modern houses with concrete and glass interiors in gentrified neighborhoods.

The kitchen was all stainless and Jeff spied a four-thousand-dollar espresso machine on the counter. It was way too late for coffee but as he leaned back on the leather couch, Azriel handed him a heavy crystal whiskey glass with two fingers of the smoothest bourbon he had ever tasted in it.

Jeff emptied the glass with a single tilt. Azriel must have known because he was standing there with a matching crystal decanter and poured another two fingers in his glass. He sat the decanter on the glass coffee table with a soft *thunk* and dropped into the oversized chair across from the couch. He took a sip and stared at Jeff for a moment with slightly narrowed eyes.

"What do you know about your ancestors?"

Jeff slowly rotated the glass in his hand as a half-grin spread across his face.

"Huh, you know the conundrum, right? Our guess is Madagascar. But short of giving a company I don't trust a DNA sample there's no way to know for sure. Even that would only give you a region. It wouldn't tell you about your people. That's a part of the crime perpetrated against us. Our names, family history, generational knowledge – all lost to time and barbarity."

Azriel nodded and sipped.

Are you in the clergy?"

Jeff tilted his head to the left. Took another swallow and said, "I was. For about fifteen years. I tried to help people be better versions of themselves, to follow the philosophy of the brown-skinned, Mediterranean Jew people claimed to believe in. But it was all smoke and mirrors. People just wanted to be excused so they could continue to be who they already were."

"Yeah, he would be disappointed."

Jeff noted the odd tone. It was the way you talked about someone you knew personally. But that was obviously not the case. So, he shrugged it off.

"I get that reasoning, Jeff. What I'm trying to ascertain is whether you were consecrated?"

Jeff shrugged. "Sure. Twice, in fact. Once, as what the church called a Deacon and the second when I became an Elder."

Azriel made a satisfied grunt. "That's it then. I suspect you are from a long line of Guardians."

"Guardians?"

"Yes. They had many names depending on the region of the Continent. The Yoruba called them *Babalawo*, while the Igbo used the term *Dibia*. The Maasai called them *Laibon*. But behind the veil, a small number of them were recruited from across the Continent to serve as Guardians."

Jeff said, "Ok. I'm with you so far. Guardians of what?"

Azriel sat there for a moment, took a deep breath, and placed his glass on the table.

He stood, crossed over to the couch, and said, "There's an easier way."

He touched Jeff's forehead with his finger and the world went white.

217

They stood on a small outcropping. The ground stretched out, unendingly, before them. It was sandstone and rocks for as far as the eye could see with a singular exception. A few hundred yards ahead was a mound that filled the rest of the horizon. The only sound was the wind blowing across the empty plain.

Azriel's now familiar voice broke the spell.

"It's called the Eye of Africa and it's as old as life itself."

Jeff had heard of it. It was so large it could be seen from space. It looked like a giant blue bullseye from orbit. He had no idea it was so old.

To his right a short line of men and women made their way to the mound.

"Who are they?"

Azriel glanced over at the handful of people and said, "They are why I brought you here."

"So, where is here?"

Azriel smirked and said, "More when than where."

"Huh!? What do you mean when?"

Jeff twisted around at the thought of it but there was nothing to see except more rocks and flat earth.

"For as long as there has been memory, the Infernal scratched at the veil that separates their world from this one. And sometimes they find a thin place where their efforts are rewarded."

"And this is a thin place?"

Azriel looked up at the sky. He put a hand over his eyes to shield them from the sun.

"In the present, people think the Eye is the result of geological factors like pressure and movement. Before that they thought it was the aftermath of a meteor strike. They would never believe the truth. The Infernal have been scratching at this spot for millennia hoping to break through. And the only thing that kept that from happening were the Guardians."

Azriel indicated the small of group with a nod of his head.

Jeff said, "So how did they do it?"

"Simply put? Magic."

Jeff immediately opened his mouth, but Azreil held up a hand and continued, "Now, before you say something asinine like magic doesn't exist, you need to understand that it's just a word. It's a word that has been used to describe forces that people didn't understand and as is the human penchant, that frightened them. It's a shorthand. Rather than trying to explain the use of energy, direction, and intention to you in a few minutes let's just say, magic."

Jeff's mouth clamped shut and he nodded.

Azriel continued. "They created a set of wards that reinforced the veil in this spot, making it impossible for the Infernal to break through."

Jeff watched the small group of men and women climb the mound and begin making strange motions in certain spots.

"So, what happened?"

Azriel nodded again. "Good question. You surmised that the wards failed and some of the Infernal were able to scrape their way through into this world, including Hardgraves."

"Hardgraves? Is that the name of the one I encountered tonight?"

"Yes."

Jeff continued to watch the Guardians do their work.

"So, how did they break through?"

Azriel sighed. It was audible and long. Jeff looked over at him and saw the sadness painting his face like the ravages of a long-fought sickness.

"They broke through because sometime in the early to mid-sixteen hundreds the Guardians stopped making their yearly pilgrimage from across the Continent to strengthen the wards."

Azriel hardly finished his sentence before Jeff said, "What? Why would they ...."

He did not need to finish the sentence. The rest of the words caught in his throat. A chill washed over him. He knew exactly what had interrupted the work of several thousand faithful years – a work that kept what he could only describe as evil at bay. Heart stricken, he turned and looked at Azriel.

Jeff swallowed hard around a lump in his throat and forced the words out.

"The slave trade."

The disgust in Azriel's voice was just as evident.

"Yeah, the slave trade."

The Trans-Atlantic Slave trade had wholly disrupted the lives of millions of African people, destabilized the African continent, and caused horrors like rape, child abduction, murder, and all kinds of brutality against Black people at the hands of white.

Jeff had never liked the term Trans-Atlantic Slave trade. It masked who was responsible for it, namely white people in Europe and the Americas, and it dehumanized African peoples by labeling them slaves. They stopped being Mandé, Gbe, Akan, Wolof, and Makua, with rich histories and innate claims to humanity and became chattel.

He preferred using the term Euro-African Enslavement Trade. It had destroyed language, culture, family history, and traditions that were tens of thousands of years old. And now he knew that one of those traditions had been guarding the world against evil. It made sense that one evil had made a way for another.

Jeff said, "We should go tell them what is coming so they can prepare."

"We can't."

Jeff looked at Azriel with scrunched eyes and his mouth agape. "Why not?"

The world turned white again and Jeff jerked upright on the couch.

"Because we weren't actually there. I'm an immortal not a time traveler."

It took him a moment to adjust to the softer lighting in Azriel's living room.

His mind flitted from the mound, to the guardians, to what he had just experienced and—"Wait. Did you just say immortal? You're an immortal? How is that a thing?"

Azriel smirked, "It's a curse, really, but that's a story for another time."

He slumped into the chair across from Jeff and wiped his hand across his face.

"You know, there is so much about the world that would be better without the sins of Europe. That's not to say that the world would be a garden of peace and tranquility—because I don't think human beings are capable of that. But so much of the world's ills can be traced to how they rampaged across the map without a conscience – and believe me, I've seen it firsthand. But that's not our immediate problem."

"And what's our immediate problem?"

"Our immediate problem is that the Infernal, particularly Hardgraves, now know about you. And you are ill-equipped to defend yourself."

Jeff leaned forward. "But he wasn't able to touch me."

"Oh, he'll find a workaround. And as dangerous as Hardgraves is, there are more dangerous things that go bump in the night in this city."

Jeff's lips pressed together firmly, and he said, "So, what do we do about it?"

Azriel stood up and said, "The amazing thing about Black folks, the real magic, has always been the ability to reinvent ourselves on the other side of the horror of enslavement. We find ways to mend what was broken."

The seat beneath Jeff stopped vibrating when Azriel turned the key. They sat outside a barbershop on a narrow street next to a tattoo parlor. It was still so early that the streetlights continued casting their warm glow at the darkness.

A street cleaner whirred by blowing leaves against the car window. Azriel waited for it to disappear down the street before hopping out of the car. Jeff followed him across the empty thoroughfare and onto the sidewalk in front of the barbershop. The windows were dark. The street was quiet.

Azriel looked left, then right, before ducking around the side. The walkway between the two shops was only wide enough for one person at a time. Halfway down it they had to squeeze past garbage cans. It ended in a brick wall.

Azriel paused and turned back to look at Jeff.

"There's no easy way to tell you this so I'm just going to explain it very briefly. You'll be tempted to ask questions, but don't. We don't have the time."

Jeff grimaced and said, "Hardgraves."

Azriel nodded and said, "Hardgraves. And probably his boss."

Jeff opened his mouth and Azriel said, "Ah, ah, ah, no time."
He stared at Jeff until he threw up his hands up and nodded.

Azriel returned the nod, took a deep breath, and said, "There's another city behind the one you've always lived in. It's a place where the gifted, the cursed, and the Other live their lives just out of the corner of the eye of human beings. Our hotels, bars, grocery stores, and coffee shops, are just behind theirs. And *behind* is just a figure of speech."

Azriel reached out to the wall and turned a knob that had not been there. The wall opened like a door, and he ushered Jeff in with a wave of his hand. When the door closed behind him Azriel pulled back a thick crimson curtain and Jeff's eyes widened. It was part barbershop, part tattoo parlor. But he knew there was nothing on the other side of that wall but a hedge, a driveway, and the first house in a small neighborhood. Where was this place?

The shop was empty save for one woman hunched over a table with a lamp beaming over her shoulder. She was working on a tattoo gun.

She didn't even look up when she said, "Well, well. The cursed immortal who found his way. What have you dragged in off the street demon hunter."

Azriel said, "He's one of the Ashkandar. Confused, bewildered, and untrained – but a Guardian of the Old Blood none the same. I need to speak to Oshun."

The woman spun around in her chair. Her sleeves were rolled up revealing dragons, sprites, and something with wings coiling up her arms in brilliant colors. Her hair was done up in Bantu Knots and her skin was as dark as Azriel's.

She reached down and opened a draw in the table. After rummaging around in the draw with her hand, she pulled out a monocle and held it up to her left eye. She looked Jeff up and down and then tossed it on the table.

GERALD L. COLEMAN

"Yep. Poor bastard. Just living his life and now the world has been pulled inside out. But what's the hurry?"

That, she directed at Azriel.

They both said, "Hardgraves."

And Azriel added, "And likely his boss. Medusa, you know what they can do if they get ahold of him before he's been trained."

Jeff shot a hard look at Azriel and started to ask what he meant by *what they can do* but the immortal held up a hand and Jeff swallowed the question. He did, however, mouth the word *Medusa* to himself and tried not to stare at her. She looked like she could've come from Atlanta or Brooklyn, not a mythical tale.

Medusa said, "Ok, ok. Bless his heart. Hold on."

She disappeared through another curtain in the back before Jeff could get his mind to stop spinning. Even he could tell he was spinning out. He managed to get his shit together by the time she returned. She was leading a small, bald, black man. He was wearing a white shirt—buttoned to the top—a vest, and pants in a green, gold, and black striped pattern. Jeff thought his black, dress boots were John Varvatos. The man was, as his uncle used to say, clean as the board of the health.

"May the sun shine upon you."

His voice was deep but comforting. His eyes were brown, and his handshake was warm.

Like Azriel, he held his hand for a bit, looked him in the eye, and then said, "I'm sorry you found your way to us like this. Has the immortal explained to you how your hereditary line was broken?"

Jeff nodded.

"Yes. He ... he showed me. I used to think that watching movies like Mississippi Burning or video of cops killing Black folks in the street was the most infuriating thing I could see. But I was wrong."

224

Oshun shook his head and said, "I understand. So much of what we knew and how we held the world together was lost during enslavement. However, we believe in finding ourselves again. Even here, in this blood-soaked country. Their sins are theirs. Refusing to take up the mantel of what was lost to us would be ours."

Azriel said, "That's my cue. Good luck, Jeff. I'll see you on the front lines."

Jeff watched him go. The things he must know - all the amazing things he must have seen. One day he'd have to visit Azriel again, when there was time for questions.

He turned back to see Oshun waiting.

"What now?"

"Now, we begin your training. There are things to be hunted. But one last thing before we get started."

Oshun produced a small knife with a curve as wicked as the smile he was wearing.

"Have you been circumcised?"

Jeff looked from the knife to Oshun's smile and said, "Fuck."

THE MYSTERY
WATCH

"The concept behind [a] Mystery ... watch⬚ is to hide the mechanics from view, creating a 'mystery' of functionality."
  ~Meehna Goldsmith

One ever feels his twoness, -- an American, a Negro; two souls, two thoughts, two unreconciled strivings; two warring ideals in one dark body, whose strength alone keeps it from being torn asunder."
  ~W.E.B. DuBois, The Souls of Black Folk

L exington in the fall was Bob's favorite. The leaves were a lovely jumble of yellow, orange, green, and red. The temperature was a dopamine-inducing seventy degrees.

GERALD L. COLEMAN

He had been thankful for the balmy temperature when the cop slammed his face into the hood of his car.

His crime had been driving a 1964 Aston Martin DB5 while black, and an acerbic witticism concerning whether the cop had time to harass him and get to Dunkin Donuts before all the jelly-filled were gone. Bob sat on the curb in handcuffs. His heart beat wildly in his chest like the hooves of the thoroughbreds that pounded the turf track at Keeneland while the cop ran his registration. His hands weren't shaking because there was anything for the cop to find. They were shaking because he was black. And this is America.

Nothing said Lexington quite like the seven cruisers that showed up for an innocuous traffic stop. Bob's window-paned, navy blue, three-piece, Tom Ford suit, and his impeccable manners hadn't mattered. They never did.

What mattered was the cop's high school education, the trailer-park sized chip on his shoulder, and a certain kind of ineluctable bias that came with seeing Bob's expensive wingtip brogues. He sat there, outwardly calm, like his mother taught him when he was seven. He knew the game. It did not stop his running commentary on everything from officer Cavanaugh's flop sweat to his heavy breathing. If he had to sit there, he might as well do something with his time.

Cavanaugh came back frowning. "Well, Mr. Robert Saffell—" he said, as he squinted at Bob's license. "You're free to go."

He stood him up, removed the cuffs, and handed him his license and registration.

As he walked off, he called over his shoulder, "You drive safely now, you hear."

Bob couldn't resist as he rubbed at his wrists.

"Mad you didn't find anything, huh? I got your badge number, Cavanaugh. Pick me up a cruller, will you?"

The cop stopped for a moment and stiffened, but then kept walking. It was all he could do. Bob learned early on not to ride *dirty*. You never gave them any ammunition they could use against you.

An expired tag could get you killed. He took satisfaction from the fact that the cop would sulk all day. It was satisfaction the size of a grain of rice, but satisfaction, nonetheless. He took a long, deep breath and let it out slowly. And then he took another one. There was a reason black men died from heart disease and high blood pressure. And it wasn't all from a bad diet or hereditary predispositions.

As he walked slowly back to his car, he noticed two black women with their cellphones aimed at him as white folks passed behind them on the sidewalk without so much as a sideways glance. He smiled at the black women, gave them the nod, and held his hand, palm up, in their direction. They returned the gesture. He could almost hear the unspoken, *we got you.*

When he slid back into the black, leather seat of his car, he rested his hands on the wooden steering wheel. The shakes had subsided to a mild tremor. He sent a quick text message before turning the key and hearing roar of the pristinely restored engine as he revved it.

He closed the text app and opened the music app, cued up a song, and turned up the volume. The FM transmitter that allowed his classic radio to receive a signal from his cellphone relayed the sound. Bob smiled at the cops milling about by their cruisers as he slowly pulled off.

His speakers boomed, *"Fuck the police comin' straight from the underground, a young nigga got it bad cause I'm brown …."*

He waited a few blocks before he turned the volume down to a respectable level and switched the song from NWA to Digable Planets. He fast-forwarded the song until he reached Ladybug

229

Mecca, the only woman in the three-person group, rapping the chorus from her verse: *"I'm chill like that, I'm chill like that, I'm chill like that, I'm chill like that, I'm chill like that, I'm chill like that, I'm chill like that, I'm chill."*

He leaned back in the seat, letting the jazz-style thrumming of the upright bass in the song slow his heartbeat and unclench his teeth. His head started to bob unconsciously to the beat.

It was early afternoon, on a Friday, and he was just pulling into town. Twenty years had passed since he'd been home for more than a few days at a time. Kentucky in general, and Lexington in particular, hadn't changed much. The city's layout was a little different, here and there, but not the people.

Spalding's Bakery, the purveyors of the best glazed donuts on the planet, had moved from Third Street to Winchester Road. He hadn't been there yet, so he didn't know if they had taken the bell over the door with them. The jangling sound it made when you opened the door made your mouth water. It was downright Pavlovian.

Whole sections of the city had been gentrified. Rose street, which ran the width of the University of Kentucky's campus, was permanently closed to traffic. It was once a quick thoroughfare that would connect you to Limestone, headed toward south campus, the hospital, and the mall. Now, it was a plush walkway lined with flowerbeds and manicured shrubbery.

North Park was gone. He'd seen Flash Gordon and Eddie Murphy's comedy specials at the movie theater that once occupied that strip mall. He immediately regretted trying to watch Raw there. The audience was so loud he couldn't hear half the jokes. Even Tolly-Ho, a college rite of passage, where you ate at Ho burger at one in the morning on a Friday night, after stumbling across the street from the Student Center, had moved.

But Lexington still smelled the same. Instead of coming in on I-75, a straight shot from Atlanta, he passed through Chattanooga, Nashville, and made his way onto the treelined Bluegrass Parkway. It was his favorite way of driving into his hometown. When he exited onto Versailles Road, he always rolled down his window and took a deep breath. It was like he could smell the horse farms and casual racism. It still made him smile. It was home.

Bob didn't have to be on campus to give his first philosophy lecture until next Wednesday. He reserved the weekend to move into his apartment and reacclimate to the city. Being pulled over, ten minutes after getting to town, was a start, even if it was an unwelcome one. He was still looking forward to a dozen glazed donuts and a plate of Hoppin' John at Alfalfas. But first, he needed to get the keys to his new place. The movers were scheduled to arrive in a few hours.

A quick turn onto main street took him through downtown, past Triangle Park with its full-length fountain and Rupp Arena on his left and shops on his right. There had been slave jails where some of those shops were on his right. Lexington was born on the back of enslaved Africans. In 1860 a little under half of the population of the city was enslaved.

The city underwent a massive facelift in the early eighties when they bid on hosting the NCAA's Sweet Sixteen. To win the bid, they'd been forced to add parks and other accommodations. While they were doing that, they also cleaned up some of the remnants of the city's dark history.

He turned right onto Jefferson Street. He past Harrison Magnet School on his right. When it was his elementary school, it had simply been Harrison. Another four blocks and he turned right onto fourth street. Halfway down fourth he glanced to his left and took a quick look at the small apartment complex where he had lived up until sixth grade. It looked so small.

231

He crossed North Broadway, passing Transylvania University's main campus on the right, and turned right onto North Upper. Another quick right put him on West Third, and a left brought him to North Mill Street and Gratz Park. Halfway down the block, just before reaching the Carnegie Center, he pulled into the driveway of his new home. It was a lovely little neighborhood made up of expensive houses on narrow treelined streets. He turned off his car and got out. Margo Underwood was waiting for him on the porch with a set of keys.

It was three stone steps up from the front yard, covered, and ran half the width of the red, brick house. The small, front yard was perfectly manicured with a black, wrought iron fence around it. When he stepped onto the porch he was greeted with a bright smile.

Margo Underwood was small, plump, and dark brown. Her hair was long, thick, and sprung up off her head and down to her shoulders like a park fountain. She was wearing a smart, navy blue, pinstriped suit and black heels. She smelled like honeysuckle. Her handshake was firm. Her voice was soft.

"Good afternoon, Mr. Saffell. I hope your drive up was nice."

Bob smiled down at the small woman and replied, "Yes, it was pleasant – for the most part. Thank you for meeting me here with the keys. I hope I didn't keep you waiting long?"

Underwood shook her head and said, "Oh, it was no problem. I love Gratz Park. I just sat on the steps at the Carnegie Center and enjoyed the weather until I got your text."

She handed him the keys to the house and said, "I don't usually pry, but may I ask you something?"

She was holding her head at a slight angle and softly biting her lower lip.

Curious, he said, "Sure. Ask away."

Underwood grinned and leaned forward just a bit.

"In all the years I've been selling properties, I've never seen someone go through, or put up with, the amount of vetting that you have. I was shocked at what the former owner was asking for. I actually thought I was going to lose the sale. I heard he even hired a private investigator to check into your background, your politics, and your family. Do you have any idea why?"

He smiled and chuckled softly.

"Ms. Underwood, I have absolutely no clue. I chalked it up to eccentricity. I only put up with it because I love the location. Having Gratz Park right out my front door was a big incentive. I also like invading this small enclave of white privilege. The former owner has a quiet, but honored reputation in our community, so I indulged him. I can only imagine what he's lived through in eighty years as a black man in Lexington."

Underwood nodded her head and said, "Mmmhmm. I know exactly what you mean."

She went on to ask if he'd like her to walk him through the house, but he decided he would rather experience it for himself. He'd seen all the pictures of the interior, but it was nothing like actually seeing a place with your own eyes. She handed him the keys with a smile and excused herself.

He opened the front door and entered. The faint smell of bleach and something citrusy greeted him. It was a large house with high ceilings and big windows. The first floor was what you'd expect.

There was a small foyer with archways to the right and left leading to the front rooms. A hallway straight ahead, leading back to a bathroom, dining room, and kitchen, was bordered on the left by the staircase leading to the second and third floor. He headed upstairs.

The second floor contained three bedrooms, two bathrooms, and a sunroom. After a quick circuit he headed up to the third

233

floor. It was the third floor that had convinced to buy. It had been remodeled into a single, massive bedroom with room for a sitting area, a small dinette, and a desk for work.

There was an extremely large walk-in closet with an island and a bathroom with a glass-encased shower, a glorious, modern, glossy, wood bathtub that looked like the side of sailboat, and enough room to take a small stroll. The only oddity he found was the white door opposite the door to the bathroom. He did not remember seeing that in the pictures.

Not one to leave an oddity unexplored, Bob crossed the bathroom and opened the door. To his surprise it was another walk-in closet. He turned on the light and saw a small island in the middle, plain walls, without actual bars to hang clothes, a standing mirror covered in a long sheet, and an oversized, leather chair. His shoes clacked softly on the hardwood floor as he crossed to the island.

Sitting in the middle of the island was a small, blue, leather box with a small manila envelope next to it. He picked up the envelope and opened it. Inside was a small, manila card. It said, *Enjoy.* That was it. It wasn't signed.

He put down the card and opened the leather box. Inside was a magnificent pocket watch. Immediately, he could tell it was old. It was silver, or white gold—or maybe platinum? The bow over the latch release was larger than normal. He pushed the latch release and opened the case. It was breathtaking.

The edge of the face was covered by an inch-wide band of embellishment surrounding the dial with the numbers and the hands. Diamonds were encrusted around the outside edge. The truly wonderous part was the interior area where the hour and minute hands were. It was perfectly clear.

The hands looked as if they were floating in mid-air. He couldn't see a single movement or watch complication. It had a double albert chain made of whatever silver colored metal the watch was made from. It was also encrusted with tiny, sparkling diamonds.

Bob just stood there holding it. Elias John Jackson Toussaint was a quiet and eccentric, elderly black man. Bob only knew him by reputation. It was said he loved the black community and was always there to support it, though he liked to work in the background, out of the spotlight.

He was instrumental in helping the cause during the civil rights movement, though no one really talked about exactly what he did. He had money and a clear point of view about how to use it. But he hadn't ever been ostentatious. In a lot of ways, he reminded Bob of his grandfather, Elwood—but without the money. Had the old man left the pocket watch as a gift? It looked like it was worth as much as the house.

He pulled out his phone and googled pocket watches with invisible complications. It took a minute, but he found out what it was. It was called a Mystery Watch.

A mystery watch, according to Wikipedia was, a watch *whose working is not easily deducible, because it seems to have no movement at all, or the hands do not seem to be connected to any movement.* Bob had no idea that was even a thing.

He closed the case, slid the watch into his vest pocket, and fixed the double albert chain across his vest, sliding the T-bar through a buttonhole, and putting the fob in the other pocket. The double albert was meant to hang across the front of a vest like a "w." A small bit of change hung from the T-bar in the center of the chain. On its end was a small, diamond encrusted medallion. He almost missed the anvil engraved on its face.

With the pocket watch in place, He left the odd little closet, turned off the light and closed the white door. By the time he made his way back downstairs the movers were knocking on the door. Bob grimaced. The white men he'd hired were a handful.

They reminded him of that quote from Lyndon B. Johnson about convincing the lowest white man that he's better than the best colored man. They had acted like they were doing him a favor taking his money to move him. If he hadn't discovered that attitude at the last minute, he would've fired them.

As it was it took all his patience to deal with it. He had made it abundantly clear that he'd sue them to within an inch of their financial lives if they damaged his things. Some of it was irreplaceable, like the antiques that had been in his family for generations.

He took a deep breath and opened the door. He was determined he wasn't going to let them ruin his homecoming. The supervisor was standing there holding a clipboard with a sour look on his face.

Before he could even open his mouth, Bob jumped into the void.

"Listen, I don't care what your disposition is, if you want to be paid you will unload this furniture according to the labels and you'll do it without a single word. Do you understand me? Because, so help me god, if I have to correct a single attitude there'll be hell to pay."

The man stood there in shock, before snatching his cap off his head and stuttering, "My, apologies, sir. I had no idea. I'm very sorry. It's just that—"

Bob cut him off saying, "Nope. No. I don't want to hear it. Just get to work."

The man ducked his head in a weird, half-bow, slapped his cap back on his head, turned and began bellowing orders. It was like night and day. In Atlanta, Bob had to constantly look over their shoulders, and berate them to pick up the pace.

It was unnecessary in Lexington. They moved quickly, but carefully. Each man ducked past Bob like he was going to strike them at any moment. He watched in amazement as their condescension melted into humility.

As he watched, something the supervisor said started to nag at him. What did the man mean by, *I had no idea*? No idea about what? That Bob wasn't going to put up with their shit anymore?

Over the course of the next few hours, the men moved him into the new house, putting everything where it was supposed to go with efficiency and care. By the time the sun was going down they were sweeping up behind themselves and tipping their caps as they passed him on their way out.

It was odd, but he was too tired to think about it anymore. He was just glad his things were where they were supposed to be, and the white men were gone. He closed the door behind them and went to the kitchen. His study wasn't set up yet, so he grabbed a bottle of bourbon from one of the boxes in the kitchen and rummaged through the other boxes until he found a heavy, crystal whiskey glass.

He made his way out onto the porch and sat in one of the chairs he'd purchased in Atlanta for the purpose. Darkness was falling on Gratz Park. The lights in the Carnegie Center to his right flickered on and he could see the lights in one of the buildings on the edge of Transylvania's campus down to his left.

The round streetlamps that peppered the landscape in the park were glowing to life. He poured a couple of fingers of bourbon into the heavy glass and sat the bottle on the porch next to his chair. He pulled a cigar out of his suit jacket's inner pocket. He retrieved his cutter and lighter from another pocket and in a matter of moments he was blowing heavy cigar smoke into the evening air and sipping on bourbon.

For the first time all day he was able to relax. He sat there for a few hours, smoking, drinking, and enjoying the evening. A few of his neighbors passed by his house as they walked through the neighborhood.

Bob didn't expect much from them given he was invading their little white preserve. But, to his surprise, they smiled and waved at him as they went by. He just smiled to himself and enjoyed the rest of his evening.

When he reached the end of his cigar he headed back in the house. It had been a long day, so he found his sheets, blankets, and pillows, made up his bed, and crashed. He slept the sleep of the dead.

When his eyes slowly blinked open, he reached for his phone on the bedside table and checked the time. It was almost ten in the morning. He smiled at the amount of sleep he'd gotten. He rolled out of bed, hit the shower, and got dressed.

It was Saturday so he threw on jeans, a tee shirt, and grabbed his Chuck Taylors. He was hungry and didn't feel like cooking, so he decided to go out for breakfast. A couple was walking by when stepped out the front door and made his way to his car.

The man stopped by his driveway and said, "Hey, uh, are you the new owner?"

Bob said, "Yes, I am."

The guy looked like he might have gone to Sayre. It was the khaki pants and black penny-loafers.

He looked at the Aston Martin in the driveway, then back at Bob with raised eyebrows and said, "Is that your car?"

Bob opened the car door and said, "Yes, it is."

Sayre looked like he had sour milk in his mouth. He grabbed the woman's arm and dragged her down the sidewalk. He stopped a few feet away and watched Bob get in the car, start it up, and pull out of the driveway.

He stopped the car over the sidewalk and gave the man his fakest smile. Sayre turned around and walked on down the sidewalk, pulling the woman along with him, as his loafers made a slapping sound on the concrete. Bob shook his head, pulled out into the street, and drove off. The more things changed, the more they stayed the same.

He drove down North Mill to Vine and turned left. He tried not to think about the difference in the waves and smiles from the night before and the disdain this morning. White folks were like that. You got used to it.

Main was a one-way street so he had to drive up past where Alfalfa's was located before he could turn onto Main and make his way down to the restaurant. By some miracle, there was an open parking spot right out front.

He parked and used his credit card to pay the meter. People stopped on the sidewalk to ogle the car. It was just something he had gotten used to.

One guy came over to him with a look of surprise on his face and said, "Is this your car?"

This was the other thing Bob had gotten used to. It wasn't the question that bothered him. He usually enjoyed talking about his car and a fully restored classic Aston Martin drew attention. It was the occasional white guy whose tone said *this couldn't be your car.*

The guy continued with a feigned chuckle, "What'd you do, steal it?"

Bob raised his American Express black card in a slow, exaggerated motion, and slid it back in his wallet. He dead-faced the guy as he slid his wallet in his pocket. He silently brushed passed the guy and went inside Alfalfas.

He took a deep breath and rolled his head around on his shoulders to release the tension as he waited for the host or hostess to return to their station to seat him.

Let it go, Bob, he thought to himself.

At least the Hoppin' John didn't disappoint, and he was back in his car in an hour and a half. Part of him wanted to drive around the city but he decided to go back home. He spent the day unpacking and putting things into place.

Before he knew it, night had come again. He showered and changed into a navy polo, jeans, and dress boots. He'd heard about a new place called Creaux in the city and he was hungry again. He decided to grab the pocket watch on his way out.

He put it in his front pocket and hooked the chain onto his beltloop so it would be inconspicuous. Lexington wasn't a large city, and his new house was very close to downtown, so it didn't take long for him to get to Creaux. This time he had to park around the corner and walk the half a block to the restaurant.

As he turned the corner, he saw the same cop from yesterday hassling a young black guy on the sidewalk. Something in Bob flipped, like a switch. Before he could think it through, he was in the cop's face yelling.

A lifetime of anger spilled out of him. He poured all the resentment about social injustice, abuse of power, and racial bigotry on the cop's head like an erupting volcano. Bob added a list of citizen's rights to his flaming denunciation of the cop's behavior.

When he finally stopped, he realized the cop had steadily backed away from him as poked him in his chest, punctuating every objection and grievance with a stiff finger. For some reason, Cavanaugh was still calmly asking him to understand that he was *only trying to do his job*. Bob froze.

Why wasn't he on the ground with the cop's knee in his back? Why didn't he have a gun trained on him? Why was officer Cavanaugh being so polite, so solicitous?

His mouth must have been silently agape because the cop took it as an opportunity to extricate himself from the situation. As Bob stood there, frozen to the sidewalk in shock, Cavanaugh raised his voice and told everyone to go on about their business, including the young black guy he'd been harassing.

He looked at Bob one more time and slowly made his way to his cruiser, adjusting his gun belt and scowling at everyone except Bob. The sound of the cruiser door slamming shut and the car pulling off with that two-note siren blip snapped Bob out of his shocked stupor. What the fuck had just happened?

Someone slapped his shoulder. He turned around to see the young black guy.

He said, "Thank you, sir. I really appreciate it when someone like you steps in to help. I don't know what would've happened if you hadn't been here. I just wanted to say thank you."

Bob smiled and nodded. They shook hands and Bob said, "No problem. Don't even worry about it. I got you, fam."

The young guy chuckled and said, "Oh, it's like that? Then, I appreciate it, fam."

He added an odd emphasis on the word fam. But Bob ignored it. Sometimes younger folks find slang from someone his age humorous.

He just stood there and watched the young guy go into Creaux and meet his friends who must have been watching from the front windows of the restaurant. They looked out at Bob as the young man pointed to him and spoke. They nodded and smiled.

One young woman waved at Bob, and he waved back. Then she smiled and threw up a fist. He chuckled and repeated the gesture. She giggled and turned back to her small coterie of hip youngsters. He realized he'd lost his appetite.

He went back to his car and drove home. He kept going back over the incident again and again in his mind. Why wasn't he in jail right now? Or dead? It was the look on the cop's face that puzzled him the most. It was – Bob fished for the exact word. It was *deferential*.

He parked his car and went into the house like he was on autopilot. He made his way upstairs and sat on the edge of his bed. He hadn't been sitting for more than a few seconds when he realized he needed a drink and a good chair to do the drinking in.

He went back downstairs and grabbed some bourbon and a glass. He was about to sit in one of the chairs in the front room when he realized that the perfect chair was upstairs.

He went back to the odd closet, behind the white door in the bathroom, with the plush leather chair. When he sat down, it was like the cushioned leather reached out and hugged him. What a great chair.

He poured some bourbon and sat there sipping. All the while he was trying to figure out what had changed between Friday and Saturday that made the cop react so differently. It puzzled him and he just sat there drinking.

After a while, he decided he wanted to finish drinking on the porch. When he stood up, he realized the only thing in the closet he hadn't really looked at was the mirror.

It was still covered in a long, white sheet. Maybe it was as an antique. If it was nice, and the right shade of wood, he could put it in the bedroom.

Bob crossed the room and grabbed a handful of sheet. With a flick of his wrist, he pulled on it and watched it slide away to the floor. He nearly dropped the glass in his hand.

"Holy shit."

He stared at his reflection in disbelief.

It must be a trick, he thought.

He walked into the bathroom and looked in the mirror over the sink. It was just his normal face. He went back into the strange closet and stood in the front of the mirror again.

"No fucking way."

He ran his hand through the blond hair reflected in the mirror. He leaned in close to see the blue eyes and thin pink lips. The thin nose and white skin was all a shock. He was a middle-aged white man.

"How the fuck is this happening?"

And then he remembered the pocket watch.

He took the watch out of his pocket and laid it on the island. Then he turned back around and looked in the mirror. It was him—dark brown skin, full lips, shaved head. It was still him. But when he put the pocket watch on, he looked like a white man.

It was crazy—unreal.

He must have put it on and took it off a dozen times and each time his reflection in the mirror changed—but only in this mirror. He ran up and down the stairs going to each bathroom in the house. Everywhere else he looked like himself.

He walked back into the strange walk-in closet and stood in front of the antique mirror. Suddenly, it all made sense.

He stared into the mirror and muttered, "Holy shit."

And then, he smiled.

A BIRD IN THE HAND

—

There is no fire like passion, there is no shark like hatred, there is no snare like folly, there is no torrent like greed.
~Siddharta Gautama

An ox shits more than a hundred mosquitos.
~Mozambican proverb

A thousand years ago, Azriel would have turned up his collar. Instead, he let the heavy raindrops cascading down at a forty-five-degree angle from the artificial clouds drifting overhead fall on his head and neck unabated. The wind was blowing so hard the rain appeared to fall sideways. The fat drops beaded up and rolled off the synthwool of Azriel's blue overcoat.

He muttered a curse aimed at whomever programmed the weather for tonight. The replicated-leather soles of his black boots splashed in a puddle pooled in the middle of Mnemonic Street as he crossed to the pub. Bright neon in red, blue, and green lit up the night and cast its luminous glow on the sulking denizens of *Eden*. Once a bright, towering, up and coming megalopolis on the terraformed moon of Saturn, Titan, it was now a forgotten sprawl festering under a malfunctioning dome.

Azriel liked the periodic flicker of the life-saving geodesic shield caused by power surges in the antiquated grid and faulty emitters. It had meant a slow but inevitable exodus of the faint at heart and a paucity of new visitors. When he learned about its fleeing residents, he hopped the first transport leaving earth. The ticket clerk, conductor, and pilot asked him three times if he was sure he wanted to go to Eden. It was the first time he could recall laughing in months.

The *Thousand Faces* was always open, but it looked so depressing in the light of day that Azriel only came at night. Minimal, multi-colored lighting, a crowded bar, and shadowy corners kept you from seeing the trash on the floor or the graffiti on the walls. Some nights he felt like getting a multi-spectral booster from the nearest med-comp when he left.

He wiped his hand across his face to remove just 246noughh water so he could see as he stepped inside. His twisty afro and thick beard would take a while to dry. A quick scan of the main room showed it was filled with the usual mix of people trying to get lost at the edge of the solar system. An old sign hung on the wall that read, *Last Stop for Gas for 100 miles,* in faded red paint. The place smelled like sweat and regret.

Only one other person had an active scan-dampener. It blocked a data-lens from harvesting any information with its scan. Azriel knew how expensive they were—and how illegal—because his was running too. While he couldn't get a bio-read or Network index off the man he could still zoom in on his face.

He let his data-lens home in on the man's features. He checked the corners of his mouth, the tiny lines around his eyes and across his forehead, the pace of his breathing, and his nostril dilation. Then he zoomed back out and checked his posture, the angle of his shoulders, and how he held his hands.

Once he was satisfied, he raised two fingers in a "v." Medusa answered with a nod. She met him at a table in the corner with a bottle of vodka coated in thin layer of ice and a heavy, crystal, shot glass. He downed two shots before she made it back to the bar. Three more shots had him well on his way to the state of merciful obliviousness that was his constant companion.

The man wore a dark-gray, chalk-striped suit that appeared to be actual wool. It was tailored to within an inch of its life. The jacket had double rows of gray buttons running from shoulder to waist and a high collar. His blond hair was cut short on the sides but high in the middle. Azriel caught the glimmer of light in his eye that indicated a data-lens as the stranger tried to scan him on his way over to the table.

"I approve. A man who likes his anonymity. May I join you?"

He was of average height and looked like he could use a sandwich or three. Even in the dim color-dappled light of the Thousand Faces he could tell that the man had the palest complexion. Azriel poured another shot.

"I'm not looking for friends."

The man's thin lips parted into a wry grin of white perfectly straight teeth.

"How about clients?"

247

Azriel raised his shot glass and quirked an eyebrow.

"Now why would I want a client?"

The man pulled a chair from a nearby table, pulled out a white handkerchief, laid it on the seat, and sat across from him.

"You know what? You're right. Let's just keep this all very casual."

The stranger stared at him for a moment. He was watching everything from Azriel's posture to how he held his shot glass. Azriel ran a hand slowly over his face.

"I'm so very tired. Just leave me alone."

The stranger said, "Ah, now I understand. You didn't get much sleep."

Azriel waved the statement off.

"No, not that kind of tired. The kind you'd have no way of understanding."

The man leaned forward and lowered his voice.

"I think the thing I'd like to hire you to do is something you'd be interested in."

Azriel growled, "How do you know what would interest me?"

He produced a small data pad from his pocket and gingerly slid it across with his fingertips while being sure not to touch the table. Azriel downed his shot and picked up the pad. A file was open onscreen, so he began scrolling through it.

"It was incredibly difficult, and very expensive, to piece together your past. Even with our resources, we only managed bits and pieces. I commend you on how you've managed to wipe nearly every trace of yourself from the Network. But as you must know, if you've got a sufficiently talented Net-ranger, bits of data can be recompiled even if it's been erased. Data is forever."

Azriel slowly lowered the data pad to the table with his left hand. His right unconsciously clenched into a fist. He took a deep breath and unclenched it.

"You must have a death wish."

"No, no." The man raised empty hands with his palms facing forward and smiled.

"Before you do something hasty, hear me out. My apologies if our information gathering has insulted you. That was not our aim. We simply needed to be sure that we had the right person for the job. Your name is whispered in fear or awe, and sometimes both, in the dark corners of the Network. It was difficult to learn much of anything substantial. But accumulating bits and pieces was sufficient to glean that you were responsible for the Hardecourt Affair, the Pegasus Incident, and that Kensington Royale business. Serves them right if you ask me. But it made it very clear that you were the person for the job."

The man turned his palms toward the ceiling, shrugged his shoulders, and pursed his thin lips as if to say – *Do you blame us?*

"Look, I don't care what the job is, I'm done helping. I tried for a very long time to … help. A very, very, long time. And I'm done. I'm tired and I just want to be left alone."

The man produced another white handkerchief, laid it across the table, and rested his intertwined hands on it.

"I get it. I absolutely get it. You came to this outdated backwater so you could be alone and spend your days in the bottom of a bottle and here I am interrupting your proverbial brood. I'm not judging. And if it were up to me, I'd leave you to it."

He made a fist and pumped it vaguely in the air over the table before continuing.

"More power to you. What did Thomas Hobbes say about human life without political community? That it would be 'solitary, poor, nasty, brutish, and short.' So, let me just run the particulars by you, so that when I get back to Terra-Prime I can say I did my job, and I'll leave you to your vodka and existential crisis."

Azriel poured another shot, raised the glass, and looked at the man for a moment.

With a deep sigh that began in his bones he said, "Fine. If that'll get you to leave me the hell alone, spin your little tale and then leave, or you'll definitely regret sitting at my table."

The man nodded his head and said, "Perfectly reasonable. Now, have you, by chance, heard of New Rosewood?"

—

New Rosewood was an homage to an ancient settlement from a time when Terra-Prime was called Earth. The original Rosewood, like Wilmington, Elaine, Atlanta, Tulsa, and many more towns and cities, was the site of racial violence culminating in the mass murder of people of African descent, and the looting and burning of those communities by white inhabitants. Azriel had been in Elaine and witnessed the atrocities. He had gotten bloody that day. He had still believed he could help back then.

He'd visited New Rosewood before settling in Eden. Even draped in his melancholy, he managed a smile at the sight of it. It was covered by clear aluminum dome infused with solar tech and overlayed by a high-density energy field. One of the city's founders had created the tech that amplified solar energy by a factor of thousands making it capable of powering an entire planet.

Inside it smelled like flowers and forest air. The buildings were covered with horticulture. The streets were wide and smooth and everywhere he looked he'd seen bright black and brown faces. It was a marvel. The idea that someone was going to threaten it had gotten his attention, even through his malaise.

Azriel tried not to spill his coffee in his lap as the hop-car came in for a landing. It was forty minutes across Titan to

Neuromancer but it seemed like a trip into the future. The dome glistened a translucent blue. There wasn't a piece of trash or a jot of graffiti anywhere. The buildings were glass and polymorphic alloy. Synthetics held open doors and carried boxes as they trailed behind people. When he exited the hop-car he actually stepped onto the sidewalk past an apple tree.

He sipped his coffee and waited for Harlan to join him. The man took a deep breath, exhaled, and smiled like he'd been gone a decade. After gawking at his surroundings like he couldn't believe he'd ever left, he motioned for Azriel to follow him.

Three streets and two blocks later they entered a building through the back door. He followed Harlan down a narrow hallway and two flights of stairs.

"So, tell me again about this planned attack on New Rosewood."

"Ah, yes, well, a group of Earth-Firsters don't like the fact that New Rosewood is doing so much better than some of the settlements on Terra-Prime."

Azriel grunted. "And how much of that dislike has to do with the fact that New Rosewood is a settlement made up mostly of people of African descent?"

Harlan coughed into his hand and said, "Uh, well, sure, it's probably a substantial consideration."

Azriel looked into his cup absently and said, "I'm sure it is. As much as civilization changes some grimy corner of it always stays the same."

I'm tired, he thought. This was why he'd found a forgotten corner of a leftover city on a distant moon and gotten lost in it.

He stepped onto the elevator with Harlan and watched the numbers tick off as they headed up. It took a minute, but soon enough they finally reached the top.

As the door opened with a soft *ding*, Harlan ushered him forward with a flourish of his hand and said, "After you. My benefactor awaits."

When Azriel looked up from Harlan's hand, he saw the two rows of gunmen arrayed like the walls of a long hallway, aiming energy-pulse weapons at him.

As Harlan stepped past him, Azriel reached out and snapped the man's neck. He dropped to the plush, purple carpet like a burlap sack full of potatoes. Azriel raised his hands and held them in the air as the body thumped on the floor. The gunmen took a step forward with their pulse rifles locked on him.

Azriel closed his eyes and waited. *Would pulse rifles be able to kill him?*

"Now, now, let's all calm down, shall we?"

The man's voice was too smooth by half. Azriel sighed, opened his eyes, and lowered his hands.

"Let me guess. Rosewood isn't in danger?"

The man looked a lot like Harlan, except shorter. Azriel hazarded a guess that his blue suit was a fine blend of wool and silk. Where Harlan's hair was blonde, his was jet black. He was as pale as Harlan was, but his eyes were green not blue. They both had the same self-satisfied grin.

He pointed a manicured finger at Azriel and smiled with the same kind of perfect, white teeth.

"There's the man I've read so much about! Brilliant, calculating, deadly, and very, very, very old."

Azriel shook his head as he sighed again.

"Please, tell me this isn't about you trying to figure out how to live longer. I've been here and done this before, so many times. Some asshole wants to live forever and they think experimenting on an immortal is the ticket to their longevity. It's like the plot of an old movie. Please tell me that's not what this is?"

"My name is Dankworth Fernsby and I can assure that is not what our little meeting is about. If you would?"

Fernsby motioned to a table near a wall that was clear glass. They could see out on the entire city to the dome that protected it from the atmosphere of Titan. Azriel crossed the room and took a seat at the small table across from him. The gunmen made a wide ring around the table while Fernsby busied himself with shot glasses and a bottle of vodka.

"I'm told you prefer vodka. Well, this is the best vodka on the entire moon."

It was ice cold and much better than what he was drinking at the Thousand faces.

After two quick shots, Azriel said, "You went to a lot of trouble to get me here." He nodded his head in the direction of Harlan's body and continued, "So, what do you want?"

Fernsby downed a shot of the incredibly good vodka and dismissed Harlan's body with a wave of his hand. He licked his lips, leaned over, steepled his fingers together, and said, "What do you know about the Bureau of Economic Policy for the Commonwealth?"

Azriel squinted his eyes.

"In 2042 the old congress of the former United States of America passed the Bezos Act outlawing the amassing of extreme wealth. It made provisions for seizing and redistributing the vast wealth held by a handful of individuals. In order to complete that task and to police wealth acquisition moving forward the new law established the BEPC. Once the united government of Terra-prime came into being it adopted the BEPC and made it global, eventually extending it to territories offworld as they were established."

"Very good, Azriel. Do you mind if I call you, Azriel?" Without waiting for him to agree, Fernsby continued. "I'll take it from here. While most of the amassed wealth was seized and extreme wealth was policed going forward, people were still allowed to become rich – to a point. And like water finding cracks in a foundation, the rich began finding ways to hide wealth. These days we use everything from billions of microtransactions to intermediaries, and couriers. I personally know a woman who has an interplanetary transport moving through the solar system at all times carrying encoded data-strips worth millions of credits. It's cloaked and always moving."

He leaned back in his chair and wiped imaginary sweat from his brow.

"The lengths we go to."

Azriel grunted. "I'll say it again. What do you want from me?"

Fernsby opened his mouth and widened his eyes in feigned shock.

"Why, how you hide your money of course."

Azriel blinked. *Did he hear him right?*

"Oh, close your mouth and stop playing coy. You're an immortal. From what I can tell you've been around for at least three thousand years. And I know you were extremely wealthy before the BEPC came along. And don't try to tell me that you don't have any money. I spent a lot determining that you're one of the richest people in the solar system. I just couldn't figure out how you keep it hidden. And that's what we're here to discuss."

The whine of pulse-rifles powering up punctuated Fernsby's last sentence.

Azriel chuckled.

"Wow. I have to hand it to you, Dankworth is it? You've managed something that hasn't been accomplished for years. You've actually surprised me."

Azriel stood slowly, so as not to alarm the thirty or so gunmen in the room, stepped over to the glass wall, which was likely an impenetrable transparent aluminum, and gazed out on the view.

"It's never enough for you people is it? You've got this view, retainers, armed guards, the expensive clothes on your back, but that's not enough. You're right, I've lived more than three thousand years and I still don't understand that level of greed."

Fernsby said, "Come on now. You're one of us. You're probably worth three times what I am. Don't play the noble citizen with me."

"No, you're wrong. I'm nothing like you. And to prove it, I'll tell you what you want to know. I just have one question."

"Yes?"

"Do you want me to reveal it in front of all these gunmen?"

Azriel turned from gazing out on the city and looked directly at Fernsby. The man jerked his head around to look at his hired lackeys and then back at Azriel. Azriel watched him come to the realization that he didn't want anyone else in the room to know what he was about to discover.

Azriel chuckled again and said, "Here, Dankworth, let me help you out. I'll sit here and you can have one of your men put restraints on me."

Azriel returned to the chair, took off his coat, rolled up his sleeves, and waited for two of the gunmen to place his arms behind his back. They wrapped long metal cuffs around his forearms connected by a metal rod. Then they handed Fernsby the controller.

Fernsby dismissed them all and held up the small gray remote and said, "Just so you know it's also an incapacitator. The cuffs will produce enough juice to leave you drooling on the floor."

He looked at Azriel's arms and chuckled.

"How quaint. Tattoos. Do you regret getting them? Are they still fashionable after all these years? Now, tell me how you hide your money."

Azriel pursed his lips and raised his eyebrows.

"Wow, Dankworth. Very thorough. I'm impressed. But, before I tell you that let me explain a few other things to you. First, the tattoos aren't an aesthetic."

Azriel took a deep breath and said, "Azurath ketreyal vendulah essuthtrak!"

The ancient, divine words scrolled around his arms changed from black ink to white light. The cuffs opened and dropped to the floor behind his chair. The light faded and Azriel stood up and rolled down his sleeves.

Fernsby shouted, "Guards! Guards!"

The gunmen came rushing back in from the other room.

Azriel made a tsking sound with his tongue and said, "Dankworth, we weren't finished. I also wanted to tell you my favorite drink isn't vodka, its bourbon."

"Now, Medusa."

A large drone dropped into view outside the clear wall from above. Azriel was already rolling across the floor toward the elevator when it opened fire. Heavy red pulses of energy burst through the wall and cut through the gunmen. It only lasted for a few seconds. By the time Azriel was back on his feet they were all down. The only sound in the room was the wind whipping through the opening where the wall used to be and whimpering of Fernsby from the far corner of the room.

Azriel walked back to the opening in the wall, saluted the drone, and said, "Thanks for the backup, Medusa. I owe you."

A disembodied voice spoke through a com-channel on the drone.

"No worries, old friend. We immortals have to stick together."

With that, the drone sailed up out of sight and disappeared. Azriel grabbed one of the chairs, picked his way through the bodies on the floor, and sat down by the corner where Fernsby crouched with his arms wrapped around his legs.

"So, listen, Dankworth. I know you're wondering how this all went so bad. When I saw Harlan in the Thousand Faces, I picked up on deception by reading his microexpressions. And I knew he was there to see me because he couldn't hide the recognition on his face when I entered the pub."

Azriel leaned over and lowered his voice.

"I ordered vodka instead of bourbon, which is what I normally drink. That was a signal to Medusa that something was wrong. When I left, she launched the drone and followed me, and she looked into Harlan. He was right. A gifted Net-ranger can find a lot on the Network. On the ride here she downloaded it all to my data-lens. And you know what I discovered Dankworth? You've been a bad, bad boy."

Azriel stood up, moved the chair aside and took three steps back.

"I mean, you've done things that can only be called evil. And because of that, I'm going to tell you one last thing."

Azriel waved his hand to his right and said, "Lamna wyllroth gallna ornith!"

A jagged red line appeared in the air. It was six feet long like someone had cut through the fabric of the universe. The smell of sulfur filled the room. Faint screams echoed from the other side of it.

"People used to think heaven and hell were spiritual places. What if I told you that they were actually dimensions inhabited by creatures of realms so different from ours that the people who got

257

glimpses of them struggled to understand what they were? And what if I told you that one of those dimensions is home to benevolent creatures that welcome those of us who cross over and whose denizens sometimes come here for the purpose of pouring good into our universe?"

Azriel took three quick steps to the corner and grabbed Fernsby. He dragged him to the jagged line suspended in the air.

"And Dankworth. What if I told you the other dimension was filled with ravenous creatures with an insatiable desire for pain and suffering? And that they relish the chances to grab us and carry us to their dimension where they can torment us unendingly? Would you believe me?"

He held Fernsby next to the jagged line. A pair of clawed hands reached through and grabbed him. Fernsby's scream hung in the air long after the line disappeared.

Azriel took one last look around the room, put on his coat, grabbed the bottle of vodka that had miraculously escaped the carnage wrought by Medusa and got on the elevator. He was tired. And it was time to get back to drinking.

ACKNOWLEDGEMENTS

This labor of love wouldn't be possible without the support of a lot of people. I want to thank everyone who contributed to the Indiegogo project that made this collection a reality: Dana Cameron, Robert Hilliard, Hillary Monahan, K. Cofrin, Kathy Gosnell, William Akin, James Liang, Jason Denzel, Thom DeSimone, Rachel Brune, Sean Hillman, Danyelle Denham, Jeff Jarvis, Seth Lockhart, Jess Lewis, Ashley Chappell-Peeples, Jennifer Halbman, Allison Charlesworth, Katharina Wesel, Liz Allen Giordano, Jeffery T. Johnson, Sarah J. Sover, Rachel Little, Linda D. Addison, Thompson Terry, A.J. Hartley, Brian C. Hawkins-Bailey, Robert Saffell, William M. Feero, Michael Lucas, John Hartness, Milton Davis, Ross Newberry, Claudia Wair, and Jessica Key.

Why Captain Kirk Must Die first appeared in Apex Magazine issue 127

A version of *Fool's Errand* first appeared in the Rococo Anthology by Roaring Lion

Planet 113 first appeared in the 2022 JordanCon Anthology Neither Endings Nor Beginnings

A version of *The Messiah Curse* first appeared in the Terminus Urban Fantasy Anthology by MVMedia

A version of *A Bird in the Hand* first appeared in the Cyberfunk! Anthology by MVMedia

A version of *Consecrated* first appeared in the Terminus 2 Anthology by MVMedia

A version of *The Mystery Watch* first appeared in the Weird Fiction Anthology Whether Change: The Revolution Will Be Weird by Broken Eye Books

A version of *Hunter's First Rule* first appeared in the Cyberfunk Anthology The City by MVMedia

A version of *Perilous Falls* first appeared in the Dark Universe Anthology The Bright Empire by MVMedia

ABOUT THE AUTHOR

Gerald L. Coleman is a philosopher, theologian, poet, and Science Fiction & Fantasy author. He was born in Lexington and now makes his home in the Atlanta area. He did his undergraduate work in philosophy, english, and religious studies, followed by a master's degree in Theology. He is the author of the Epic Fantasy novel series, The Three Gifts, which currently includes *When Night Falls* (Book One), *A Plague of Shadows* (Book Two), and the upcoming *When Chaos Reigns* (Book Three). His poetry has appeared in: *Pluck! The Journal of Affrilachian Arts & Culture*, *Drawn To Marvel: Poems From The Comic Books*, *Pine Mountain Sand & Gravel Vol. 18*, *Black Bone Anthology*, the *10th Anniversary Issue of Diode Poetry Journal*, *About Place Journal*, and *Star*line Vol. 43, Issue 4*. His speculative fiction short stories have appeared in: The Cyberfunk Anthology: *The City*, the Roaring Lion Anthology: *Rococoa*, the Urban Fantasy Anthology: *Terminus* and *Terminus 2*, the 2019 JordanCon Anthology: *You Want Stories?*, *Dark Universe: Bright Empire*, *Cyberfunk!* by MVMedia, the JordanCon 2022 Anthology: *Neither Endings Nor Beginnings*, and *Whether Change: The Revolution Will Be Weird*. His essays appear in the polish language Con-Magazine: *KONwersacje*, *Apex Magazine 127*, and the Hugo nominated Fanzine: *Journey Planet*. He has been a Guest Author at DragonCon, Boskone, Blacktasticon, JordanCon, Atlanta Science Fiction & Fantasy Expo, SOBSFCon, The Outer Dark Symposium, World Horror Con, Imaginarium, and Multiverse. He is a Scholastic National Writing Juror, a Co-founder of the Affrilachian Poets, an SFWA member, a Rhysling Award Nominee, a recipient of The Hero of the Horn Award at JordanCon, and a Fellow at the Black

Earth Institute. He is currently working on new editions of When Night Falls, A Plague of Shadows, and writing book three in epic fantasy series. And his newest poetry collection is entitled, *On the Black Hand Side*. You can find him at Geraldcoleman.com.

CPSIA information can be obtained
at www.ICGtesting.com
Printed in the USA
LVHW041342221222
735760LV00001B/36